SKIATHOS

SKIATHOS

by

Boris L. Slocum

2020

Printed in the United States of America

First Printing, 2020

ISBN 978-1-7335425-1-7

3B Independent Publishers
347 W. Franklin Street
Paxton, Illinois 60957

www.3bpublishers.com

Prologue

A fter nearly 600 years of spacefaring, the humans of the known worlds had yet to encounter a single species that might even loosely be termed humanoid.

The beauty was that their tiny sliver of the Milky Way, much to the surprise of all, was replete with life. Of more than 200,000 explored systems, just over 11,000 worlds were home to some type of lifeform, and many of those spheres held such biodiversity as to rival even the fecundity of old Earth. In all, the human species had encountered 177 unique civilizations, 11 of which had mastered extra-planetary travel.

But most such lifeforms were exotic beyond the wildest imaginings of humanity's ancient ancestors. The learned and technologically advanced Dolen of Acacia IV were little more than floating bags of gas; the Leel of Phocaii IV were something akin to especially intelligent and amiable slugs; and the Eme of the Titian colonies, the species that most resembled humans in thought and feeling, were tall stick figures with a variable number of limbs and no discernable heads.

And then nine years ago, a civilian survey company exploring a terrestrial-type planet, located past the edge of settled space, had discovered the Lacertians

1: Mathilde

Nadja was still working the cobwebs from her head. The potent Lonn Drive that powered their star liner was a godsend, one that enabled humanity's spacefaring way of life, but it was not her favorite mode of travel. Even at the unimaginable speeds at which the vessel hurtled through the void, voyages the distance of the one which she'd just endured were taxing on passengers, crews, and ship's resources. She'd passed most of the four-month journey in Hibernation, an induced state of neurological and physical quiescence, awaking only three days prior to her debarkation to revive her body gradually and to begin her last-minute preparations.

The leviathan vessel on which she travelled, christened the *Mathilde*, was something of a great interstellar bus, shuffling people about that remote corner of the cosmos, picking up and discharging passengers and cargo along the way in smaller drop-ships, seldom falling from faster-than-light travel for more than the time necessary to make the exchange. Throughout the journey, both crew and passengers passed most of their time in Hibernation and were roused only as they were needed.

On the far side of a sterile partition, the purser who served her now, a sleepy-eyed woman who went about her duties as if half in a fog, was not the same who had manned the vessel when Nadja had embarked four-months before. It likely would be another crewmember or two on a different leg of the journey, depending on how many passengers and how much cargo came and went.

Their stop wasn't so much a stop as a pause in stride. A single small vessel would drop on Skiathos with Nadja and her two assistants, a small Marine detachment, and a negligible bit of cargo. No passengers were scheduled to embark before the great bus jumped back to FTL and resumed its course.

She looked around the airlocked bay after the purser had passed Ken and Janet their sealed containers of coffee and departed. It seemed like everyone was there who needed to be. Her married assistants, both postgrad researchers in linguistics at Heather Institute, were sitting patiently on a nearby canvass-strap bench and, she thought, waiting nervously for their chalk to form—it was not shaking out to be the adventure honeymoon of which they'd dreamed. She counted 15 Marines, all of whom were formed up patiently on the ground, leaning back on their rucks. Nadja had done her military service many years before, back when it was still mandatory, and the phrase "rucksack flop" came to mind. She wondered if that name was still used to describe such a waiting game.

Before she could ponder further, the intercom screeched the Skiathos drop and, as a body, the Marines came to their feet and fell in. Nadja was veteran of a dozen or more drops over the years. Loading the chalks usually was a careful procedure, except when numbers were small. In such instances, the process was more informal, and passengers just gaggled aboard. As long as everyone was onboard and in harness in time for release, no one on the crew fussed. But this time there were Marines involved.

The situation soon resolved itself and, as if by an unspoken compromise, the Marines faced left and merely filed in a familiar route-step to the secondary airlock. Nadja and her team followed, their personal gear and carry-ons in hand. It took all of five minutes for the debarkation team to scan and admit them all, and another 20 minutes found their bags stowed and their persons strapped into seats. They need only await the drop.

Despite their reputation, drops generally were uneventful affairs, little different than the shuttle rides to which most travelers were accustomed on settled worlds. But this was past the edge of settled space, the frontier. The nearest emergency services units were a hundred or more light-years distant, and *Mathilde* would make her jump to FTL the moment the drop-ship was free. The real danger was that every planet was different, and one could never completely predict atmospheric conditions on a world only a few humans had visited.

Nadja sat back and hummed quietly.

"First drop?" a male voice asked.

She looked three seats over and saw a young Marine private—or a Marine private who appeared young—it had become harder and harder to tell. She smiled back.

"Nah, I'm past a dozen," she said. "Just trying to relax."

The young man laughed. "Oh, well, you've got me beat, ma'am. This is three for me ... hold my hand?"

Nadja suppressed a laugh but heard a feminine voice from several rows back. "Leave the nice woman alone, Christian." The voice was stern, but patient.

"Aye-aye, ma'am." The young Marine was resigned, but cheerful.

Nadja forewent her usual ritual for the moment and flipped open her tablet. Release was still some minutes off, and she thought to torment herself further.

She had another two years to figure out this problem—by necessity, stays on un-terraformed worlds were long, due to the enormous strain placed on the human body by CAP, the Clemence Acclimatization Process, but it already had been seven years that she had worked this problem and was no closer to its solution than she had been on the day she started.

The Lacertians didn't appear to have a language, or they had a language that a veritable army of linguists, including Nadja, had yet to decipher. That was the problem.

Language was a constant throughout the civilizations that humanity had encountered. It was a lodestar, a keystone, a firm bedrock without which cooperation within a species was impossible. But every such system was unique; some were downright arcane. Transfer of neurons, manipulation of appendages, the shifting of inanimate objects, changes of colors all played parts in the various languages they'd encountered over the centuries. All were different, and though some few races even relied on atmospheric vibrations to transmit information, none of humanity's intergalactic interlocutors actually "talked."

The Lacertians talked.

It was that fact that had left Nadja pulling out her hair and rending her clothes most of the last seven years. Since grad school, she had been on four teams tasked with learning to communicate with new civilizations. After obtaining her doctorate, she had led one of those teams—the Forcor of Pangea IV relied on a complex system of taps and whistles of their own design to communicate with non-Forcor. It had taken her team 18 months to master that system and another six months fully to grasp the Forcor internal language, a series of protein markers that conveyed information via the exchange of aspirated gases. Exo-linguistics was a subtle, complex, and highly developed science, one that often relied far more on biochemistry than on conjugation of verbs.

The Lacertians talked, actually moved their mouths and talked. For they indeed did have mouths—and eyes, and ears, and arms, legs, fingers, toes, and … yes, a single humanoid head on top. They looked more like humans than any exo-biologist ever could have imagined, and they survived on a world the characteristics of which were not terribly different from those of old Earth.

On average, Skiathos was a great deal warmer and more arid than Earth, but the atmosphere was a familiar mix of oxygen and nitrogen, and the gravity, despite the planet's greater surface, was about 15 percent below Earth normal. More, a strong, but peculiar, electro-magnetic field protected against the worst interstellar radiation. Of course, the planet had its own slew of particles, microbes, and bacteria—against which Nadja's arduous CAP treatments should be proof—but every survey, report, and story about the planet suggested it was nearly as suitable for human habitation as any terraformed world. That fact alone was astounding.

But not so astounding as the fact that Lacertians talked and that after seven years of study Nadja couldn't understand a single word they were saying.

2: The Great Desert

A large body slid into the seat to Nadja's immediate right, pulling her from her thoughts. It was a Marine. The EV-suited gate crew was redistributing the load on the half-empty drop-ship in anticipation of departure. The whirring of the autopilot said drop was imminent.

"Where are you in from, sergeant?" Nadja asked over the autopilot and other noises that had erupted in the cabin.

"Ma'am ...? Oh, Clem's World. We're part of the 1107th Force Recon stationed there." The voice was the same that had scolded Pvt. Christian previously. "You're the new civil affairs officer from State Department?"

"Yes, sorry." Nadja extended her hand. The young Marine's grip was hard and firm. "I was still under when you folks came onboard. I'm Nadja ... Nadja Bikram."

"Mandy Lyn, sergeant type," the lean woman smiled back. The youngish Marine hesitated. "We weren't supposed to bother you ... orders."

Nadja laughed. "Don't worry. I won't break."

"I didn't think so. Did you say earlier, you've dropped before?"

"A number of times. It's usually not as bad as they say."

The young Marine bit her lip. It was a trick to avoid smiling that Nadja had often seen among military types. It only partly worked now. "The platoon planet-side lost a troop transport in the Central Desert almost five months ago." The Marine glanced to Nadja's two assistants. "We don't suspect hostile fire, but you might have your team buckle up tight."

Nadja glanced over just to make sure the newlyweds were properly harnessed and felt the sudden queasiness that meant the gravity plating and inertial negators were adjusting to the drop-ship having disengaged. A quick glance aft showed the hatch was sealed. The load crew had departed the fully-automated drop-ship without a word.

The intermittent flight instructions and safety briefing the AI had been broadcasting for the past five minutes had offered no warning of any potential danger, but a combat drop was mandatory, if even the slightest possibility of shooting trouble arose along the frontier. Real hazards were quite rare, and the precautions largely were one-size-fits-all and of doubtful efficacy, but it was what it was. The drop-ship would race for the surface and once in the atmosphere turn, pitch, and roll before shooting at near ground level to the general vicinity of their destination. A sudden ascent then would take them to the sub-orbital platform that was the planetary survey team HQ for Skiathos.

The gravity/inertia systems for the vessel could only do so much, so it would be an unpleasant experience, and it crossed her mind to warn her acolytes—she previously had assured them the drop would be uneventful. But it was a little late now. The whole mess would all be over in 10 minutes or less.

As a second thought, she reached over and snatched two sickness-bags from the seatbacks in front of her and handed one to each.

————

The disagreeable odor in the passenger compartment as they began to disembark said at least one of the Marines had not taken the drop well—it had been like a sled ride to Hell—and Nadja hoarded a secret delight that Ken and Janet both had left their bags unused on their seats. In fact, Ken had the wherewithal, albeit on somewhat rubbery legs, to ask what all the fuss was about. Apparently, despite Nadja's initial reassurances to the contrary, the drop had been much as he and his bride had anticipated.

Ten minutes later, Nadja emerged with her bags, the last off the transport, into the warm sun of Skiathos.

Her first view of the sun-drenched world below took her breath away. The platform on which they perched hovered nearly 10 kilometers above the alien land. And from where she stood, that world seemed to go on forever in subtle shades of tan, gray, and brown intermixed with occasional patches of green and sparse, but vivid, swirls of color. Skiathos, for all its brutal heat, deadly fauna, and wild unpredictability was a thing of beauty, pure and unrepentant.

Placing down her bags and stepping to the platform rail, she realized she could smell it. Even here, at 10,000 meters, masked in the platform's electronic camouflage shroud, the planet reeked of spice and perfume, flower and flora, death and decay, and raw and unyielding life. It was her first desert, her first truly wild planet. She'd never imagined a place so arid could be such an assault upon the senses. But with all that, the place smelled so … clean, the air so fresh.

"I need your hand, ma'am."

She glanced over and saw a medical corps technician and lazily reached out with her right hand for stamping. The incoming passengers would need to stay "top-side" on the platform for 30 days until the medical officer ensured that their CAP treatment had indeed acclimated them and that no debilitating side effects of the highly invasive treatments afflicted them. She crossed her heart inwardly—six months in an isolation chamber (or, worse, a trauma pod) until she could be evacuated was not something she hoped to experience, not after all this. But she couldn't take her eyes from the planet and scolded herself for having placed her field optics in her hold baggage.

"It's not going anywhere, ma'am," said the technician, a smile in her voice. "I was the same way, when I first got here. The beauty of the whole thing makes up for not getting to go planet-side."

Of course. Only a small number of personnel were permitted to descend and risk interacting with the locals. Encounters with the Lacertians during the last seven years had been perplexing. The natives showed no outward signs of hostility, were actually quite friendly, but the socio-cultural teams that had ventured down to meet with the humanoids had been sorely disappointed. Their hosts mostly had restricted their movements to the lesser of the race's two caste strata, the study of which had been fruitless.

"It's just a joy to watch." Nadja couldn't contain herself.

"Part of that's the gravity," the medic corrected. "Everyone feels it when they get here."

"Oh, right." The gravity on space-liners customarily was set at 20 percent above old Earth normal to compensate for heavier planets, of which there were many, and Skiathos was 15 percent below normal. The sudden release of gravity stepping from the drop-ship had left Nadja feeling slightly buoyant, both physically and otherwise. On Skiathos, she weighed barely 50 kilos.

The medic appeared to have completed her bio-stamping, and from the sound of it, the young woman was putting away her gear. "Ma'am, keep hydrated. It's cool this high up, but the sun is still powerful. Eat. Most important, sleep. CAP won't reset your body clock, so get to bed early tonight and force yourself to get up in the morning. Don't worry about the sticker on your hand; we'll let you know if there are any problems. Oh … and, don't step over the rails. The gravity eddies holding this place up are fun to bounce on, but they fluctuate. That first step is a doozy."

Before Nadja could reply, a male voice came from farther down the platform.

"Dr. Bikram?"

Nadja turned to see the other passengers had gone, probably below for in-processing, and a young man was approaching with his hand extended. She took the proffered hand with a squeeze. "Sgt. Matthews," she said after glancing at the etching on his uniform. "Is Capt. Carruthers available?"

"Dead, ma'am," said the NCO, as he might comment on the weather.

"Sorry to hear that. Report." It was many decades since Nadja's naval service, but she'd worked occasionally with the military since. If the sergeant was surprised by the brusqueness, he made no sign. Soldiers and Marines responded best to direct language.

"Marine 3-1 dropped from 600 meters at grid 2663-442-10 on 4-4-28. The time was about 1100 hours local time, and the transport was returning from a survey of a potential engagement site for the linguistic team. There were 11 PAX aboard, but we only recovered four bodies."

"The rest?" she asked.

"Dunno, ma'am. No survivors, and those power cells burn hot when they've been damaged."

"Who'd you lose beside Carruthers?"

"Gunny … Gunnery Sergeant Nice, that is ... Dr. Downey and both of her assistants, and six Marines from first squad."

"Well, piss," Nadja muttered. She and Melissa Downey hadn't been friends, but she'd known the woman for close to 20 years and was supposed to be her replacement. "What happened?"

"Unclear, ma'am. Maintenance says they likely had engine trouble—there's a silicate in the sand here that plays hell with the power units and converters, and the electromagnetics of this rock are fucking bizarre. But Chief Eddy couldn't be certain the vehicle didn't take particle weapons fire, so we've been on alert since."

"Where's Dr. Wray?"

The young Marine cleared his voice. "He went planet-side two months ago ... alone ... and we haven't seen him since."

"Oh, for chrissake," she whispered. Gunter Wray was a bio-anthropologist and ostensibly the civilian project manager. "Who's in command now?"

"That'd be you, ma'am." The young Marine caught the glare Nadja shot him. "Chief isn't an unrestricted line officer, and Dr. Sokay is a contract employee. I've been running things since Dr. Wray skipped off ... well, even before that."

Nadja felt her temper rise but suppressed it. Her assignment had been to work a single problem, one that haunted her. She had no intention of getting bogged down with a mountain of extra duties, but she was a State Department officer. And though this was a military-led mission, she was obliged to iron things out and, if necessary, to take charge. *Piss*, she thought to herself. *Piss*.

"OK," she sighed. "Point me toward the CP and have the squad leaders join me there in 20."

3: The Marines

Sergeants Matthews, Lyn, Fernandez, and Bisbee were at the appointed time and place, a large and airy room near the aft section of the platform. She'd learned in her brief walk that the enormous platform, designed for long-term use by a cadre of 200, had scarcely 100 personnel. The room used by the Marines as a command post was broad and airy and likely was intended for loftier purposes.

"OK, who's senior?" asked Nadja, once all were seated. The non-commissioned officers all held the same rank and swiftly engaged in the time-honored practice of comparing dates of rank. Lyn won out. Rather than rankle, the news seemed to please Matthews.

Nadja continued, looking at Lyn but pointing to Matthews. "Listen to everything Sgt. Matthews has to say until you get your feet wet … and stick around after we break up here. I have some things I want to discuss. Matthews," she said, turning to the NCO, "have you been running any sort of staff meetings since Wray departed?"

"No, ma'am. I've just been going to each of the research and support sections and getting their input for my SITREPS."

"Notify all section heads: staff meeting at 0700 tomorrow. There'll be an all-hands later this week, so folks can register their gripes, bitches, and complaints." Personnel on stations such as this did not do well without structure and discipline, especially out on the frontier. She felt her anger rising that things had been allowed to go to hell. The urge to skin Gunter Wray suddenly leapt up.

Nadja looked again to Matthews. "What have you done to find Dr. Wray?"

The young sergeant again cleared his throat. "He … um … he told us not to come looking for him, ma'am … said he was 'going dark.'"

"What the fuck does that mean?" barked Nadja, no longer trying to hide her annoyance.

"It's anybody's guess, ma'am," volunteered Sgt. Fernandez. "The professor was a bit theatric."

"He's chipped, isn't he?" All members of the survey team had transponders imbedded more easily to find them if separated.

"He turned it off, ma'am," said Matthews. "Anyway, there's a lot of EM interference on the planet, and it is one big planet."

"Ma'am," said Fernandez, "if we could put some satellites up…."

"Nah, sorry folks. For political reasons you may or may not be aware of, dropping satellites is a no-go … at least for the time being. Sgt. Lyn, sit down with your fellow NCOs and come up with a plan to find Professor Wray. Don't execute until you run it past me, though."

She looked again to Matthews. "What's the ETA on getting a new platoon leader and platoon sergeant here from Clem's World?"

The naval station at Clem's World was the nearest military facility to their location. It was three and a half weeks for a message to reach there via Pinpoint comms, the same time it would take a vessel from the station to arrive.

"That'd be you, ma'am," the young Marine repeated.

It took Nadja a few moments to soak in that information. *Fucked right in the ass*, she nearly said aloud. Well, it made sense. If the Marine Corps was going to send a new command team, it would have come with Sgt. Lyn and her squad on the same transport as Nadja and her team. She sighed inwardly.

"OK…," she sighed aloud. "I suppose you should know a little about me. I'm not one of the contract academics you've worked with in the past. Dassault University does keep me on the faculty books, and I teach the occasional class, but most of my time is spent with State. Before that, I was a naval officer, had command of *The Dread*, an Entebbe-class destroyer for two years before leaving service."

She looked again around the table.

"I'm usually not a stickler, but if we're going to do this thing, we're going to do it right. Sgt. Lyn, I want to see a duty roster by 0800 tomorrow and a training schedule 30, 60, and 90 days out by the end of the week. I expect Marines to act like Marines: so, discipline, grooming, physical training, and professional development for young Marines … and for NCOs. What have you folks been doing for arms training?"

"We have a range in the southern desert, ma'am," Matthews replied. "It's hot but uninhabited."

"OK. We're starting planet-side ops again in 30 days. Lyn, make sure weapons are on the training schedule. We can resume flight training then, too. How many vehicles are up and running?"

Again, Matthews spoke. "All the skiffs are online, and Chief has our two remaining troop transports refitted for the desert. First squad's replacement vehicle and fourth squad's vehicle came as cargo on your drop-ship."

"Great. Is there an operations cell?"

"No, ma'am," said Matthews.

"Lyn, that's you. Get with Chief and pick an assistant from one of the naval personnel. Is there an intel cell here?"

"State has a couple of analysts in the SCIF on the middeck," said Bisbee. "The captain had me working as unofficial S-2."

"Keep doing that. Sgt. Lyn, you're also platoon sergeant. The four of you figure out the best corporal to take over fourth squad. Let me know your decision. Look, team … we're short command staff, and I have other things to do. You're all going to be pulling extra duty for the duration. Any questions?"

"No, ma'am," they said as a group.

"Dismissed. Except for you Lyn; stick around a few."

———

"What do you need ma'am?" asked the tall young sergeant after the others had departed.

"Nothing much. I'm going to be relying on you pretty much to run the Marine detachment. Just wanted to make sure and get to know you. Where you in from, originally?"

"Harvest World, ma'am."

"Farm girl?" Nadja suspected as much. The young noncom was tall and strong.

"No. Dad's a doctor, but I grew up in a farm community near Land Fall."

"Married? Kids?"

Nadja had to ask. The human lifespan had increased steadily over the centuries, and the latest techniques in genetic manipulation, a process that scientists termed "Allele Stacking," had slowed the outward expression of age so radically that it was difficult to discern how old someone was and, consequently, how much experience that person might have. It was a phenomenon with which people Nadja's age were still coming to grips.

"None, ma'am. I'm 24. Six years in the Marines."

"Nice." She smiled back. The youngster had read her intent. "Someone who looks 24 who is 24. How well do you know the other Marines?"

"The sergeants I know well. We all came through the ranks together. Clem's World was our first posting."

"Good people?"

"The best. It broke our hearts when we lost Gunny Nice and the others."

"And the captain?"

"I never met him, ma'am. He came in just for this project."

14

"You're all of the same platoon. Why was fourth squad so long getting here?"

"Truth ma'am? ... I think the commander of the 1107th thinks this is a waste of resources."

"Which is why he doesn't want to replace the command team," Nadja muttered. She continued in a normal tone. "What do you know about Skiathos?"

"Um ... it's named after a Greek island?" the young woman ventured. She didn't begin laughing until she saw Nadja had. "No, seriously, ma'am. I've read all the socio-cultural briefs ... and every SITREP that came through. Was there someplace you wanted me to start?"

"Yeah ... yeah," Nadja was suddenly interested. "Tell me about the Lacertians."

"They're not really lizards. I know that much. And doesn't the name actually come from some clever bastard in cartography realizing the system would be in the Lacerta Constellation as viewed from old Earth?"

"Yes, it would, but only barely. There are far too many clever bastards in cartography." That last part was a truism. Nadja reached over and flicked on the holographic projector, synching it to her tablet as she did.

In the middle of the room an enormous and fearsome figure appeared. The Lacertian was all of 8 feet tall and was a mass of long, lean muscle and elegant sinew, across which was stretched a hide that lightly rippled several shades of green and brown. The being's chest and shoulders were broad, the waist tiny, and its four long limbs suggested tremendous power. The being stood on two legs, its large head high and erect on a lean and muscular neck.

It was from that point the similarity to humans stalled. The long legs, corded with muscle, seemed to have one joint too many: there was a knee that seemed placed for forward kneeling, but also a second joint that arched slightly backward, from which extended a narrow foot that held three long and powerful toes, upon which the great weight of the giant seemed precariously balanced. Each toe was capped with a long, ebony nail like something from nightmare; higher up, just behind and below the leg's lower joint, extended a long and wicked dew claw or spike that was perhaps 25 centimeters long.

The Lacertian's arms from shoulder to wrist were long and powerful, with but a single elbow, and jutting from the wrist was a short and broad hand with three long and powerful fingers and what might be a thumb. Each was capped with the same formidable claws as the foot.

Nadja had examined this precise figure and others like it a thousand times over. The resolution was remarkable, and as she stepped forward, she pointed to the being's broad chest.

"Come take a look at this," she said. "Skin, not scales." She heard the young sergeant move behind her.

"I've seen this holograph before, ma'am, but never to scale. It is to scale?"

"It is."

The NCO let out a sigh. "Wow. I knew they were big ... but ... wow!" The young woman took a step forward and looked up. "I can't stop looking at the face. It isn't human at all, but just...."

"Seems so human," Nadja added. The being before them had a short and powerful muzzle with clearly defined muscles and bone beneath. The holograph was on a one-hour loop, and as the two women watched, the giant before them moved casually, turning and tossing its head as if in curiosity—or what would have been curiosity for a human. The being's enormous maw revealed a set of long and sharp teeth. A pair of longer fangs, smooth and curved, flanked the upper and lower rows.

"I think it's the eyes," said the sergeant. "And ... yeah, I know they don't look human. But they are eyes ... and they seem so, I dunno ... intelligent."

The two large golden orbs, set just below a heavy brow ridge, looked more catlike than human or reptilian, with dark slits set in a blue iris. There appeared to be two additional, clear sets of eyelids beside the heavy opaque lid that would occasionally flick from top to bottom.

"How do they poop?" blurted the sergeant. "I always wanted to ask someone that."

Nadja couldn't completely suppress a smile. "I don't think they do." Other than the mouth and thin nostrils set just above it, the body before them had no type of external orifice, nor any hint of genitalia.

"How is that possible?"

"They're not like us."

"How do they, you know...?"

"We think they aspirate their waste. People who've been around them say they give off a strong odor, and one that's not terribly unpleasant."

"But no solid waste?"

"Nope," replied Nadja. "They must have incredibly efficient metabolisms."

"But what if they eat something they can't digest?"

"I don't know, honestly. Dr. Wray has some ideas, but they're just hypotheses."

"Aspirating smells. Is that how they communicate?"

"No." Nadja suspected the NCO might have read up on her work with the Forcor, but said nothing of it. "They talk. Every research team that's hit this rock in the last seven years has seen Lacertians yammering away at one another. We just can't figure out the language."

"Not at all?"

"Not a single word." She turned to the sergeant. "And yet they have a civilization, so they must communicate in some way. Tell me what you know about Lacertian society."

"Ma'am, well ... um. It appears to be primitive or tribal. They forge crude metal, work with hides and fibers, and build with stone and local plants. We haven't charted the whole planet, but there appear to be a handful of smaller cities and larger towns and scads of villages. There are a few small seas, which I guess are little more than large lakes. Along those and the few river valleys they farm, in the mountains they keep flocks, and in the deserts, which is most of the planet, the natives hunt and gather and keep a few animals. They have trade networks, and there's some sort of caste system, with the warrior caste being larger and differently colored. The smaller caste seems to do most or all the manual labor and are kept like chattel by the warriors. In fact, didn't the first survey team conclude the smaller caste was a separate species altogether?"

"They could be for all we know. We haven't had much luck getting any of them to submit to medical exams or scans and moving in and snatching a body for exams wouldn't exactly endear us to the locals."

"Why should that...?" The young Marine appeared to catch herself. "Ma'am, why are we even here? This planet doesn't have anything unique by way of natural resources, and the natives are interesting, but ... don't we usually have some sort of non-interference policy?"

This kid is smart, Nadja couldn't help but think. She suddenly felt better about having her as platoon sergeant. "You're right. For people like me, it's about curiosity, but the government has never been interested in exploration for the sake of exploration. It's either about natural resources or security threats."

"And there's a security threat here?"

"The Marine Corps apparently doesn't think so, but the Lacertians have interacted with at least three other civilizations—there's plenty of physical evidence for that. And none of those civilizations are native to this rock. There's a star cluster, the edge of which starts just about 200 light-years beyond Skiathos. State thinks there might be a civilizational pod located there like the one we found near Cygnus 227."

"What's a pod, ma'am?"

"Civilizations sometimes nurture one another, through trade, conquest, or other interchange. We've met fewer than a dozen spacefaring races in 600 years, and the appearance of another three in such a brief time could be ... well ... good or bad."

"OK, ma'am. So, we're here to what? Recon on these three civilizations?"

"That's part of it. Dr. Wray was the first to see signs of non-Skiathos presence, when he got here three and a half years ago. Unless one or more of these species decides to make an appearance, finding out about them will be hell without cooperation from the natives. And ... also, there's no clear proof the Lacertians are even native to this rock."

The young woman gave a look of surprise. "They don't look like they're spacefaring caliber, ma'am."

"But they're also not like the other fauna on this planet, at least not in a significant way. Wray's team has logged over fifteen-hundred unique species, all of which share similar genetic codes and broadly similar phenotypes. Six legs seem to be the norm ... of those animals that do have legs. The few tetrapods we've observed have tails and are kept by the Lacertians, either as livestock or pets. Beside those few, no indigenous species have physical similarities to the Lacertians. In fact, on any other planet we likely would've presumed the two Lacertian castes were separate species. They only resemble one another by being humanoid."

Reaching up, Nadja tapped her tablet and a second, smaller humanoid form appeared beside the huge being that they'd been regarding. The smaller caste Lacertian had a lighter hue, a significantly smaller head, and slighter frame. It's appearance, overall, was less menacing and more docile. It was otherwise about the size of an adult human.

"How do they reproduce?" asked the Marine.

"It's anybody's guess. None of the species Wray has examined have genitalia. There's no discernable gendering ... or young, for that matter. Some type of parthenogenesis is our best guess. Perhaps young gestate outside the womb in some way and emerge full grown." She chuckled before muttering, "maybe they grow from a severed thumb. I dunno."

The Marine smiled but spoke sternly. "Ma'am. You're looking a bit tuckered. You need to hydrate, eat, and get some sleep."

Nadja agreed.

4: The Platform

The staff meeting the following day went easily enough. All in attendance had been nearly five months without any real structure and were cranky at having to adhere to the schedule of a new boss, but no one groused too much. For the time being, staff meetings would be daily; if all went well, Nadja intended to roll that back to once or twice per week.

She next took a stem-to-stern tour of the platform from the maintenance and operation chief, Mr. Eddy. He was like the thousand other naval warrants she'd ever met: hardworking, efficient, and jealous of his turf. But Nadja had been on many such tours. She knew the questions to ask, the forms to examine and annotate, and the right things to say to the harried chief to show him she was on his team. Naval service had not been so long ago that she didn't understand the importance of winning loyalty.

The vessel, the length of three football pitches and half as wide, looked great. It was old, but in top trim. In addition to the four Marine troop transports, there were four naval skiffs and enough escape pods for a full crew. Though lacking an FTL drive, the platform itself was space-worthy once buttoned-up and was resourced sufficiently to maintain a full complement for two years.

She spent the rest of the day learning procedures, inspecting stores, and signing forms. She needed to reset all the security protocols with her biometrics and give each crewmember his or her new access. It was a tedious and obscene spectacle of bureaucratic ritual, and she was happy for the day to come to an end.

On the good side, she had an admin assistant who was smart and efficient and to whom she intended to delegate much of her administrative work. The young man, Alejandro Payton by name, joined Nadja, along with Ken and Janet De Novo, for dinner late in the evening.

"There are a lot of enormously talented people on this survey mission," said Nadja. It shouldn't have been a surprise. Scads of people came to the frontier, bored at the sedate and docile lives they lived on the settled planets.

"I'm just surprised to hear people calling you 'ma'am,'" said Janet. The young woman was usually a chatterer, but being out on the edge of settled space was still sinking in with her. The young bride had seldom spoken on the trip and was only just beginning to talk since their arrival.

But the young woman had a point. When Nadja had left the Navy, she'd eschewed all things military. She was one of those professors who wanted her students—certainly her grad students, if not her undergrads—to call her by her given name. Even on her many State Department assignments she'd seldom been in charge and preferred greater informality. Slipping back into boss mode was going to take some doing.

"As I recall, Janet, it took you more than a year to stop calling me 'professor.'"

"No," the young bride objected vehemently.

"It was more like 18 months," said her other half.

Janet changed the subject out of the blue. "You know," she said, lowering her voice, "I think Gunter Wray and Melissa were having it on before she died."

"It explains a lot," said Nadja, not attempting to modulate her tone. It was a small station; people knew. "Especially why he went walkabout."

"Any sense on where he is?" asked Ken.

"Dropped planet-side not far from where Melissa was lost and sent his Marines away." That was something about which Nadja was still stewing. "I have the Marines working on a plan. It's a dangerous planet, but if he's still alive, he couldn't have walked far in two months. Have you made any sense of Melissa's research?"

"Just scratching the surface … ma'am," joked Janet. "She left her usual encyclopedia of notes and hundreds of hours of vids. She spent almost all of her time with the lower caste and didn't seem to be making any headway."

"Keep plugging and make a chart of all the places she visited. I'll be wrapped up in admin stuff for the next few days. Then I can jump in and help." Nadja thought. No, there was nothing to add that she hadn't already said. "I know you both heard it all before, but keep hydrated, eat, and sleep. It'll take a few days for your body clocks to adjust. Skiathos has a 21-hour day. Give it a few days before you dive in full-force."

"Will do," said Ken.

They chatted a while longer before Nadja suggested they all call it quits and get some rest. She insisted Alex Payton walk her to her quarters, partly because she couldn't quite recall where they were located, but mostly because she wanted to pick his brain. Administrative staff always knew things their bosses did not. And Alex had been on the station nearly three years.

"How are things going on site … really?" she asked him as they left the mess hall.

20

"People are getting along OK," he confided. "It was a big kick in the nuts for everybody when the transport went down. The captain was pretty popular, and Gunny Nice was a wonder, really kept things running around here."

"And Gunter Wray?"

The young man hesitated. "He got here six months before I did. The guy seemed enthused about his work, but … I dunno. He was hard to read." Alex looked at her as they walked. "Was he a friend of yours?"

"I knew him more by reputation, but he and I crossed paths."

"Mmm … he struck me as sort of fragile. His work seemed to be humming along—you should talk to his team about that—but I heard him say a couple of times he wasn't getting anywhere with the 'lizard people,' as he called them. That must have irked him. And he was pretty fond of Melissa."

"I understand that," mused Nadja. "She was likable. What about everyone else?"

The young man snorted pleasantly. "I've seldom worked with better people. As near as I can tell, no major substance abuse problems, not much excess drinking, and as far as I know, not a single fight in three years. That's a pretty good record."

"No fights? Even among the Marines?"

"Even among the Marines," he confirmed. "And I'm sure I would've heard about it."

The news gladdened her. There was always the outside possibility that affairs, serious problems, had gone untended of which Alex wasn't aware, but it was unlikely they would be those volcanic problems that might blow the top off their tiny community. Interpersonal problems were ubiquitous; a good manager handled them without letting it destroy the mission.

After she bid Alex a goodnight and settled into her quarters, she began to feel better. There was a veritable mountain range of work in front of her, including a great deal that she hadn't anticipated prior to her arrival. Her admin assistant's word had made her feel better about the 28 days that now stood between her and getting down planet-side.

5: The Search

To Nadja's delight, the days flew by. On day 30, she held a full showdown inspection of Marines and all their gear, from A to Z—it had been preceded by less-thoroughgoing inspection of all other departments—and everything was to her liking.

The inspection was followed by a station-wide kegger and barbecue. It was a practice she intended to implement regularly. Once-a-week barbecues and, in a tradition borrowed from Britain's Royal Navy of old, once-a-month costume carnivals would become part of station ritual. Mandatory fun was a morale builder and an ancient military custom she did not intend to forsake. All hands, both civilian and military, were required to attend.

Over a freshly tapped keg in the middle of their lovely gala, Nadja talked to Sgt. Lyn about the finishing touches of the next day's mission, the search for Wray. The young NCO had meshed well with the rest of the crew and had risen to the job of platoon sergeant beautifully, but even the five beers she'd imbibed couldn't hide her slight anxiety over the upcoming search. The troop transport incident that had killed 11 of their number may have been the result of equipment failure, but Skiathos was an enormous planet. None had lost sight of the fact that they might not be the only visitors on it. The Lacertians did not possess particle weapons, but others did.

"I think our plan is a solid one, ma'am," Lyn concluded about the proposal she and the other NCOs had submitted two weeks before.

Nadja agreed it made sense. The intel cell had earlier moved a drone into place to begin a low-level search pattern for Wray on the off-chance he had reactivated his transponder.

The next morning's search would have two troop transports begin a grid search of Wray's last known, using sensors to seek human bio signs at close range—the planet's dodgy EM patterns would allow little else. A third transport would fly above in overwatch. Only the pilots and gun crews would be onboard any of the transports. Even farther above, a naval skiff would fly additional security. The skiff wasn't a combat vehicle, per se, but it was designed better to absorb particle energy and had been refitted by the maintenance crew to search out any incoming vehicles or weapon signatures. If anyone else was out there, they would know about it in advance.

As Nadja and Sgt. Lyn finished their conversation, Nadja spied a head she'd scarcely seen since her arrival. The blond mop of Dr. Reem Sokay, head geologist, appeared on the stairs from down below and, after catching sight of Nadja, made its way toward the keg.

The two had spoken seldom since Nadja's arrival. She didn't blame the geologist one bit; rather, she was seized by a small fit of envy. Had circumstances gone as Nadja had hoped, she too would have been knuckled down with her work to the exclusion of all else. As it was, she'd only been able to help the De Novos review Melissa's work a few hours per day. The effort had availed them nothing.

"Reem, I'm happy you made it up," she said with a smile.

The scholar smiled back. "Well, when the boss says, 'mandatory fun,' it's hard to say no. Still, it's nice to see structure. Everything's just felt so ... hinky, especially since Gunter left."

"I hope we can bring him back. Did you know him well?"

"Yes. No. He was a tough guy to read, and he and I didn't always get on well. I don't think it's a secret he and Melissa had something going on. He didn't go immediately nutty after she died, but you could see him start to unravel. I'm with you. I hope he's still out there."

"After this long...." Nadja left the rest unsaid. "Look ... I can only justify giving three days to the search, but Melissa was working that general area, so I plan on picking up where she left off. If Gunter is still alive, there's a chance he's taken shelter among the locals. We'll hit all the villages and hamlets thereabouts over the next month."

"Would they do that?" The geologist's work didn't place her in direct contact with the natives of Skiathos.

"The locals? For reasons I can't even begin to guess, the Lacertians appear to like humans. Even the warrior caste seems more curious about us than anything, despite that one little incident."

Nadja had learned that two years earlier a Marine had panicked and fired his weapon when one of the warriors had reached down and picked up an anthropologist during a planet-side visit. The warrior's injury had not been fatal, and beyond grabbing the Marine, disarming him, and giving him a good shaking, the warrior had not retaliated. The entire team thereafter had been restricted to a kraal in which the worker caste was housed and had slipped away two days later, never to return to that village.

"I was here when that happened," said Reem. "Gunter came up with a dozen different theories about what motivates them ... and shot each one of those down in succession. He finally decided their focus should be on this worker caste you folks talk about, but I never figured any of it out. I'm just having a tough time puzzling out why there's so much electromagnetic interference on this rock. The patterns don't seem to extend from the planet's poles. It would help if we could deploy the satellite net."

"That's something everyone says, but State says 'no.' It would seem too much like we were staking a claim to the planet."

"Yeah, I know. Treaties. But drones have their limits and … ugh, they are slow."

"Make up a list," said Nadja, "and I'll see if I can get you some more resources. But either way, it looks like we're doing it the old-fashioned way, low and slow."

————

The search kicked off at first light the following morning, and it took about 30 minutes for their small convoy to ascend into low planetary orbit, swiftly travel the distance to the search area, and then descend in a leisurely loop to their destination. Sgt. Lyn was back at the CP to coordinate their efforts, and Nadja had opted to take an additional skiff along to begin a low aerial survey of the few villages in the vicinity. Socio-cultural teams had visited none of the places, and Nadja wanted an eyes-on to get a sense of what they had in store when they began their surveys three days hence.

Beside the pilot and a door-gunner, the skiff held only Nadja and the high-resolution scanning equipment Chief Eddy had placed within. Throughout the slow arc of their descent, the system would take a series of visual scans of the surrounding area; the scans would automatically be relayed to Sgt. Lyn at the CP for the intel cell to run through the AI. If as much as a single desiccated human bone was visible in their search area, the AI would find it.

"'Going dark,' my ass," Nadja muttered under her breath. She again pondered the wisdom of having waited a month to commence the search for Wray, but came to the same conclusion. The man already had been off the grid for more than two months, and she'd needed the extra weeks to acclimate herself and, just as important, to ensure that the crew she had inherited was working at close to optimal level. She didn't regret waiting, but considered ringing Wray's neck, if they ever did find him alive.

Still, it was a splendid day. Skiathos was a place of incomparable beauty, especially from high above, and after they'd popped the hatches, the air was remarkably fresh and breathable even at 15,000 meters. The rush of air was cool, but the planet would warm them as they descended.

24

The EM disturbances that the teams had experienced in the past were local and random—at least they'd appeared to be—and usually only effected less robust systems. She'd made the decision to have the first skiff keep a visual lock on the troop transports as the Marines searched, just in case. Even if comms crapped out, they would at least know the location of each transport. As she thought of that precaution, she could hear the occasional crackle and glitch in her earpiece as the Marines and support personnel chattered back and forth, giving orders, sharing information, and occasionally cracking wise.

"Keep the chatter down, ladies. The boss is listening in," Nadja said over her link. A moment's silence followed before the chatter continued, sans the joking. But the crackling and glitching continued. There definitely was something odd about this planet.

Their search continued for the next four hours without interruption. As Nadja's skiff skimmed from one village to the next, she kept one ear and half her mind on the search. The Marines soon fell into a rhythm that saw their search go by at a startling rate. Throughout, Lyn's voice could be heard from time to time, 'focus,' 'cut the chatter,' 'move to next grid.' It was all remarkably well ordered, and Nadja was even more pleased that they'd taken the extra month to train.

The Marines were competent, but there was no sign of anything other than sand, native flora and fauna, and the occasional Lacertians who popped up to regard the passing skiffs and transports with what appeared to be curiosity.

At the end of those four hours, Nadja had seen all she wanted to see and had come up with a tentative plan on how to proceed in coming days. She shot her notes to Ken back at the platform and sat back to enjoy a few minutes sight-seeing, one leg dangling out the skiff's cargo door. Three days hence, they would begin a series of engagements with locals at three small hamlets Melissa had dubbed 'London,' 'Paris,' and 'Madrid,' in honor of three great cities of old Earth.

Gunter had convinced Melissa that the worker-caste was a more productive avenue for understanding the Lacertians, and the socio-cultural teams had devoted their energies to that group. Nadja suspected a certain bias in their decision.

Certainly, the workers were more docile and easier to engage, but everything she'd read and observed said they were less intelligent, with weaker attention spans. And though the warrior caste was amiable and inquisitive, they tended to bore quickly of their would-be interviewers and to shoo them off to the worker-caste living areas.

It all smacked of convenience rather than good research design, especially given the members of the warrior caste truly were fearsome and intimidating. Often armored and always armed with an assortment of crude blades, bows, and cudgels, the gigantic warriors had no respect for personal space and would often pat, hug, and even pick up humans who they had only just encountered. Such overweening familiarity was enough that even an experienced field researcher, such as Wray, might find it daunting.

Time enough to sort that out later.

The Marines on search duty would be working 10-hour shifts for the next several days, so Nadja didn't see it as good leadership to return to the platform after her survey. The next six hours passed with her trailing after the troop transports, following up on anomalies they'd sighted and building a clearer picture of the area in which they'd soon be working, often skimming along the terrain at barely 50 meters above dunes and flats. At that elevation, especially during midday, the heat of the planet was like a pulse, but the place smelled even more delightful, like mystery and spice. It was an intoxicating environment, and to Nadja's surprise, she could make out occasional patches of green that dotted the desert floor like a thin fuzz.

On three occasions that day, the observation skiff detected what might have been movement of other vessels on the extreme edge of their sensor range. On each occasion, the Marines responded rapidly and properly by dropping below the horizon and concealing themselves behind a sand dune or hillock until the anomaly was confirmed as an anomaly.

It was a gut-wrenching 10 hours. There existed any manner of technology that could conceal or shroud a large ship from visual or sensor detection—the platform from which they worked had such a system—but none of those worked perfectly and all were costly. They would keep their eyes open, attempting to discern any patterns in these 'anomalies,' for they might well be just that.

There was always the perfectly reasonable possibility that the rock's peculiar EM pattern was merely teasing, making fun of their anxiety and naivety, but the mission had lost a dozen people in less than six months. Nadja would be damned if they lost more.

———

It took precisely 30 minutes for the Marine crews to switch out, for the maintenance team to PMCS the transports, and for the next shift to launch from the platform to continue the search. Second shift would be doing

26

most of their work at night, so Nadja decided it would be prudent to have an extra vehicle along to play the role she had during daylight. Sgt. Matthews took a fresh skiff and played foreman on site, and Sgt. Bisbee took over for Sgt. Lyn in the CP.

The first-shift Marines endured a short after-action brief, before heading to their berths to rest; Nadja stopped into the CP for 30 minutes to observe shift-change, before heading to meet with the De Novos in the office the three shared. She wanted to get a little bit of work in before sleep and a return to a second day in her observation skiff.

The heat had drained her, and it was unlikely anyone expected her to be out on the search for Wray on the second and third days. It was one of the perks of being boss: the person in charge wasn't expected to do the legwork. But Nadja was still new and wanted to set a good example. And, yes, she was sometimes like a dog with a bone, unable to let go.

So, she would weather the heat again tomorrow and then the day after. The odds were incredibly slim. But if Gunter Wray was out there, she intended to find him.

6: A Rescue

N
adja awoke with a start, her breathing tortured, and her chest on fire. Pain seemed to cloak her entire body. It was dark, and when she sat up, she nearly screamed. The torment was unimaginable, unlike anything she'd ever experienced, and her head swam so wildly, she felt herself again slipping toward unconsciousness.

"*Fuck*," she finally managed to half scream and half rasp in a pathetic mewl.

There was a flurry of motion when something large occluded what scant light there was around her, and something cool pressed against her forehead.

The darkness took her.

Three more times she swam up from the inky depths, her chest killing her from the pressure. Three more times she was pulled back down after breaking the surface. Each time gave her just a scant view of the light and a return of the pain. She just couldn't breathe. And her body ... she'd never hurt so much.

"What's your name?" she heard on her fourth or fifth time at the surface.

She tried to speak, but something pathetic came out. How much time had passed? Where was she? Where were the Marines?

"You need to drink this."

Nadja felt something behind her, a human hand, and felt herself lifted half to sitting. There was something else, something bigger, harder, cooler.

"Nadja," she squeaked out. "Nadja Bikram." She wanted to cry, mostly because of the pathetic blubbering she heard in her voice when she said those few words. Some recess in her mind snapped to attention, and an inner voice screamed at her. *Bikram, you are not going to fucking cry.*

Something hard pressed against her lips, and she found herself drinking. It was bitter and cool, and the vessel at her lips continued to rise until she began to cough. The pain continued, but was no longer searing, and as the vessel moved from her lips, she glanced up into the darkness. Two enormous golden cat's eyes stared back at her.

She later flattered herself that it was the concoction she'd just imbibed that caused her to faint away.

———

28

When she next stirred, it seemed like a millennium had passed, and the pain that before had tormented her nearly was gone. What remained was a dull and raspy ache that would allow her to sleep no longer. She had a difficult time opening her eyes, and when she did, there was the same scant light around her as before.

The first thing she saw was a figure moving toward her. Nadja blinked, tried to lift a hand to clear her eyes, and failed. Wherever she was, it was hot—she was burning up. A hand rested on her shoulder, and she felt something cool and damp applied to her forehead and eyes. She endured these ministrations until she could bear it no more.

"Where am I?" Her voice was weak and raspy, but sounded otherwise her own.

"At a camp in the central desert ... or at least that's what the map calls it," the woman replied. "Here, take a drink of this."

A flask came to Nadja's lips, blessing her with more of the bitter concoction from before. At the woman's prompting, she took two more gulps of the stuff.

"How did I get here?" she asked after a few tepid coughs.

"Stig brought you ... four days ago. You were a mess."

"Who's ...." Nadja, eyes now open, caught a clear glimpse of the young woman to whom she'd been speaking: dark hair, olive skin, strong face. The woman's Marine Corps uniform said it all. "Gunnery Sergeant Nice. You're supposed to be dead."

The woman reached behind Nadja and helped her sit up. "I thought I was a time or two. But Blacky's band rescued us."

"Bl...?"

"He's chief here. Me and Lance Corporal Spiros survived impact, but Spiros was a mess. Blacky and his people helped him like they helped you."

It took a moment for Nadja's confusion to clear. "Wait ... why didn't you wait at the crash site?"

"Blacky's band got there first. We were taking some vids of a few of them when we got hit. Dr. Downey was thinking about stopping for a chat."

"You were shot down?" Nadja let out a slight gasp. Memories of what had transpired on the second, no, third day of their search for Wray hit her. From nowhere, a sudden flurry of panicked transmissions from Marines in the transports, "COUNTERMEASURES. COUNTERMEASURES. COUNTERMEASURES," signaling incoming weapons fire, followed by

29

the rapid staccato of commands, "'HARD PORT,' 'HARD STARBOARD,' 'DECK. DECK. DECK.'"

Before she could even respond to seek clarification, her skiff had taken fire. The door gunner's arm had disappeared in a flash of light and blood, and she, foolishly, had popped her harness to move to the man's aid. A faint sensation of falling followed and then nothing. A sudden maneuver by the pilot must have pitched her out the cargo door beside which she'd been stationed.

Nadja was an idiot, and it was a wonder she was alive. *God protects fools and children.*

"You OK?" the gunnery sergeant asked.

"Yeah. I had a moment. Tell me what happened the day you went down."

"Like I said, we were taking a few vids, and Dr. Downey said it might be nice to stop and chat—she was like that sometimes. Next thing you know, proximity alert went off, and the planet was corkscrewing up toward us. I don't know how, but I was able to get up and out of my harness. As near as I could tell, Spiros was the only other one still alive after the dust settled."

"Chief Eddy said a fuel cell ruptured."

The gunnery sergeant made an ugly noise. "I think that's what it was meant to look like. Blacky and a few of his people were there in no time. Fortunately, they had the common sense ... or instinct to pull us behind some of that high brush you sometimes get out here. A small skiff of some sort slipped by a minute or so later and dropped some kind of incendiary device on the crash site."

"Human?"

"Ma'am, I couldn't tell. I was in a state, and it was mostly shrouded."

"What about your transponders?"

The young NCO looked down at her left wrist. "I think it's still online, but the EM fields around here are fucked. These little contraptions aren't powerful enough to push through a signal."

"And the locals took you away right after the crash?" Nadja was still tired and dizzy, but her thoughts were clearing.

"They are downright protective. I didn't understand that until I spent some time with them. But I see why now." The NCO took Nadja by the elbow. "That stuff they gave you works wonders, but it's at its best if you get some exercise between doses. Take a couple of turns around the hooch with me, and you'll need to rest some more. It'll be a day or two before you're feeling better."

Nadja was soon on her feet and wobbling an unsteady course around the large and hot tent in which she'd been sleeping. Her exercise lasted all of five minutes, by the end of which she was exhausted and trembling. Gunnery Sergeant Nice helped lay her back down.

Then it occurred to her tired brain. "Wait. How do you know how their medicine works??"

"They told me," the young woman replied moments before Nadja fell into slumber.

7: In Loco Parentis

'Ready for a turnaround camp, ma'am?"

Nadja had awoken only a few minutes before, and to her surprise and delight the pain that had beset her was all but gone. It had been replaced by a stubborn stiffness throughout her chest, ribs, and lower torso. In the gloom of the tent, a pair of hands helped her sit up. It seemed like another day or more had passed, but she wasn't sure. Nor did she care. She needed to know something more important.

"Yes," she replied in a normal voice. "So, you can talk to them?"

A faint smile formed and disappeared on the NCO's face as she offered Nadja a drink from a small flask. "Dr. Downey spent all her time trying to communicate with the smaller ones," said the Marine after Nadja took three more swallows of the bitter blend. "They're not really talkative."

It was like a freight-train hit Nadja, one that slowly had been coming toward her for the past seven years as she'd stood on the tracks and stared vacuously at its approach. She wondered whether her professional reputation would survive at all. "The little ones are children, aren't they?"

"They are."

"But…," Nadja attempted to backpedal, "they speak the same language as the warrior caste … the adults, that is."

"You've never been a mother, have you ma'am?"

"No … does it…. Oh, jeez."

"I crapped out six little darlings before I joined the Marines. Evidently, the parents on this rock speak baby-talk to their toddlers, too."

"So, I've been trying to translate goo-goo, gah-gah for the last seven years?"

"If it makes you feel any better, ma'am, I was here a month before I figured it out. And the little ones do make the same basic sounds as the adults, but they don't actually start forming real words until right before their change."

By that time, the two had stood and made it to the opening of the tent. Nice continued hesitantly.

"How much time have you spent among them, ma'am?"

"None."

"OK, they can be a little overwhelming at first … you know, touchy, feely, may try to pick you up and cuddle. But they all know you've been injured. Just be prepared. Oh … and don't worry too much about the claws.

They're always very careful with those. But watch out for their heel spikes. Those things are like razors."

The young woman pulled back the tent flap. The heat, which had been oppressive in the closed tent, was diminished by a sudden spot of breeze, but the sun was startling. The young Marine led Nadja to what appeared to be a bench just outside the tent opening and motioned her to sit.

"Thanks," Nadja said. She felt much better, but the fatigue she'd experienced earlier was still there, and her body still trembled slightly. As her eyes grew accustomed to the glare, she saw several colossal forms busying themselves around camp. The sight took her breath away; there was no preparing for such a thing.

"I try to be proactive," said the Marine. "They bore more quickly that way." She turned to the nearest Lacertian and called out. "Hey, lunkhead, c'mere!"

Taking three long strides, the fit and trim Marine planted a foot on the top of the giant's knee—if it truly was a knee—and launched herself into the being's awaiting arms. Soon, the smiling NCO, one arm draped over an enormous shoulder, was playfully tugging on one of the two lethal canines on the top row of the Lacertian's teeth.

To Nadja's surprise, the Lacertian began making what she could only imagine were contented and happy purrs, whirrs, and peeps. At least, they would have been contented noises made by a terrestrial being. Even as that thought came to her, the creature's levity increased as Gunny Nice began friskily using the fang as a handle to jostle her playmate's head back and forth.

How could Gunter and Melissa have missed this? And there were other teams before them? "No," she said aloud. The sound that came from the native was in no way human, but there was something about it. "That can't be laughter. I'm just projecting."

"They're a lot like us, ma'am," came a voice to her right.

Glancing over, she saw a lean and tall young man standing a few meters away enjoying the same spectacle as her.

"Lance Corporal Spiros." She extended a hand, and the young man took a step closer and accepted it.

The Marine, who rested lightly on a walking stick, smiled. "I'm going out on a limb and saying you must be Nadja Bikram. Is it doctor, or should I call you something else?"

"Doctor's fine. I'm Melissa Downey's replacement."

"That's what Gunny figured. How's the rest of the detachment doing?"

A kilowatt jolt shot through Nadja, and she couldn't squelch a short-tempered, "*fuck*." In her stupor, she hadn't even thought of her team of Marines and civilians. She wanted to kick herself.

"If there is a God in heaven, and if Sgt. Lyn listened to my orders, they should have buttoned up the platform, pushed it into low orbit, and got on the Pinpoint and called for naval support from Clem's World."

"You mean Sgt. Lyn from fourth squad? She's here?"

"She and her squad came in with me last month."

"Nah, ma'am. She'll do as she's ordered. Sgt. Lyn is good people."

"If she doesn't, there are going to be some hides tacked to my wall."

"Don't do that, ma'am. I used to have a crush on her back in the day."

Whether prompted by Nadja's short-tempered outburst or by Spiros's goofy laughter, Gunny jumped down from the Lacertian's embrace and led the giant by his lethal looking paw over to where she sat.

"Ma'am, this is my boy Stig. He's the one who dragged you in six days ago."

Stig reached his free hand over and playfully tossed Spiros's hair, but the giant made no move to approach Nadja, only regarding her carefully while occasionally cocking his head at different angles. The being's multiple eyelids flicked from time to time.

"How do you say, 'Hi'?" she asked of the Marines.

"That was the great breakthrough, ma'am. Me and Spiros understand a couple hundred of their words, but can only pronounce some of them. They can't say our words much better, but they're clever and quick learners."

"So … just say, 'Hi'?"

The Marine nodded.

Nadja swallowed her heart, stood, took two steps forward, and, hand extended, said, "Hi, Stig."

The native gently took her hand in his, and two slight pops emanated from the back of his throat.

Nadja had learned her first word in Lacertian.

———

After a few nibbles of jerky, which Gunny guaranteed was unpleasant, but perfectly edible, she had another dose of the bitter mixture Spiros named the "good stuff" from a bronze-shouldered Lacertian, who Gunny called Greta. The two human women then spent many hours talking with the camp doctor—for that's exactly what Greta was—and everything was full steam ahead from that moment.

34

The seven years Nadja had spent studying the language had not been totally fruitless. She had learned the various phonemes, the grunts, purrs, whirrs, growls, chirps, and pops, and, even without her translation AI, was able to emulate virtually every one with a high degree of felicity. She needed only to apply meanings to the various sounds and to divine the syntax of the various utterances.

By the time the excited linguist began to grow weary two hours later, she'd already amassed a lexicon nearly to rival Gunny's.

"I should've made you come back to the hooch when Spiros did," warned the gunnery sergeant, as she steered Nadja back to the tent the three shared. "That stuff is good for you, but it sometimes knocks you out after a bad injury."

"I was having too much fun and learning too much. Jeez, seven years. I feel like a dolt."

"Well, ma'am, there's nothing like just jumping in feet first. What Spiros and I learned, we learned out of necessity."

But wasn't that the reason Nadja had travelled the four months to Skiathos, at least in part? Subtle doubts about the type of research being done there was certainly part of it. But there also was that hidden notion that living comfortably on a settled world took a certain something from people. Risks had to be taken, otherwise there was never any real reward.

She opted to philosophize at another time.

At the tent, Gunny produced a tiny lamp and began to lay Nadja down for bed.

"Gunny, I'm not a cripple."

"Ma'am, soak it in. Greta thinks you'll be better by tomorrow. And Blacky wants to be on the move first light."

"Move? To where?"

"They're nomads, ma'am. They follow the rains to graze their critters and can't afford to stay here much longer."

Nadja was seized by another upwelling of curiosity. There was so much about these people she didn't understand. And she didn't know where to start. The livelihood she would ask about later. One thing she decided she needed to know first.

"What's in the 'good stuff'?"

"Ah, ma'am, you're talking deep and dark magic there," the Marine teased. The young woman paused, the only sound inside the tent being the light snores of Spiros across the way. "It's this root that grows hereabouts. They use it for all sorts of things. Greta somehow mutters some mumbo-jumbo over it and turns it into some sort of medicine. Truth be told, I'd rather be in a proper med-bay with a Class IV trauma surgeon, but that stuff ... wow."

"Like how 'wow'?"

In the half-light of the tiny lamp, the Marine's features softened, and her tone turned serious. "You were pretty bad off when you got here. Greta wasn't sure what to make of you. You were stove up pretty good." She made a slight motion with her head. "But Spiros there ... ma'am, I swear to God. I had no hopes he was going to make it. Plasma burns, bad internal injuries, really bad, and missing a couple hunks of him."

"How?"

"I dunno, ma'am. Greta knew nothing about human physiology, but whatever is in the stuff helped her stitch Spiros back together. He's damn-near a hundred percent now."

"That's amazing." Human medical science had advanced in leaps and bounds in recent centuries, and there weren't too many traumatic injuries short of complete decapitation that couldn't be healed with the proper surgeon and necessary equipment. But it amazed Nadja as much as it did Gunny that a native healer with no knowledge of human anatomy could accomplish such a feat. There was something there; she just hoped they would have the time and opportunity to figure it out.

"Ma'am, when are we getting out of here?" The Marine's face was now serious.

"And go where? If Sgt. Lyn followed orders, the platform should be in orbit. In any event, we have no way of signaling for help."

"Ah, ma'am. I've been thinking about that." Gunny reached into her pocket and procured a small tube. She rolled it out on the sleeping pad between them. The three-dimensional chart gave off a slight glow. "Beside my pistol, I only had a few things in my pockets and on my BV that weren't damaged or destroyed when we went down. This here lovely map tells me that we are right there." The young NCO pointed to a low and broad valley at the middle of the map.

"Gunny, I'm assuming you've got a plan." A Marine was a Marine, and clearly this Marine had thought out everything and wouldn't be bringing it up if she hadn't.

The young woman smiled. "See this highland area here? About 400 klicks away, grid north by northwest?"

"What about it?"

"Not every region on this planet has the same EM problems as the place we're in right now. In fact, we're in one of the worst spots, especially at ground level. It doesn't screw up everything electrical, but it totally mutes our transponder signals."

"And this area over here?"

"I took Dr. Sokay on a couple of surveys there, before things went sideways. Damn near normal EM signature there, ma'am. But Spiros and I haven't quite gotten to the point where our language skills are strong enough to ask Blacky whether he can help us get there."

Nadja sensed a hint of hesitation. There was something else. "So, what's the other problem?"

"The Lacertians are a fighting and feuding people, ma'am. And I reckon the place we need to reach is far outside the territory of Blacky's band. Whoever owns that patch would see them coming through as an invasion. The band has already had a couple of dustups with their neighbors since we've been with them. They don't joke around when it comes to war. It is no bullshit bloody and violent."

"What if we went alone?"

The Marine again thought. "I don't know if that's an option ma'am. I mean, I'm sure Stig would give us a riding animal, and both Spiros and I have become pretty handy at the reins, but there's something about these people. I think it's hardwired into them to not allow a cub, or any small humanoid, to come to harm. It's the reason they rescued the three of us and brought us back here to heal. I think, if we tried to go, they would either stop us or feel compelled to come along."

"OK, what do you propose?"

"These folks are smart, ma'am. Really smart. They know we're not their children. They just have that protecting impulse. Neither Spiros nor I have the chops, but you might be able to reason with them."

Nadja barked a laugh. "You've learned more of their language in six months than I have in seven years."

"No, ma'am. You know the language better after two hours than I do after six months," the Marine corrected. "Ma'am, don't make me have to pull rank. You know as well as I do that no one outranks a gunnery sergeant when she's pissed.

"OK, what's our first move?"

"Stig. He lets us ride one of his mounts, and he is far and away the most patient with us, even more patient than Greta. Let him teach you Lacertian."

"OK. Let's do it." An exhausted Nadja was asleep before Nice had even shut off the lamp.

8: The Band

The next morning, they were up with the sun and breaking camp. The whole affair was remarkably swift, but required a great deal of muscle. Several times, Nadja stopped passing Lacertians and sought their assistance reaching something she couldn't or helping her lift an onerous bundle. The 60-ish academic was strong, as strong as state-of-the-art genetic manipulation could make her, but the power of even the lower-caste Lacertians (as she still thought of the children) was remarkable. And the adults were always helpful.

Once camp was broken, many score large and hardy six-legged beasts, not unlike some demented artist's version of a water buffalo, but with a heavy tail and long body, appeared from behind a slight hillock where they'd been picketed. The creatures were the only things she had so far encountered in camp that exuded an unpleasant odor, and over the next 30 minutes, all present loaded the beasts with the camp's various shelters, riggings, and instruments.

One of their hosts, whom Gunny had christened Phillip, showed Nadja how to lash the pack saddle to the animal and several times required her to repeat the process, though she was certain she'd replicated his knots and cinches properly on the first try.

"It's the way they have of teaching the young," Gunny said in response to her inquiry about the episode. "The cubs don't start to talk until right before their change, so there's a lot of demonstration and drill. The little ones are remarkably smart, pick the stuff right up."

"You said something about a 'change' before. What's that mean?"

"Oh," the Marine chuckled. "See those tiny little rug rats running around camp?"

Nadja looked and saw several small and lean animals racing about that she'd assumed to be simple livestock or pets. The largest weren't much smaller than an adult human, the smallest barely 60 centimeters at the shoulder. All had tiny heads, long thin necks, feeble arms, powerful legs, and heavy tails, the last of which seemed to stabilize the animals as they jetted about.

"Not pets, ma'am," Gunny continued. "Those are infant Lacertians."

"What the...?" she whispered and felt a smile begin to form on her face. Things were beginning to come together.

"I don't know how they breed, exactly. But every few months, some of them disappear for a time. When they come back, they have a bunch of those little gizmos with 'em. They ain't much bigger than chickens then, but they grow fast. When they get big enough, their tails just drop off." The Marine pointed to one of the larger of the infants, not quite so thin and with a slightly larger head. "See that one. His tail is about ready to go."

"Oh, my gosh," whispered Nadja. She didn't know where to begin.

"Usually about that same time," continued Gunny, "a hunting party will take a few of the adolescents, the cubs, with them on a hunt. When they bring them back a few weeks later, they've all completely changed."

"Changed? How?"

"They're bigger, better developed, not quite the size of adults yet but close. They need another few weeks of filling out, but by then you can't tell them from the rest. And they can talk."

"It's that quick? Is there some sort of...? How does it work?"

"That part, ma'am, I can't tell you. But I do know it involves a change in diet. The cubs eat nothing but greens until right before they change. Then for a time it's all meat."

An annoyed squawk by Phillip reminded them there was work to be done, and at that same time Spiros appeared leading another animal, this one a leaner version of the beasts of burden they'd been loading with gear. Stig was a few steps behind.

"Our ride," said Gunny.

The creature was lovely in its own way, but exuded the same pungent musk as the others, and when it drew closer, Stig took Nadja gently by the shoulder and steered her toward the bench on which she'd sat the day before. He motioned to it.

"*What?*" she asked in Lacertian. She already had learned another two dozen words that morning and was committed to immersing herself.

"*Move.*"

"*Where?*" And then it struck her. "Oh, saddle?"

The Lacertian peeped pleasantly.

To her still weakened body, the thing felt like it weighed a metric ton, and wrangling it the short distance to their mount caused her to strain, grunt, and groan. It helped not at all that the heat of the day had made its appearance.

Arriving at the skittish and shifting beast, Nadja paused to catch her breath. Stig stood beside her patiently. After a few moments, she took the weighty contraption, which appeared to be constructed of some sort of heavy leather over a metal frame, and pulled it up to her chest. Tossing one knee underneath, she managed to chuck the ungainly thing in one move onto the back of the enormous beast. It was a lift of two meters. She breathed a sigh of relief.

Stig promptly pulled the thing back to the ground, spun it once, and pointed to a thick metal ring that appeared to be the front of the saddle.

"Oh, crap," she whispered. Her next try was less fluid, and after raising the saddle, she stood breathing even more heavily.

Stig again pulled the saddle to the ground. This time, he moved immediately behind her and, using the back of his knuckles so as not to cut her with his enormous claws, guided her right hand to a point at the rear of the saddle and her left to a spot near the metal ring. When she again lifted, it was with the slight assistance of his hands, again turned so as not to nick her.

The saddle rose and fell several more times before Stig, still behind her and his great hands extended before her, showed her how to cinch the saddle properly beneath.

"Done," he said. *"Food."*

She stood a moment longer, regarding the side of the smelly and freshly saddled beast. She wanted to kick Stig over the whole exhausting and ridiculous display. She still shook slightly from the exertion, and her stomach growled, her having ingested little since her arrival but the "good stuff," which was healing but not especially filling.

Instead of slugging Stig, she turned toward him. He was mere centimeters away and gave her a loving pat on the shoulder. His gentleness was indescribable, and she had to fight down a lump of something inside, an emotion as foreign to her as was the creature standing before her. She resisted, and instead grabbed him by the wrist and dragged him toward where Gunny and Spiros were gathered with a knot of Lacertians eating some sort of greens from a large plate on the ground.

The CAP treatment they'd received couldn't protect them from every pathogen or toxin, especially on a planet not completely surveyed, but the Marines had assured her the food in camp was edible. That alone was a wonder. She knelt and examined one of the morsels before picking it up. The green was a tad larger and wider than a human thumb. It looked like an especially stubby and thick blade of grass.

"What's this?"

"Life," said Greta, who squatted to her left.

From the corner of her eye, Nadja saw Gunny and Spiros nibbling away and threw caution to the wind. The moment after she took her first bite, she found herself sitting flat on her ass. A gale of laughter, both human and Lacertian, assailed her.

"What the fuck?" As she sat back up, it occurred to her something had coursed through her body.

"Sorry, ma'am," said a still chuckling Gunny. "We couldn't resist."

"What was that?"

Gunny held up a green and squeezed the short crescent stalk lengthwise until it popped, releasing a slight spark of electricity. "It's got a kick. You have to nibble them slow, or you'll get a shock."

"Assholes," Nadja grumbled, resisting a smile. "This is how you treat the sick and dying?"

"You're not dying, ma'am," said a still smiling Gunny, "but you need to eat. It'll help in the healing."

She did eat and enjoyed the companionship and humor of her practical jokers, and as they continued their meal, the words in Lacertian flew at her like a hailstorm.

When breakfast was done, Nadja placed a timorous foot on the top of Stig's proffered thigh and mounted the smelly beast she'd earlier saddled. He was soon on the beast behind her, and with a thunderous call from Blacky a hundred or more meters ahead, the long column of the band slowly lurched into motion and made its ponderous way to new pastures.

By her count, there were about 300 adults in the band and around half that many cubs, as Gunny referred to the adolescents. The small and extremely lizard-like infants numbered many hundreds more, and these dashed in and out of the column, dodging, jumping, rolling, playing, and grazing as they went. The youngest Lacertians were disorder incarnate, and the adults made no effort to temper or stem their anarchy.

The cubs were the subject of careful supervision though, as was Nadja. Throughout their long morning's ride, Stig showed her the reins and how to handle the animal while pointing out items of interest along the way, giving words to every manner of item, both special and mundane.

During one of her riding companion's few lulls, she found herself pondering him, and it struck her that she'd come to think of Stig as 'him.' She wondered why that was so; her new friends appeared thoroughly devoid of gender. Perhaps it was the names Gunny had given them, each of which was the best human rendering of the Lacertian's appellation. Perhaps it was Stig's powerful physique, which resembled that of an enormous human male in so many ways, from the thick shoulders and powerful arms to the ridiculously muscular thighs.

But, no. Greta had the same powerful body, but somehow in Nadja's mind Greta was a "her." Was she projecting? Maybe. But there was that one moment when Stig regarded her earlier in the morning after watching her with the saddle, and there was … what? Was there something in that gaze a loving and approving father might give? Or a doting mother?

Nadja felt something coil inside her. It had to be her injury and the shock of their current circumstance; she was never sentimental or emotional. But the feeling she'd experienced with Stig that morning came to mind.

She'd never been close to her parents. Both were in finance and when she was young had often been away on business or pleasure or … just to get away. After leaving for college, she only occasionally saw or spoke with them. It was that way for many of her friends too. Family gatherings were rare and often had the flavor of a reunion of old college chums, people with whom one might get together every five or 10 years for a beer and for a rehashing of old times.

Science had given them long lives and impeccable health, but what had all that taken from them? Or was it something else? Was it just something in her?

She shook all that off. It was just the injury talking.

Leaning back into Stig, she pointed to a distant range of hills and asked him its name.

9: The Path

A t just past midday, they crested a low ridge, and a broad valley lay before them. Here and there were patches of green fuzz, but Stig pronounced those insufficient to meet their needs. Still, it was a bit of fodder, and there was sufficient water at a small tank to keep the band moving. It was also a good place to rest during the heat of the day.

Nadja was sore, but she'd learned much during her turn in the saddle with Stig. He was thoughtful and generous and answered her questions freely. It was remarkable how easily the language was coming to her. To acquire anything approaching working facility in a language, at least any human language, required about 1,500 words of basic vocabulary. She was confident she already was about 20 percent there. Her tablet, which haply had survived her fall from the sky, would help chart her progress.

The language, as she'd come to realize, was mostly topic and comment with a variety of sounds to represent moods, states, desires, and degrees of certainty. There were very few proper verbs. Pops and cracks formed in the back of the throat represented the finer emotions; anger and aggression were signaled by deep barks and growls (but those phonemes also signaled doubt, humor, and intense curiosity), and most proper nouns were enunciated using a variety of coos, barks, and whirrs. There seemed to be a deeper system as to what sounds signaled what types of noun, but Nadja hadn't yet teased out that detail. It would all come.

If Stig was surprised at her ability to enunciate Lacertian sounds, he said nothing of it. Gunny and Spiros could only replicate a tiny handful of words. Nadja fancied that given a month or three she would be able to converse with Stig and his companions with a fair degree of fluency.

That simply wasn't soon enough. As much as the linguist in her wanted to lean back and bask in this experience, there was something dangerous afoot. Someone else clearly was on this planet, and she and her people were in danger. She, Gunny, and Spiros needed to find some way to contact the platform—she gulped at the thought—if the platform still existed.

Who had attacked them? And why?

She and Gunny went over those topics during their midday break, while all present nibbled on some greens and Spiros goofed around with Stig and some others. The group appeared to be trying to teach the young Marine to wield Stig's cumbersome sword, a curved and razor-edged blade of some 180 centimeters.

"I spent most of the last six months out of my gourd worrying about the rest of the Marines," said Gunny at one point. "And there were no other attacks before you arrived?"

"Not a one, but Matthews had the place locked down before I arrived. The only mission off the platform was when Wray flipped out."

Gunny laughed. "The frontier ain't for everybody, and Dr. Wray always struck me as sort of...."

"Fragile? That's the word I've heard."

"Yeah. Like I said. Ain't for everybody." The NCO hesitated again. "I would have tried getting out of here on foot earlier, but was too banged up that first few weeks, and once I figured out these guys wouldn't do Spiros any harm, the band had already moved a few hundred klicks farther south. This is actually the closest we've been to a feasible extract point since I've been with these guys."

"Which is why we're not going to miss the opportunity," Nadja added. "And stop beating yourself up. According to Stig, there are a lot of predators in this part of the planet that would happily eat a cub ... or a stray Marine. You were right to stay put and form a plan."

The woman nodded. "Agreed, ma'am. The band doesn't keep count on the infants, I think, but they've lost a few cubs since we've been with them. Gwyneth took some of the lads for a hunt after one got snatched. The critter they brought back looked like an especially big and greasy tiger ... if a tiger had too many legs and a shitload of eyes. This is a wild-ass country."

"Have you heard them talk about other outsiders?" asked Nadja on an impulse.

"Nah. My language isn't that good, ma'am. But they didn't seem terribly shocked or frightened when they first encountered Spiros and me. I mean ... beyond that impulse of theirs to protect us, which I really think is hardwired into them, they're smart people. They must know we're not from the neighborhood. It doesn't seem to shock them."

"Good point, Gunny." She pursed her lips. "Ugh. I have to powder my nose. What's a person use for ...?" It was her first bowel movement since regaining consciousness.

"Hold on." Gunny walked over to a pack and returned with a small wad of what looked like cloth. "Leaves, but they actually work pretty good. Have you urinated since you woke up, ma'am?"

Nadja realized that she had not. "No ... I should drink more water."

44

The Marine took her by the arm and steered her to a clump of dried brush 20 or so meters away. "Yes, always. But don't fret that you haven't peed. It's one of the effects of the 'good stuff'. It'll wear off in a day or so." Gunny looked around as they reached their destination. "I'll keep watch, just duck down low. They are endlessly fascinated by our pooping and peeing. First time I pinched a deuce, half the band showed up to watch."

It had slipped Nadja's mind the Lacertians appeared to leave no waste behind, and as she voided her bowels, it also occurred to her that she didn't smell as bad as she might. Someone must have bathed her when she was unconscious, likely the woman beside her. She'd never been modest in that way, and it didn't seem worth mentioning now.

When Nadja stood to zip up, Gunny stepped closer and began toeing sand over Nadja's night soil. "As funny as they think it is, the smell really drives them crazy."

The two turned and headed back to the group.

"How is their sense of smell?"

"Ma'am? Oh ... good, I think ... really good, in fact. Their sense of hearing is a little poor, but it's directional. They can tell what direction a sound is coming from better than us. And their sight is better than the average human, especially in the dark."

"You've been paying attention."

"Not much else to do out here, ma'am."

"How far did we travel so far today, Gunny?"

"About 15 klicks."

"Is that average?"

"It depends, ma'am. It's faster than usual, but I think they're in a hurry to get to new grazing. That's the problem. They follow the rains, and rains are scanty. Once we find green pasture, we might be there a while ... or they might change direction entirely. I don't know."

The two resumed their original seats near the animals, and Gunny produced her map.

"What's the longest you've stayed in one place?"

"Since we've been with them, about a month. But there've been a couple other stops for around two weeks each. A week seems average."

Nadja thought. "What's the longest the band has gone without stopping?"

"I think it was five days ... again, the pace was a little faster then, too." The Marine looked at her map and traced a path with her finger. "We've been travelling roughly north all day. If we keep this pace up for five days,

45

we'll be about … right here. That EM free zone we want to reach isn't due north, but from that spot," she tapped the map, "we'll be about 40 klicks closer."

Something occurred to Nadja. "Can you zoom in? I remember there being a village near there."

Gunny fiddled with the map, zooming in and zooming out and shifting the screen about. "Good call ma'am. There's a little ville not far from there."

"It's the one Melissa called Madrid. It's sort of an oasis with what looks like a tiny fort."

"That's right," the Marine whispered, before continuing hesitantly. "Might Sgt. Lyn send a search team there?"

"Not if she's following orders. And that area has the same EM problems. Still … we might bump into Gunter Wray there."

"You need to talk more with Stig, ma'am."

"I do. I don't like not knowing … but what about Blacky? You said he seems to be chief."

"Nah, ma'am. Blacky's a good guy, just like the rest. But he's a lot less patient. He's dropped me in the kraal with the cubs a few times when he's gotten bored with me." The Marine thought. "No, ma'am. Stig is patient. I got the sense he has a bit of clout around here too. You can always try out Blacky once you've learned to confab a little better."

Nadja hesitated. "What makes you think Stig has clout?"

"Oh, he owns lots of animals, most of the others seem to defer to him, and his weapons and armor … that sword of his is a work of art. It sure wasn't forged by the village smithy."

"Damn, Gunny, you're good at this." It all made sense.

"You don't need to speak the language to see the lay of the land, ma'am."

"So Stig is some sort of knight?"

The gunnery sergeant laughed; the sound was somehow sweet and girlish. "He might be, ma'am."

10: The Southern Tank

The next four days were productive, if also occasionally frightening.

The three humans took turns riding with Stig on his trusty steed, and many of the intricacies of the Lacertian language fell bare before Nadja's constant barrage of questions, queries, and carefully structured conversations with the band's adults. She needed to build a broader understanding of the language, but also concentrated on developing competence in topics that would enable her to make a persuasive case to enlist the aid of the band and its chief.

As much as Nadja enjoyed her time with the band—and she truly relished the experience—each passing day left her more anxious over what was going on elsewhere on the planet and in orbit.

But onward the band travelled, and the sedate pace of their progress was ruffled only slightly when, on the third day, they caught sight of the first of several riders from rival bands skirting the skyline. From that point forward, the adults, each and every one, went about in their full martial panoply, and Stig began riding solo, so as to respond more readily to any attack.

The situation was not an inconvenience for the humans. Their patron offered to bring up an additional mount, but the three opted to take turns walking. Despite the onerous heat, the planet's gravity was light and the air clear and fresh. And many of the Lacertians walked, or walked and rode in turn, to spare their mounts or merely to stretch their legs.

Nadja took a secret joy in seeing Stig and the others in their war attire. Their hosts usually went about thoroughly naked but were now clad in eclectic suits of leather, chain, and plate armor. Stig wore a light helmet and segmented metal plate across his shoulders and arms, beneath which was a heavy mail shirt. His lower half was protected by a long leather kilt and studded leather greaves. His heavy falchion dangled from a baldric to his side, and a long and thick spear was ever in his hand. Nadja wasn't sure she'd ever seen such a heroic figure.

By the end of the fourth day, however, no attack had been forthcoming, though Nadja sensed the threat had not yet diminished. As the band stopped and made camp for the night, unloading the beasts, erecting shelters, and kraaling the cubs, she discussed it with Stig. Her ear still missed far more than it caught, but the intent was clear: The band was near

47

an important goal, one that might bring them a certain amount of peace, albeit temporary.

Later, as Stig and some others played a game that involved rolling stones and balancing sticks amid bouts of wrestling, she tried to explain to Gunny and Spiros what she'd learned.

"Apparently we've been making for Madrid the whole time," she told them. "It's some sort of market town they visit once or twice a season, where they can get things they can't make themselves."

"So, we're to have a holiday, then?" said the lance corporal with a smile.

"I dunno. Stig didn't go into any details that I could understand, but it appears to be more than just a market town. It's also some sort of neutral ground—no fighting allowed. It's the one place members from all bands can come together."

"I thought they were looking for pasture," said Gunny. The band had found only bits of grazing here and there over the last days, and the small tank at which they now camped was the first water they'd seen in that time.

"That's the wonderful part, Gunny. Evidently, the area around Madrid is unique. It gets rain twice a year like clockwork. For upwards of a week—well, nine days by their counting—there's enough pasture and water for everyone. After that, everybody goes back to their regular turf."

"Where the fighting and feuding over pasture, water, and livestock begins anew?"

"It's almost like Spring Break." Nadja smiled at the two.

"It's got me feeling nostalgic, ma'am." The unamused NCO again pulled out her map. "So, we should reach this place by sometime tomorrow?"

"Maybe not, Gunny. Stig says we'll have to wait here, maybe for a day or two, for the rains to begin, and then they'll spend another day or two ambling to Madrid to give the livestock time to graze."

"When does the feuding end, ma'am?" asked Spiros.

"When the rains come. Until then, our friends are going to stay on alert." She gave Spiros a playful cuff to the shoulder. "But don't worry. Stig assured me we cubs are thoroughly off limits. No adult would ever consider harming or molesting one, not even cubs of a different band."

"What about that other thing, ma'am?" Gunny again was using her grownup voice.

"That I'm not sure of. They measure time differently than we do ... and they think about time differently, too. I sometimes have a hard time figuring out whether Stig and the others are talking about the present or the past. And sometimes it isn't clear if they distinguish between recent past and distant past."

"So, they've seen other alien races?"

"No, Gunny … I don't know. They've seen flying machines before, but it isn't clear whether Stig is talking about ours or those of another group … or both. And he sometimes talks about 'others', but today I got the sense he might be talking about another sentient race on Skiathos."

Gunny made a disillusioned grunt; Spiros sat while twisting his lips, as if in thought. The three watched their Lacertian friends at play a few minutes longer.

"Is that possible, ma'am?" asked Spiros finally.

"What? More than one sentient species on a planet?" She saw the lad nod. "It's uncommon, but isn't unheard of. And we haven't surveyed the entire planet. There might be another civilization here we don't know about."

"What did he call this species?" asked Gunny.

"I dunno. Like I said, he sometimes uses the name 'others.' Sometimes he says, 'black rock.' He gets a little excited when he talks about it, and I can't always follow the conversation."

"What do you think he's trying to say?"

"Devil only knows, Gunny. I'll sort it out somehow. It isn't even clear if 'other' and 'black rock' are the same thing." Nadja made a growling sound. "The learning curve has been so sharp since I got here that I just felt like I was getting nowhere most of the day."

"That's easy, ma'am. Just back off and talk about something else. I'm eager to get back too, me and Spiros both, but if what you say is true, we might be in this area for another 10 days or two weeks. That's more time to convince our friends here to get onboard," she said, nodding toward the still wrestling Lacertians."

"Ah … shit, Gunny. That's actually one place I think I made a little headway today. I'm pretty sure I've convinced Stig that we're part of a different kind of band and that the three of us want to get back to our people."

"Ma'am, that's good news. Does he have any suggestions … offer any help?"

"Not yet. But I'm hopeful. He wants to know why our band doesn't just fly in and pick us up—a good question. I got a little hung up trying to explain that whole situation, but I think we might have a meeting of minds in the next few days."

The gunnery sergeant grimaced then smiled. "Oh, jeez … why didn't you lead with that, ma'am? That's the best news I've heard in months."

"I didn't want to get your hopes up until I was certain. In any event, we're still a long way from getting out of here."

"A lot closer than we were just a few days ago, ma'am." Gunny glanced over at Spiros, who, as they'd spoken, had drifted off to sleep on a blanket next to them. "I'm grateful for the 'good stuff' and for Greta putting him back together, but I'll be really happy to get him into a proper medical bay."

It was obvious the young Marine had shown signs of flagging toward the end of each day's walking, his slight limp becoming more noticeable as he did. "Does he always use that stick?"

"The stick? No, ma'am. Not as much as he was even a month ago. But he's still mending. Greta comes around every few days and looks at him and gives him a dose of the 'good stuff' every week or two. That right leg of his was damn near torn off during the crash." The gunnery sergeant shook her head.

The advanced and highly durable field uniforms the Marines wore doubtless had kept the lance corporal from bleeding-out, but Nadja realized there must have been something more. "You said that stuff is from some sort of root?"

"Yeah. I've seen Greta go out and dig them up. They look something like a gnarly black potato."

It was another hour or more before sleep time, and Nadja felt the urge to indulge herself on topics totally unrelated to their rescue. "Where does she find them?"

"She just walks out into the desert and, every once in a while, stops to dig. I don't know how she knows where, but she digs down about half a meter and pulls one out, pops it in half, and puts one half in her bag. The other half goes back in the ground and gets covered up."

"No shit," Nadja whispered with a smile. "You said they use them for other things?"

"Mostly it's for health-related stuff. Her and the others grind it into a paste and slather it on open wounds, sometimes without even sewing them up first. It seems to work wonders." The gunnery sergeant smiled broadly and tapped her tongue lightly behind her bottom teeth. "Phillip lost an arm in a fight with another band about two months after we joined them. Greta patched him up and kept dosing him. Three months later, he was as good as new."

50

"No shit," Nadja repeated, pondering whether regenerating limbs might not simply be a trait of the Lacertians.

"They burn the stuff occasionally too … as part of some sort of ceremony. I never figured that part out. Other than that, they use quite a bit of it to spice their meat when they dry it. I dunno, it might be some sort of preservative too."

"Where do they keep this stuff?"

"Ask Greta, ma'am. It's the one thing in camp that isn't shared around pretty freely. And …." The Marine hesitated as if uncertain.

"What?"

"I just … you know, I don't think they get sick. At least I haven't seen any sign of it."

Nadja scratched her ear. Was such a thing possible? Every species humanity had encountered among the stars had some notion of illness, even if that illness was something humans hadn't immediately recognized as such. "They put the 'good stuff' in their food, don't they?"

"They do, ma'am. And they do eat a lot of prepared and spiced meat. But the cubs only eat greens, at least they do until right before they change, and I haven't seen a sick cub, either."

It was a thing worth pondering but not a matter they would likely solve that evening. Something else dawned on Nadja. "What is that meat they feed us?"

"It's tail, ma'am."

"Tail of…?"

"Their livestock. The big smelly fuckers, six legs, long tails?"

The band had a thousand or more such animals. They all appeared to be of a kind, but used for different purposes, some for riding, some for cargo, and others still were herded as kine. "They only eat the tail?"

"Sometimes they'll slaughter a whole animal, ma'am, but usually they cut off the tails once they're fat enough. It only takes a few months for them to grow back."

"No shit," said Nadja a third time.

Gunny began laughing uncontrollably. "Hey, gimme a hand getting Spiros back to the tent, ma'am."

11: Razzia

The three humans woke to thunderous screams and the deafening din of steel on steel. As alien as this world was, it took no time at all for them to realize the camp was under attack. Gunny was up and moving toward the tent's opening, pistol in hand, before Nadja or Spiros were even off the ground.

"Spiros, strike a lantern."

"Gunny...," Nadja began.

"Ma'am, the natives see good in the dark, but we're not in the kraal. I don't want any of us skewered because one of these big bastards doesn't get a clear look at us."

Even as the NCO spoke, the sound grew louder and closer. The battle now was right outside their closed tent flap, and even to the human ear, the cries of defiance, anger, and pain were unmistakable.

Dread and anguish coursed through Nadja. She'd been in fights before, but never as an observer, and the rules against involvement in local conflicts were clear. Still, the sense of affection and camaraderie she'd come to feel for their hosts twisted inside her. As frightened as she was, the thought of standing aside while those who cared for and sheltered them fought for their lives was like a poison inside her. *This is not our fight*, she inwardly admonished herself.

Before Nadja could move or speak further, an enormous form lunged through the tent opening, swinging a massive blade in a wild arc at head-level to a human. The edge only just missed the top of a crouching Nadja's head and thoroughly missed Spiros, who was just rising from where he'd lit their tiny lamp. The intruder's momentum carried it past Gunny, who dropped to a knee and put three rapid pistol shots into the back of its head.

The enemy warrior dropped flat on its muzzle, but its presence brought the battle into the middle of the tent. In one sudden rush, the entire structure collapsed and ripped as a mob of screaming, slashing, and grappling warriors poured into their sanctuary.

In the chaos, something enormous and writhing dropped right on top of Nadja, and suddenly she could no longer breathe. The weight was excruciating, but lifted almost immediately, leaving her wheezing and fighting to extricate herself from beneath a flap of tent.

As if by magic, she was free, up, and running, or nearly so. Human hands grasped either arm, and though the breath had been utterly knocked from her, her ears still made out a powerful Lacertian voice above the commotion: "*Gunny, kraal!*"

Her head was clear enough to realize the kraal was nearly a hundred meters away, and she tried to speak, uncertain whether Gunny and Spiros knew to make for the safety of that destination, but she couldn't get out a single peep. As they ran, her feet barely skimming the ground as the Marines rushed her onward, enormous swirling, spinning, and gyrating forms danced around them, now more farcical and hellish bathed as they were in the ruddy-orange light of burning tents.

It was like something from *The Inferno*.

Unsurprisingly, the Marines knew to make for the kraal. A dozen times along the way, they ducked, dove, or were knocked to the ground by the screaming and hurtling combatants. On their last trip to the deck, Nadja attempted to rise only to feel a furious tug on the nape of her blouse. Glancing back, she saw Gunny, flat on her ass and heels dug into the dirt, dragging her desperately toward a clump of dry brush five or so meters distant.

With all her strength, Nadja rose, took two steps, staggered forward, and rose, took two steps, and pitched again to the ground, before she, Gunny, and Spiros lunged forward as one and landed at their destination in a great heap. The three then crawled frantically under a hollow in the brush, turned, and pressed their backs against the base of the foliage with all the might their fear could muster. It was never clear what was more disconcerting, the excited laughter of the Marines or Nadja's own trembling.

It was another 20 minutes before the tumult of the battle abated, ending nearly as rapidly as it had begun. And there were an indescribable few moments of absolute silence throughout the camp before the cries, chirps, and whirrs of victory began. Moments later, Phillip strode by their impromptu refuge, a naked blade in his hand and a severed Lacertian head in the other. Their friend bellowed a guttural victory cry.

Gunny's voice was raspy but relieved. "I told you, ma'am. These guys don't bullshit when it comes to war."

"No shit," she whispered.

"Come on." The NCO tapped Spiros's leg and gave Nadja's ankle a squeeze before duckwalking from the safety of their shelter. "Greta can use our help right now."

———

Nadja spent most of the morning with Stig and some others meeting with Blacky. Gunny had rightly prognosticated Stig was among the leaders of the band, along with Greta, Gwyneth, Phillip, and another half dozen.

All of those present with Nadja had a similar characteristic—all possessed a dark amber or deep bronze coloration of their skin that formed a cowl that ran from the crowns of their heads back to their shoulders and upper back.

Her first thought was this represented some class or family marker, but she dismissed this notion immediately. Blacky had similar markings, but, appropriate to the name Gunny had bestowed on him, his cowl was of the deepest ebony. He was a tall and powerfully built warrior, larger even than Stig and Gwyneth, and all in camp were noticeably deferential to him. Her conclusion was that such darker colorations were a sign of maturity and age.

Despite the brutality of the attack, all present seemed in high spirits. The event was clearly a victory in the eyes of those assembled, and as they chatted, a charitable Blacky occasionally would reach over to where Nadja sat beside him and offer her a tiny slice of the bitter, but otherwise quite palatable, pemmican that formed an important part of the warrior diet. To her other side, Stig whispered throughout the conference short summaries and simplifications of what was being said. She otherwise only caught one word in 10 being uttered in Blacky's spacious pavilion.

The first order of business was what to do about Gunny. The idea that any adult might harm a cub was anathema, but the notion that a cub might kill an adult simply had never occurred to anyone. The assembly at first was at a loss. Finally, Gwyneth (who much to Nadja's surprise had not been present for the battle, because she'd been off with 40 or so others raiding the camp of their attackers) made the simple observation: If the warrior Gunny killed hadn't been where it shouldn't, it would still be alive.

All agreed that Gunny committed no crime, and after some more discussion Blacky decided the fallen warrior's mount, weapons, and armor would go to Gunny, as was the custom of their people. He made the added proviso that, at least for the time being, the gunnery sergeant's sidearm should remain with Stig, before asking all assembled, in turn, if they agreed with his decision.

Nadja wasn't certain how surrendering her weapon would go down with Gunnery Sergeant Nice, but she would smooth it over somehow. She knew the NCO liked and trusted Stig and, if push came to shove, she could always order the Marine to surrender the sidearm. She hoped it wouldn't come to that.

The assembly chatted further on a variety of topics, many of which went beyond Nadja's ken, even with Stig's whispered guidance, but it was a good encounter. She spoke several times during the assembly—Blacky seemed amused at her broken Lacertian—and even toward the end made a short statement expressing her hope to return to her people.

She refrained from making a direct appeal for the support of Blacky and the assembly; her language skill simply wasn't sufficient to make such a request persuasively. Only about half of Blacky's response to her final statement was clear to her, but she intuited that it was something along the lines of, "these are dangerous times, little cub. We will keep you safe."

It was not ideal, but it was another step in the right direction.

To her surprise after the assembly broke up, Stig reached down and scooped her up and began walking with Greta at his side toward the medical tent. Both Gunny and Spiros were experienced Lacertian medics by that time and continued to treat the minor wounds received by the camp's warriors while Greta was in assembly. That their hosts so trusted the humans with such a critical task both moved and confounded her.

The realization that Stig's highhanded behavior at snatching her up didn't really bother her confounded her even more. The adults were stern taskmasters with the cubs, wordlessly drilling them and re-drilling them on tasks both simple and complex. In the moments in between, though, they were attentive and affectionate parents, often playing and goofing shamelessly with their smaller wards. None seemed to have unique attachments; adults tutored whichever cub happened to be handy. The young were special to all, particular to none.

Perhaps the three humans should be flattered that Stig and others took such particular interest in their welfare.

Stig and Greta chatted amiably as they walked, and as they did, a distracted and thought-filled Nadja paid them no mind. Her huge chauffeur jostled her playfully as they went, and when they reached the medical tent where Gunny and Spiros lounged without, Stig lightheartedly spun her once and deposited her feet-first on the ground, before striding off wordlessly toward the animal pens. Greta patted her two human helpers gently on the head on her way into the tent, uttering a muted, "*Hi.*"

"That was a long one, ma'am," said Gunny as she rose from the pile of saddles on which she lounged. "Good news?"

"Good and bad. Which do you want first?"

"How about bad news this time."

"Once we get the tent sewn back together, Blacky wants us closer to the kraal."

Both Gunny and Spiros grimaced. "Oh, they are so noisy," said the former.

"It beats the alternative. He first wanted us to sleep in the kraal, but Stig and I talked him down. Apparently, we've got some special status, but it ain't completely special."

"I suppose that's not too bad."

"There's worse, Gunny."

"How worse?"

"Blacky wants you to surrender your sidearm."

The gunnery sergeant seemed physically taken aback. "My 10-millimeter, ma'am?" she said after a long breath.

"I need you with me on this, Gunny. You don't have to get rid of it, but Blacky agreed to let Stig hold onto it for the time being. Apparently, they're not sure of what to think of a cub capping an adult."

The NCO hesitated. "OK. I trust Stig … but I joke not, ma'am. This hurts. Is there more bad news?"

"No. Just the opposite. It appears you're a woman of property now." She explained to the NCO the assembly's decision on the fallen enemy's belongings. She finished as Stig arrived with a long, lean riding animal in tow. Its saddle had been piled with the weapons and armor of the slain warrior.

Gunny stepped forward and took the proffered reins from Stig. "Wow."

"*Victory*," said their enormous friend. He pulled a steel helmet from a hook on the saddle and placed it ceremoniously on Gunny's head. The headgear, small by Lacertian standards, enveloped the Marine's head and face.

"*Oh, boy*," Nadja heard from within.

Gunny moved around and shifted the helmet several ways, trying to see from its eye slits. Passersby paused to gape and chuckle, and the sound of Greta's laughter emanated from the tent.

"I don't see this working," echoed Gunny's voice from inside the helmet. Lifting it off her head, she pointed to the three bullet holes in the piece's left rear. The rounds formed a tight pattern that could have been covered easily by a human palm. "But I gotta say, that's some damn fine shooting."

A laughing Stig drew an enormous sword from its sheath on the saddle and handed it hilt-first to Gunny. The weapon was not so grand as Stig's own, but it was a thing of great beauty, and a gentle brush with the side of Gunny's thumb showed it had a razor's edge.

Moving two steps back, the NCO took the hilt in both hands and raised the blade at length before her. The tip of the curved and lethal weapon wobbled noticeably. "*Kak.* This thing's gotta weigh more than 20 kilos." Placing the tip of the weapon in the sand a half meter before her, Gunny peered down the length of the blade. Even at that angle, the pommel of the enormous weapon rested against the Marine's chin.

"I don't think it's your size, Gunny," offered Spiros. "Anyway, it's out of regs for a bayonet."

Gunny cracked her first true smile, but Stig spoke first.

"*Gareth needs a sword,*" he said to Nadja. The Lacertian in question was another of Gunny's favorites, one of the small number to whom she'd given human names for convenience's sake—the true name, the one that Stig used now, was difficult even for Nadja to enunciate properly.

But their friend's words seemed to set something into motion, a choreography of exchange and trade obviously well known to the locals, but not unpleasant for the humans.

Over the next hour, with Nadja working as translator and Stig as informal auctioneer, Gunny disposed of most of her war booty. The Marine noncom at first thought merely to give Gareth the sword, but Stig explained things simply weren't done that way. Still, Gunny was generous in her parting with the weapon. In exchange, Gareth gave her a handsome double-edged dagger nearly the length of her arm, two nicely made blankets, and agreed to help them rebuild their shelter.

Other bits of the fallen warrior's kit went in exchange for odds and ends the humans might need: a few water flasks of assorted sizes, some leather satchels, and a spare harness and picket rope. Gunny opted to keep only the mount, saddle, and tack. A small curved dagger she gave to Spiros.

The last piece on the chopping block was an elaborate breastplate of what appeared to be leather and segmented steel. One warrior, whose name Nadja couldn't quite master, seemed especially keen on the item, but several times Stig had pronounced it a thing of great worth, one that might fetch 40 or more animals if Gunny opted to wait and barter it at the market in Madrid.

They hemmed and hawed over the item for some 15 minutes—the truth was the humans didn't need anything the warrior had to offer—but at the end of that time the warrior excused himself, promising to return momentarily.

Minutes later, he was back, bearing what appeared to be a leather tube of about one meter in length and of roughly 25 to 30 centimeters in diameter. Uncapping one end, the warrior gently pulled forth the item's innards and handed them to Gunny. It was what appeared to be several hundred rolled sheets of fine, but sturdy material, upon which was etched what only could be some sort of writing."

"*We'll take it*," said Nadja and Gunny simultaneously, each in a different language.

12: The Oldies

They spent most of the next two days at Greta's tent, tending to the wounded and poring over the large manuscript they'd obtained from the Lacertian who Gunny had taken to calling Trixie—a designation that was a feeble, but close-enough, approximation of the warrior's actual name.

As the band awaited the rains, and the cessation of hostilities they would bring, more bands arrived in the area and fighting continued. Still, though the stream of wounded was steady, it wasn't the overwhelming onslaught it had been. The first night's battle had cost the band many score wounded and 11 dead—eight at the camp and three during Gwyneth's raid on the attacker's encampment. Their attackers had lost nearly three times that number.

With an additional five or so bands now within 10 kilometers of camp, a situation elbow-to-elbow by Lacertian standards, the band had suffered four more dead and a handful of critical injuries. Greta explained that the first attacks had been for booty, but the more recent skirmishes (which were far less likely to take a rival band unawares) were mostly demonstrations of force meant to keep adversaries on their toes and at a distance.

Several times on that second day, large mounted companies had approached the camp only to be driven off by Blacky at the head of a strong party of warriors. Those melees had been quick and relatively bloodless affairs. Attacks on the band's livestock, which Gwyneth and a large body of troops kept bunched near camp, had been more serious. Each such sortie had left dead and wounded in its wake.

The humans seldom saw Stig during that time, off as he was with the balance of the camp's warriors, riding, raiding, clashing, and skirmishing to keep their enemies off their guard and to seize any opportunity for plunder.

As evening approached on the second day, Spiros assisted Greta in grinding roots and preparing for the next round of casualties, and an exhausted Nadja and Gunny idled outside for a breath of fresh air. As she had throughout the preceding days, a tired but voracious Nadja stole another opportunity to peruse the manuscript, a simple curiosity Trixie had gotten in trade some seasons before and about which the warrior knew nothing. They'd had little time to investigate further.

"You make any sense of that yet, ma'am?" inquired the gunnery sergeant.

"Just a little." Nadja ran her finger along the edge of the page she was reading. "See these glosses along the outside of the page?"

Gunny peered over and then flipped through several more pages in the pile of sheets sitting before them. "They're not on all of them."

"No. Just on the first 50 or so. I think someone was beginning to translate it. They look like two different scripts ... which ... well...." Nadja's tired thoughts were suddenly jumbled. "I suppose two scripts may or may not mean they represent different languages. It isn't unheard of for a single language to have multiple scripts."

"But you think the writing along the margin and the main text are two different languages?"

"Well ... yes." The linguist in her had a moment's clarity. "Back in humanity's manuscript age, it was very common for books to have a main script surrounded by a gloss, or even a gloss of the gloss, to explain or translate the main text. It was almost always like this, around the edges. And look at the central text. It looks a little like ancient Arabic, but without the diacritic marks. The inscriptions around the outside are completely different." Nadja pulled out a second sheet. "Look here ... here ... and here," she said pointing. "The markings on the main text are all the same, as are the parallel markings in the gloss. If I didn't have access to an AI, that's probably how I'd go about trying to translate a text I'd never seen."

"Doesn't your tablet have software for that, ma'am?"

"It does, but it just doesn't have the computing power to figure out either script on its own ... not without my help. And I still need to scan it in."

"So, you think one of these languages is Lacertian?"

Nadja nodded. "The one in the gloss, I think. The little dots might represent their peeps, and the dashes might be whirrs or hums ... or both. I just need to puzzle them out; if I can do that, the marginal gloss can help me figure out what the main text says." She gave a long sigh. "If I had access to the AI on the platform, it would only take a few hours."

The Marine was gently rubbing one of the pages and appeared to have moved on mentally. "What are the pages made of? Back where I come from, they still use paper books some, but this doesn't feel like paper."

"I don't know," whispered Nadja. "If it's parchment, it's the finest I've ever seen."

"Parchment?"

"Treated animal skins. They used to be very common in ancient times back on Earth, but I'm not sure that's what this is. Of course … animal hides are different here, and who knows what chemicals they might use to treat them."

"It looks manufactured to me, ma'am. Perfect size, perfect consistency … and the script is flawless and regular. It looks like it's printed."

"That's what I thought at first." Nadja pointed to several lines of script. "But see how those characters all end? Almost identical, but not quite. Either it's been printed inconsistently in some way, or the scrivener who wrote it has a near perfect hand … again, not out of the realm of possibility. Medieval illuminators were often astounding artists."

"Well … we're not going to figure that out right now. Not with you dead on your feet. Why don't you get some sleep, ma'am, and I'll scan the pages into your tablet." The NCOs words weren't an order, but neither were they a request.

"I'm too tired to sleep."

Gunny gave one of her mischievous smiles and said out of nowhere, "You're an oldie, aren't you ma'am?"

Nadja smiled. "I am. How can you tell?"

"I can't, but the young'uns can. I don't know how. Maybe it's the way we talk. But Spiros had you pegged first day."

"So … *you're* not a young'un?"

"No, ma'am. I turned 60 my last birthday." Just a generation or two before, anyone seeing Gunny Nice would have thought her a woman in her mid-20s.

"Holy … wait. How long have you been in the Marines?"

"Fourteen years. Before that, I was a farm wife on Nuevo California."

"How the…?" Nadja had to squelch a laugh.

"Got married when I was 18, spent most of the next 10 years spitting out pups, and on the day I put my youngest on the shuttle to college, I left the spaceport, dropped the keys in the floorboard of the family car, and walked the three blocks to the Marine Corps recruiting station. They shipped me out that evening."

"Jeez … Gunny." Nadja didn't know what to think. "What did your husband say to all this?"

"Well, he wasn't so happy. He even showed up at basic training and tried to get me back. But you know what? By that time, I'd been married to Javeed for nearly 30 years. In all that time, he'd never once asked my permission to do anything: not what crops to plant, what equipment to purchase, or how to run a business we both technically owned. He never sought my permission or asked my opinion when he met with dealers, took on debt, or travelled off-world to go to conferences or meet buyers. Once my kids were grown, I wanted to see something of the universe outside Nuevo California, and I didn't feel the need to ask his blessing to do that."

The NCO's every word had left Nadja more dumbfounded, and she couldn't resist a smile of admiration. "So, you still married?"

"We are, ma'am. Don't get me wrong; I love the guy. He gave me six great kids and a good life, and when I retire in five or 10 years, I hope he's waiting for me. But that's his call."

"Oh, my…." Something occurred to Nadja. "Wouldn't the Corps have reported your death to your family?"

"They may have. Policy out on the frontier is to hold notification for six months, if no remains are found, just in case. But if I know HQ at our regiment, they'll fuck it up somehow."

"But … your poor family will be devastated."

"They'll get over it, ma'am. But I swear to God, if those greedy little bastards sell my cottage on the coast, I will flip out. I got that from my gramma."

"How many kids did you say?"

"Six, ma'am … plus four grandkids. And if my oldest granddaughter is anything like her mom, I might be a great-grandmother soon … if I'm not already."

Nadja sat thinking a moment. Hot and sweating, and still smeared with the black viscous fluid that was the blood of a dozen different Lacertians, she felt for the first time the deepest sense of camaraderie with the gunnery sergeant and the lance corporal.

"Gunny, what's your given name?"

"Really, ma'am."

"It's a fair question … unless you want me to call you 'Gunny' for the rest of our time here." It was a common theme of military humor that many professional Marines and soldiers claimed their ranks were their actual first names.

"No, ma'am … my first name *is* 'Really.'"

Nadja's brain, fogged over by lack of sleep, merely hummed a moment before kicking in. "Your full name is 'Really Nice'?" she asked at last.

"My folks are bohemians, ma'am."

"Gunny isn't really all that nice," came Spiros's voice from the tent.

Really Nice made a half turn and called back. "By gunnery sergeant standards, I'm a pussycat … Vivian."

"Vivian Spiros is an old and honored family name," replied the young'un, perhaps a skosh defensively. "And it's very masculine."

"You know," said Nadja, "let's just stick with 'Gunny,' 'Spiros,' and 'ma'am.'"

"That sounds like a plan, ma'am."

———

The rains came lightly and gently an hour before sunset that same day and continued throughout the night.

From the heavens' first tear, it was as if they all had been transported to a different world. Weapons were sheathed, armor shed on the spot, and warriors sauntered about laughing and playing with one another and with the cubs newly freed from the kraal. Several times before the sun's last rays vanished, teams of warriors from other bands sped by, waving and calling out greetings from the saddle, the blood, fury, and pitiless conflict of mere minutes past now a far distant land, foreign to all.

Mere moments after sunset, Stig's mount came lumbering from the shadows. His war party's arrival was sedate, but was not silent once they'd all returned to the lighted glow of the band's tents and joined in the celebrations.

Across his saddle, the arriving champion bore an enormous platter of food, one given him by members of the very band whose camp Stig and his companions were in the act of charging when first the rains came. The treats, which were a concoction of tail meat, nuts, and something else—and which were the closest thing Nadja had yet tasted on this strange planet to a confection—were rough and bitter, but left an aftertaste that was decidedly sweet. For hours after, the band played, laughed, and danced in a broad circle around Blacky's tent, before succumbing to the exhaustion accumulated through two straight days' combat and retiring to their shelters for a well-earned rest.

Their tent still in shambles from the first night's invasion, the human's yielded to exhaustion at Stig's airy pavilion. Amid a pile of warm cubs, the two Marines soon were fast asleep, with Nadja nodding beside them. Meanwhile their host sat patiently on a saddle near the tent's opening, humming and singing in a uniquely Lacertian way, while he expertly fletched a new arrow and regarded the light drizzle without.

Gunny had told her of the custom, of course, but it still took some time amid this dozy scene of blessed tranquility for the half-sleeping Nadja to remember that Stig's people crafted their arrowheads exclusively from the heel spikes of fallen warriors. This was Skiathos.

13: A Walk in the Garden

The next morning, Nadja stood staring in disbelief at the vast plain that stretched before them. She'd been woken by Gunny's gasps of wonder moments before and had staggered sleepy-eyed to where the Marine gaped outside the tent.

The great flatland, which mere hours before had been a parched anvil of brown and gray, was resplendent with color, from the deepest greens of the pastures to the splendor of the flowers on plain, shrub, and brush. Every color of the palette was represented; what had been a wasteland was now a garden.

"Will you fucking get a load of that?" whispered the NCO.

Nadja was speechless and continued to regard the vastness before them. The sun now shone, but here and there showers bathed the plains in the distance and twice during the next half hour the two transfixed women felt the slightest hints of rain beat down on them.

The linguist had just fixed her attention on the lazy movements of another band in the distance when something enormous glided silently past her from the rear. It was a member of the band, one whose name Nadja had yet to learn, who skimmed by in a mute pirouette before spinning twice more and gliding back in long strides toward the middle of camp.

The Lacertian's wordless flight woke Nadja from her reverie, and turning she realized there was a figure standing right behind her and the gunnery sergeant. It was Stig, and his steady gaze was focused on the very tapestry upon which hers and Gunny's had been so fixed.

She wondered how long their friend had been standing there and spoke without thinking. "*You have a beautiful world,*" she said in his tongue.

"*We are...,*" said Stig, before uttering a nearly imperceptible set of hums and whirrs.

The last words Nadja hadn't recognized, but she wondered now from her new friend's hushed tone whether he and his people didn't have a notion of being 'blessed.' On another impulse, she turned and stepped into her massive friend. Placing her head against his chest, she put her arms around the champion in a tight embrace.

With just his hand, Stig returned the embrace tenderly.

"I think you're a little stoned, ma'am."

The gunnery sergeant was probably right. The powerful bouquet of the new foliage was even more profound than the usual pleasant smell

Skiathos offered. Perhaps there was something in the air? Some special something that added to her mood and to the mood of their hosts, all of whom seemed especially exuberant. But Nadja hoped not; her temper was too good to allow it to be a mere illusion.

"Gunny, why don't you go grab Spiros, and we'll rustle up some eats."

A few minutes later found them outside Blacky's tent with 50 or so others picking gingerly at large platters of meats, greens, and yet more bitter confections. The morning was a delight, and as they chatted about events of the last few days, with Nadja occasionally acting as translator, Lacertians came and went, eating, gossiping, and playing, before going about their business.

"*Did you enjoy your new plaything, Nadja?*" asked Greta a few minutes after the surgeon joined them at the breakfast circle.

It took Nadja a few moments to realize Greta was asking about the manuscript. This was the first the healer had spoken of it. "*I enjoy it a great deal. Are there other such things in camp?*"

"*No. I don't think so. Trixie has always been such a....*" Several short pops followed.

Nadja presumed she'd discovered the Lacertian equivalent of "packrat" and mushed on. "*Do you know how to ... how to understand them?*"

"*You mean the marks? No. We don't need them.*"

"*Who does?*"

"*Traders,*" said Greta flatly.

Traders? Nadja knew the word, but wasn't certain what it meant in this situation. "*I don't understand,*" she said finally.

"*One mark for an animal. Another mark for a hide. Another mark for a tail.*"

"Of course," Nadja said aloud in English. How silly. Most every societies' first writings were merchants' ledgers. "*I understand.*"

"*I'll show you when we reach the gathering,*" said the gentle surgeon.

This news was exciting, and Nadja spoke some minutes more with Greta before Gunny announced she and Spiros were going with Gareth and Stig to repair their shelter and pack it for the day's journey.

"You coming, ma'am?"

Nadja felt a large hand on her shoulder and the gentle pull that she'd come to realize was an adult Lacertian's way of signaling they wanted the attention of a cub.

"Greta wants me for something. I'll be along later."

Gunny departed, draped over Stig's shoulders with Spiros in tow, and Nadja followed Greta to her tent, where the Lacertian recovered a large leather bag. The two next made for the edge of camp. They walked for some minutes in silence.

The sun was out for the third or fourth time that day, and the heat of the day was just beginning to show its fury. Nadja looked about and realized she should have brought a water flask. Lacertian's seldom drank water, but she was not so endowed. As if reading Nadja's thoughts, Greta reached down and plucked a green from the ground and handed it to her.

It was the first time Nadja had seen the plant harvested and was fascinated by the sound it made. She reached down, took one in her fingers, and pulled. There was the faintest resistance, followed by a slight popping sound. The green had come away cleanly from the ground into Nadja's hand. Glancing from green to ground, she felt a moment's confusion. There didn't seem to be any root system anchoring the plant to the ground. She stood and looked around, her confusion mounting.

Off in the distance, the plain looked as if it were an ocean of green, but she noticed when she looked down that the greens were relatively sparse. One poked its head from the earth every 10 or so centimeters. The illusion was further disorienting.

She noticed Greta stood looking at her wordlessly.

"*I'm not....*" She didn't know the word for crazy.

Greta resumed her walk, and Nadja followed, stepping lively to catch up. As sparse as they were, it was hard to walk without stepping on a green. When she did, they seemed to spring back up unblemished.

Was it her imagination, or was there some sort of pattern to the greens? It didn't seem so at first, but then she realized the spacing between the small buds was far too regular. There were occasional tiny wildflowers interspersed between them, but take those out of the equation, and it became clear that no two greens were closer than eight or 10 centimeters to the next. Gaps between them were seldom more than twice that distance. One would expect seeds to fall randomly. And there were seeds on this planet—she'd both seen and eaten them.

But were those seeds? There wasn't a botanist on Gunter Wray's tiny life sciences team; she'd presumed he wore that hat himself. The man was, after all, an accomplished scientist with advanced degrees in several fields. But, now that she thought of it, there hadn't been any botanical reports on the material she'd reviewed for the mission. She'd had no reason to even ponder such a matter before her arrival on planet, and once she'd arrived and realized the entire mission was hers to supervise, she hadn't had time to review things in their entirety.

Now such a gap in study seemed downright peculiar.

Still, academics generally were agreed to be irritable and self-important nut-bags. Wray was primarily a bio-anthropologist, and it would be well within his character, like that of most academics, to ignore anything that fell even slightly outside his current focus of study and to place that subject on the highest available pedestal for all the universe to worship.

It was another thing to add to the laundry list of grievances she had against the man, sufficient by that time to merit punching him in the kidney, when and if she found him alive.

Greta had stopped along a slight rise and was beginning to dig. As she watched her friend's excavation, Nadja began gently to chew and suck on the greens. They were heavy with moisture, even more so now that the rains had come.

After some minutes, Greta motioned her over and gestured downward. Reaching within the hole, the medic extracted a large dark item. As Gunny had said, the root looked like nothing so much as a large and gnarled potato—Nadja had seen only diced specimens at the hospital tent. With a single twist of her powerful hands, the doctor snapped the root in two, handing one side to Nadja and placing the other in her leather satchel.

A bizarre tingle ran through Nadja's hands when she took the proffered item, something not quite electrical but suggestive of the jolt she'd received on tasting her first green. There was something there, something more than a simple piece of vegetation. More, the noise when Greta had cracked the root in two had seemed somehow too loud. Stepping over, Nadja peered into the hole from whence the root had come. She then went to her hands and knees and looked down more closely.

In the half-light of the hole, she could see broad white tendrils extending into the bottom from every angle. In a strange way, the tendrils very much resembled old-style data cables she'd seen in videos and on holograms. A thought filled her head, and without moving her eyes from the tendrils, she reached over and pulled on a green ever so gently. The pressure wasn't enough to pull the shoot from the soil, but as she tugged, she saw the slightest movement in one of the tendrils. She tried a second and a third. Each tug was met with a corresponding movement from within the hole.

The root in her free hand had ceased its noiseless rumbling, and she remained next to the hole unable to understand the full importance of what she'd just seen. Glancing up, she saw a kneeling Greta regarding her with that look on her face Nadja had come to recognize as a Lacertian smile.

The medic motioned to the hole, Nadja dropped the root she held into it, and the two proceeded to reinter the item.

"What is that?" she asked Greta after they'd finished.

"Life," replied her friend.

For the umpteenth time, Nadja pondered whether the strange feeling that overwhelmed her at such answers was a result of her own inability to understand or her companion's attempt to be enigmatic. She found no answer.

After filling the hole, the two moved on, leisurely pausing, digging up roots, and refilling holes for what seemed hours. From time to time, Nadja would nibble on a green to hydrate herself, the hood of her blouse now raised against the sun, and the ordinarily taciturn, yet funny, Greta would tell her an uncomplicated story of this, that, or the other, expounding at length on simple lessons that the land might provide.

Nadja understood only snatches of what Greta said, but didn't care. Their gentle meanderings were like nothing else she'd ever known or thought that she could know. It was as if time stood still and the universe spun fecklessly around them. And in that endless moment, there was nowhere Nadja would rather be. Home, work, war, peace, freedom, commitment could all be damned.

Quite idly as they strolled, dug, and chatted, Nadja noticed the band was on the move, but at a pace that was as slow and ponderous as was hers and Greta's.

"What about your animals and gear?" she asked.

"Someone will tend to them," replied her companion.

It was the way of things in the band. All looked to their personal effects, but any passing adult might strike a tent, saddle a mount, or load the animal of another, without so much as a word exchanged. They were commune, band, and family all combined.

"Where do children come from?" Nadja asked on an impulse. She sensed. No, she knew that Greta was revealing the band's deepest secrets to her now. She couldn't explain the sensation, but she suddenly wanted to know more—to know everything.

"They come from us," replied Greta, without breaking her lazy stride.

"But how? How do they come to be?"

Greta slowed and paused, looking at her with an indescribable look. *"Where do your children come from?"*

Nadja literally took a step back and after a few short breaths attempted to explain as best she was able and in as few words as possible the nature of human mating, the need for a male and a female, and the incubation, birth, and rearing of a child. She paused after she finished to allow Greta a chance to think or respond. It wasn't clear she'd explained herself thoroughly or clearly.

"*We are nine,*" Greta said after a few moments.

"*Nine? You have nine ... types?*" She still didn't know the word for gender, wasn't sure such a notion existed.

"*No,*" she said. "*We need nine to make children. But one must be ready.*"

"*Ready?*" Nadja hesitated. "*Ready for what?*"

"*To make children.*" Greta's voice and affect exuded a sense of indulgence.

"*I don't understand.*"

Greta smiled. "*Once each cycle, I am ready. We are all like that ... once each cycle.*"

Nadja sensed part of what she meant. Once each cycle. Once each year. "*What does it mean to be ready?*"

"*To make children possible with the other eight.*"

It was then that Nadja understood, and over the next few minutes Greta explained further. Once each year, an adult Lacertian was "ready" and with the help of eight others, they repaired themselves to an isolated spot in the desert with a few fixings, dug a hole in that blasted plain, and each took their turn depositing the biological matter for the creation of new life. It was then that the nine waited the 18 or so days necessary for the newly fertilized young to emerge and to return with them to camp.

The remarkable part to Nadja was the mode of delivering biological material. "*So, you just open your mouth and it comes out?*"

"*Yes.*" Greta seemed surprised at Nadja's reaction. "*How do you do it?*"

The two resumed walking as Nadja tried to elucidate, pointing back to her earlier explanation of human sexuality for clarification. The conversation was strangely awkward, so she made it as short as possible.

"*And you carry it around ... inside you?*" asked Greta. The doctor obviously was doing her best not to offend, but there were telltale signs of disquiet on her large and animated face.

"*Yes, for a full cycle ... as it grows.*"

"*But ... doesn't it hurt when it burrows out.*" Greta's unease was so palpable that she again came to a halt. "*You don't look big enough.*"

"*It's not as bad as it sounds,*" she reassured her host, before further explaining the mechanics of human childbirth. It wasn't clear how much of what she'd said up until that point was comprehensible.

Greta listened patiently for Nadja to finish. The whole time, her head pivoted back and forth, her multiple eyelids clipping in unison, sometimes eyeing Nadja from the left and sometimes from the right. A few moments after Nadja finished her explanation, Greta faced her full on. "*I promise not to tell anyone about this,*" she said solemnly.

"*It's OK.*"

Greta hesitated.

"*What?*" Nadja asked.

Her giant companion's unease lifted for a moment, and she asked, "*When you and Gunny decide to make children, can I watch?*"

———

Later that evening, as the band gathered and celebrated around a new camp, Gunny asked the obvious question. "So, how did you explain to Greta that that wasn't in the cards?"

Spiros again sported on the far side of the camp with their friends, and a still amused Nadja had spent the last hour recounting to the NCO her strange day's perambulation with Greta. The medic had been shocked by the notion of human procreation, but said Nadja was free to share what she wished about Lacertian ways. Apparently, there were no points of shame or embarrassment in their culture.

Nadja suppressed yet another laugh. "I was a little vague ... didn't want to drag poor Spiros into the conversation. But that wasn't the interesting part."

"What's that, ma'am?"

"Our friends don't seem to have libidos."

"As in...?"

She turned on the blanket to face the NCO. "As in they don't have a sex drive. Having children, deciding to procreate, is a carefully planned community decision. I didn't catch every detail, but it seems to be based on how many fighters they expect to need in the future and how much pasture they imagine will be available. Too few fighters, and they can't defend their range; too many fighters, and there's the potential of starvation or conflict."

"Which is why they're always at war over resources."

"Exactly. But military success has its own price. Greta says, if a band is too successful and gets too big, there are problems. Bands like that frequently will split up."

"They've done that a few times since we've been with them, ma'am. When we come to areas of thin pasture, they'll sometimes break into two or three groups and spread out. But they always come back together."

"I guess sometimes those splits become permanent. A few of the groups the band was fighting before the rains came were distant cousins of theirs. Well, if Lacertians even have notions of cousins ... or brothers and sisters."

Gunny did her own pivot to face Nadja fully. Crossing her legs in front of her, the Marine leaned closer, elbows on knees. "So, nine of them get together, and one of those provides eggs to fertilize? And they provided this material through ... some gland in their mouths?"

"Yup."

"And they take turns being ... well ... female?"

"More or less, Gunny. I thought they might reproduce by some type of parthenogenesis, but this isn't quite the same thing. Apparently, they have a nine-month year of sorts—though I don't know how long their months are—and one month each year a Lacertian is 'ready.'"

"It sounds like a Marine beach party."

"Except eight are necessary to fertilize the seeds of the one who is ready. And it's always a different eight. It's how they maintain genetic diversity."

"Yup, ma'am. I knew there was something I liked about these big lugs. Sounding more and more like Marines every minute. You oughta see the way some of those young'uns climb on and off each other when they're on liberty." Gunny could no longer suppress her laugh. "But, hold on. Who are the females now?"

"Well, one-ninth of the band. Greta named a few, but the only one I knew was Phillip. Stig was ready last month. Greta is midway through her cycle. It's part of her job to keep track of those things, but it's all widely known. They don't have any shame or hang-ups about sex."

It was clear from the look on her face that Gunny wanted to make another wisecrack about the promiscuity of young Marines, but relented. "You're holding the best news for last again, aren't you, ma'am?"

"As always," said Nadja with a smile.

"So, what else did you learn?"

"There seems to be a fairly well-developed trading network in this part of Skiathos. I didn't press her too hard, but Greta says merchant trains travel to and from Madrid at this and other times of the year, buying hides, meat, and other products and selling manufactured goods from the cities."

"You're thinking we might hitch a ride with one of these caravans?"

Nadja nodded. "Let's just keep this to ourselves for now—you, me, and Spiros—but if we can sniff out a caravan going even in the general direction of that extract point you identified, maybe we can press Stig, Greta, and the others into helping us book passage."

"It's a little risky going with strangers, ma'am, but definitely worth a try. I like the idea that none of these folks would harm us, but...."

"But there are rulebreakers in every species. I get that, Gunny. Let's find out if this is even feasible first. Then we can lay our plans and pitch them to our friends."

"And deal with whatever risks might arise later."

"Agreed."

14: The Gathering

The next day passed in the same leisurely fashion as had the one before it.

The band made a late start, and throughout most of the day Spiros rode Gunny's mount, while Gunny switched back and forth between riding with Gareth, Phillip, and a few others. Nadja again walked the morning away with Greta, poking about for roots as well as nuts, flowers, and sundry other things to fill the doctor's bag.

Afterward, she spent some time in the saddle with Stig, who had worked most of the morning with Gwyneth, pushing the band's herds northward. Greta had tutored her on the nature of life, and Stig educated her on the finer points of what to expect at the "gathering" they were to attend.

"How many will be there?" she asked him.

"Oh, many."

"How many?" She realized it was a silly question the moment she'd asked it. Lacertians seldom kept tally the way human's might, and numbers for them were often colorful abstractions.

"Folk will number the same as our herd many, many times over," he answered to her surprise. *"They will cover the ground in every direction, from the village to past the waters."*

So? Many, many thousands. Nadja pondered her brief flyover of Madrid from days before, reminding herself that locations often appeared markedly different from the air than they did from the ground. She recalled a walled village of perhaps a few hundred inhabitants with a high stone tower. The waters, a series of sapphire blue oasis pools, extended in a green belt for a kilometer or so in every direction. It was true; to fill such an area would require many, many thousands of Lacertians.

She may have begun to think like them, for her next question came naturally. *"Will there be enough fodder for all the animals so close to the village?"*

"Oh, plenty. If the animals rest, they are nourished from their tails. They won't lose much weight in two or three days."

"What happens then?" she asked. *"After two or three days?"*

"We keep them in pens, and then we sell most. Some we will feast upon."

Stig went on to explain that the band would part with most of its animals at market and at the end of the gathering would return to their distant pastures with fewer than 200 of the stoutest beasts to begin to rebuild their herd. This week was one of the highlights of their year for a variety of reasons.

Her friend continued to speak in response to her various questions and promptings.

"There will be feasts and merchants and performers," he said when she asked about what they would do there.

What he said afterward wasn't perfectly clear; a number of words he used over the next five minutes were new to her, but another 90 minutes of questions and clarifications ironed out most of it. It required her to decipher swiftly 50 or so new phrases and concepts. The whole endeavor left her feeling exuberant but also a bit light-headed.

"So, there will be races and contests? What types of contests?" Their next week was sounding more and more like what Spiros had first prognosticated: a holiday.

"Some will race on foot, and others will race their animals. There will be contests of strength, and contests of arms."

"Will there be bloodshed in those? In the contests of arms?" Nadja was surprised there would be fighting, given the tenor of the last two days' armistice.

"Yes, but only in the proper place."

She felt her brow knit against her will. *"What if there are conflicts during the gathering?"*

"Then the residents of the village will judge them. They are...." He seemed to grope for a word. *"They are special."*

Nadja leaned back into Stig's broad chest and pondered a moment. What exactly had he meant by "special"? He seemed to have another idea in mind and to have used that word as a substitute for it. Perhaps the idea behind the word was too difficult for her to master—he was sometimes sensitive to her limitations—but might his reticence have been something else?

The conversations she'd had with Stig and the others were fascinating in more ways than she could recount. The chats revealed much beyond the information her new friends shared with her. Imparting knowledge about themselves, about their way of life, was often difficult for members of the band. She wondered. What was it like to live a life so insular and so full of certainty about all things that the very idea that things might be different

74

was an idea left unthought? A world where some things were so simple, so manifest, so obvious that they confounded explanation?

She let that moment pass and moved on to other topics.

An hour or so later, after having eked a few more dollops of information about traders and merchants from her riding companion, Nadja's eyes beheld a wonder. Their ambling mount rounded a slight hill, and on a valley floor before them lay a deep, dark emerald wreathed in startling blue.

Madrid.

The place was still about 15 kilometers distant, but from the rise on which they'd halted they could see 50 kilometers or more into the distance. From every direction, vast streams of Lacertians and livestock slowly wended their way toward the place, already ringed as it was by teeming throngs of early arrivals.

The sight of it took her breath away. *Many, many, many thousands*, she thought to herself.

—

The band made an early stop in the evening and, after a few hours of what might have passed for work (had the band's labors not looked so much like preparations for a night on the town), they were up with the sun the next morning.

Spiros and Gunny got caught up in the spirit of things, but Nadja spent most of the evening and part of the morning on her tablet catching up with her journal. She'd promised herself to be more attentive to logging everything that transpired on the planet.

It was midmorning when the band assembled in the middle of camp, and Nadja was thoroughly taken aback. Despite the armistice, all were bedecked in their full martial regalia, and the members of the band were draped with every imaginable color of sarong, sari, veil, and wrap. The colors of the gorgeous and billowing vestments were so loud and vivid that she several times felt the urge to avert her gaze lest she be struck blind. In their Sunday best, the band was a wonder to behold.

Except for the cubs and a few guards—one could never discount the chance a predator might steal into camp and grab a cub or an infant—the entire band, en masse, mounted their finest steeds, bedecked with their best saddles, and paraded as a single grand cavalcade to the carnival at Madrid some 10 kilometers distant.

The three humans, Gunny and Spiros on their mount and Nadja again with Stig, had knocked the dust from their fatigues and endeavored to blend in as best they were able, given the fact that few cubs would be present for the festivities. All were excited at the prospect of seeing a place that might be a stepping-stone to their repatriation.

As they rode, Nadja chatted with Stig. She was proud of her linguistic accomplishments in such a brief time. Among those she knew best—Stig, Greta, Gwyneth, and several others—she understood most of what was said to her. With others, she understood about half of what was uttered in one-on-one conversation, though her comprehension diminished with each new speaker who joined a discussion. Still, encountering Lacertians in their thousands was not as daunting as it might have been.

Nadja found herself glancing backward and forward several times, wondering about their numbers. Their company seemed too few. *"Where are the rest?"*

"Clever cub," Stig muttered. *"Gwyneth and some riders pushed the herd to the pens last night and will meet us there. A few went early with Blacky to find a spot and prepare a feast."*

Of course ... how silly. She might have missed Gwyneth, but the band's leader was not among them at that moment. *"Who is the feast for?"*

"Everyone."

"You feed everyone?"

"Generosity is an obligation," he said simply.

"So, all of the bands will be holding feasts?"

"All of them ... all who are able."

"What would prevent them?"

"Oh, cub. Some are poor and weak."

And there it was in a nutshell, something that had been floating around in her head as she'd watched this martial folk make its preparations for the gathering. Feasts, like everything in Lacertian culture, were public relations exercises designed to broadcast one thing: the band's great strength. Though outwardly it might seem different, that was the nub of it. Fine weapons and armor? A show of strength, even in a time of truce such as now. Sumptuous gowns for a people who generally went about unclad? A show of wealth and strength. Vast herds? A large war-party? Strength. Lavish feasts for all? Of course, strength.

The more she chatted with Stig as the road slowly rolled by, the more she was convinced of this truism.

"All the bands will have daily feasts," he said, as if it were perfectly self-evident. *"The first two days we will do little but eat and visit. Then the trading begins, and the contests. The true gathering, the gathering of leaders, will come last. But we will feast throughout."*

76

The thought of such a thing was fascinating. For their size, Lacertians were unusually light eaters. Nadja presumed, given their inability to excrete waste, that their metabolisms were enormously efficient. What would happen if one of their number overate? And what constituted feasting?

She also found herself pondering what delicacies might be on the menu. Even before her arrival on the planet, it had shocked her to learn humans could digest some Lacertian foods, and it was only with great skepticism that she'd received news from Gunny that everything laid before them was both safe to eat and sometimes quite palatable. How was such a thing possible? Precious few victuals not grown on carefully terraformed worlds ever had been found safe for human consumption. Why here?

She thought to inquire more about the feasts, as well as the entertainers and whatnot, but by that time the village was drawing nigh. And it was not at all as it had seemed from the air—no great surprise there. The tower, which was located beside the large village gates, was nearly 20 meters high and even at a distance was formidable and imposing. The village walls, or, rather, the *town* walls were more than a third that height.

The tower and walls appeared to be hewn of a smooth and bleached stone, and the closer the band came to them the more utilitarian and menacing they seemed. There were frequent hooked spikes near the top of the wall to dissuade climbers, and the tops of the wall and tower itself were capped with sturdy battlements.

As they moved onward and approached the broad field that separated the town wall from the fringe of green that formed the oases, the crowds about them grew thicker and their pace slowed. There was no hurry and no pushing, only shuffling and jostling. From time-to-time a passing Lacertian would gape or make a playful coo, but none seemed put-off or alarmed by the presence of three aliens or outsiders in their midst.

For the nth time, Nadja wondered about this strange and accepting people. Had they seen outsiders before? Was this merely their constitution? Their way of being?

Before she knew it, Stig's beast was lumbering off the trail and across some low hummocks to a broad tent in the open field before the town wall. She recognized Blacky approaching, as much as she could recognize anyone in this vast ocean of new and alien faces—even in camp it sometimes was difficult keeping straight who was who.

The band's leader patted her head and exchanged a few words with Stig when they were met, and she found herself lifted from the mount and deposited feet-first on the ground. Blacky conducted her to the tent, speaking calmly and gently with her, pointing out things here and there as he might to a young child.

"*The beast roasts beyond,*" he said, before pointing to the carpets and cushions within the cavernous pavilion, the largest such she'd seen outside a circus. "*And here our friends and guests may relax and eat.*"

Throughout the broad space were large platters of food, mostly variations on the nut and tail-meat delicacies on which they had dined in recent days. The surprisingly appealing aroma of cooking meat reached Nadja for the first time, and she could see the carcass of one of their great six-legged kine on a spit, smoking and sizzling on the far side of the tent.

Nadja felt Gunny sidle up behind her, and when she did, a now squatting and smiling Blacky gingerly reached up and fed them each a morsel of food from a large platter. For all that he lacked the gentleness of Greta and the patience of Stig, their benefactor was always kind and affectionate.

"*Eat as you like and rest. Explore as you wish and fear not; you are safe here.*" Pointing outside, he indicated the town's tall main tower, almost a kilometer distant. "*I know my kind all rise tall above you. If you get lost, wait at the tower. One of us will come for you.*" He patted them each affectionately and then reached over and lightheartedly tossed the hair of Spiros, who had entered behind Gunny. The band's leader then went about his leaderly business.

"This is a big damn tent," said Spiros, looking up and about.

Nadja was already carefully regarding the tent frame. It seemed to be shaped of the same bamboo-like material the Lacertians fashioned, glued, and laminated in some manner to make something akin to wood. Gunny flopped down and began to nibble from a tray on a low table.

"So, I guess this *is* a holiday," said Spiros as he took a place opposite the NCO. There was only a tinge of self-satisfaction in his voice.

Nadja sat cross-legged where she stood. "And it smells so damn good here. Of course, it always does on this rock."

"Cause these people don't shit," interjected the gunnery sergeant.

"That might be part of it, Gunny. But there's ... I dunno. Maybe you're right. Maybe there is some sort of something in the air." Some sort of intoxicant? If such a thing had gone unidentified, it was yet another bone she had to pick with Wray and his team. "But who would have guessed the meat would smell so good?"

"I thought it was just us, ma'am. First time they butchered an animal like this, both me and Spiros about flipped."

"And it tastes just as good as it smells," said the lance corporal. "Not that bittersweet … or bitter-bitter taste of most of their food."

"Just like chicken?" joked Nadja.

Gunny gave one of her laughs. "Y'know, ma'am. It does a little bit. Like a cross between steak and chicken. You gotta get it fresh though, right off the bone."

Nadja leaned back to get a better look at the animal on the spit. "How long till lunch?"

Gunny glanced over as well. "Oh, I dunno. It looks to be another two hours or more. Spiros?"

"Yeah, Gunny, I'd say about that."

Nadja stood. "Good. Time enough to explore."

The gunnery sergeant mirrored her rise, a hint of doubt on her handsome face.

"Blacky said it was safe." She looked at the chronometer on her tablet before tucking it back into a cargo pocket. "Spiros, if Gunny and I aren't back in two or three hours, don't worry overly much. If we get lost, our hosts know to find us at the tower. That's our rally point outside the tent."

15: A Mother's Touch

Moments later, Nadja and the NCO were pacing toward the distant tower. Before departing, she had taken a quick assessment of the band members still present.

"Gunny, did you see where Greta slipped off to?"

"I didn't." The woman looked around. Most of those within view were armed and armored, and many sported a variety of cloaks and wraps. "She shouldn't be hard to find the way she was dressed, even in this crowd."

It was true. Greta had arrayed herself in a knee-length chainmail hauberk and steel half helm and bore a long saber, over which was an elaborate wrap of the most vivid orange. Their enormous friend likely could be seen from orbit.

The closer they got to the tower, the greater was the press. From time-to-time, of course, they would get a friendly smile or an affectionate pat from a passerby. And over the next thirty minutes, their search for their friend produced no Greta but was hardly fruitless. They saw much.

On the broad trail to the front gate, they found what Nadja could only describe as a series of stalls for the sale or trade of what appeared an endless variety of items. There were weapons, armor, cloth, and trinkets. Every manner of cooking utensils and tools were to be found, as were saddles, harnesses, and tack. The amount and variety of doodads and thingamabobs was beyond counting or qualifying.

Behind each stall were one or two tall Lacertians, most of whom had the dark amber colorations of mature adults; around these, however, were the first cubs Nadja had seen at the carnival. The cubs were engaged in a variety of simple tasks and, as did the cubs of "their" band, these took their guidance from the adults in a series of touches, gestures, motions, and demonstrations. The youngsters were intelligent but pre-vocal.

"Ma'am, take a look at this." Gunny motioned to a stall about 200 meters from the town's main gate.

Within the stall, placed on a stand amid a variety of items Nadja did not recognize, was a small stack of what appeared to be writing paper or parchment. It was a rougher quality than the parchment they'd obtained from Trixie, but it seemed unlikely the material was for anything else. When she reached over to touch the material, a tall Lacertian materialized and regarded her carefully with what could only be amusement. The shopkeeper said nothing and made no motion to instruct the two humans or send them away.

"*What is this for?*" Nadja asked.

The words seemed to startle the shopkeeper, who replied with a series of pops and purrs that Nadja didn't recognize. For a moment, she panicked that she might need to start afresh in learning some local dialect, but the merchant spoke again, this time more patiently.

"*What strange cubs you are,*" it said. Another flurry of sounds followed of which Nadja understood only a few. It was enough.

"*We're not from around here,*" Nadja said. "*We are from far away.*" She pointed to the material. "*I've seen such things before. Is it for making marks?*"

"*It is, little cub. But it's poor quality, and I have no use for it.*" The merchant reached down and gently slid a single sheet from the pallet and, after rolling it in a tube, handed it to Nadja. "*Take this as a plaything.*"

There was a furious tugging on her blouse sleeve followed by Gunny's whisper.

"Greta, three o'clock, ma'am."

The merchant's kindness was touching, and she thanked the Lacertian profusely before toddling off after Gunny. Why did she feel so much like a child all of a sudden?

It was a feeling that deepened when she and Gunny reached Greta, who was perusing some items in a stall and talking rather deliberately to a merchant who stood behind a broad table. Before Nadja could even speak to announce herself, a large hand with claws carefully averted descended on her shoulder and pulled her tenderly to the surgeon's side.

Greta's conversation did not skip a beat, and she'd appeared not to have noticed Nadja's presence beyond having taken her in hand. Their friend continued to talk, and over the next several minutes as Greta dickered with the merchant over some item in the stall, she several times squeezed Nadja almost imperceptibly and once gently caressed her hair. Another hand snaked out and corralled Gunny, pulling the NCO to the same place on Greta's right as Nadja was on her left. At no time was the tall medic's attention diverted from her transaction.

It's amazing, thought Nadja, *mothers all over the universe can multitask*. She didn't know from whence that thought sprang, but she felt a sudden lump rise in her throat, a reaction that confounded her even more. She knew Greta wasn't a mother, wasn't a female at all in any human sense. But there it was.

Several more minutes passed before Greta concluded her transaction and, reaching into her bag, she recovered a small pouch that she gave to the merchant. A long flask of something from the trader disappeared into that same pocket. It was then Greta peered down at her for the first time.

"I haven't forgotten about the markings," she said to Nadja soothingly. Making a half turn, Greta steered the two women in the direction of the tower. *"Have you eaten?"*

Nadja worried that her stomach might growl in reply. She'd been in such a hurry to explore that neither she nor Gunny had troubled themselves to do more than take a few nibbles at the band's canopy. *"We're fine,"* she fibbed to her enormous friend.

Greta made not a sound, but with a slight pressure to Nadja's back changed their course to a nearby tent. The place was not so grand as the band's feast, but those within greeted them all as old friends. Food was soon shoved in their direction, and to Nadja's surprise, Greta began eating at a pace far beyond her usual delicate picking.

"Eat your fill," she told the women. *"It does great honor to our hosts."*

Gunny shrugged and began to tear into a concoction of nuts, spiced tail, and fresh meat. Nadja mirrored her efforts and within 10 minutes was feeling bloated, thankful at least that the food was tasty. Greta during that entire time made sweet chirping noises of delight that appeared to gladden those attending them.

Lacertians came and went, eating and drinking, but few words beyond simple pleasantries were exchanged. Not only was this tent smaller, but the band that now hosted them clearly was of modest means. The chirps and coos of Greta and other guests seemed to fill them with pride, so much so that Nadja imitated the noises as best she was able.

Greta ate until it was clear Gunny and Nadja could consume no more, and with no pretense she stood and ushered the two humans beneath the canopy. Not a word of thanks was spoken, but outside Greta made a great show of loudly huffing three times before disgorging an enormous spray of vomitus into a large barrel five paces from the tent.

She then moved aside and carefully regarded her two small companions. Without hesitation, Gunny stepped forward, inserted two fingers in her throat, and emptied her guts into the barrel. Howls of delight exploded from the tent, but Nadja hesitated.

"We don't ... this isn't ...," she stuttered. *Oh, fuck it.* She mimicked the gunnery sergeant, and after a few false starts began gagging and vomiting piteously into the barrel. "Shit," she muttered after, wiping the phlegm from her mouth.

82

Moments later, they'd resumed their path toward the tower.

"Christ. Gunny, you could've warned me about that," she whispered.

"First time I've seen that particular behavior, ma'am. I just followed Greta."

Nadja had to squelch a laugh. "At least we know how they evacuate waste now."

"Yes, but we need to rehydrate, ma'am. We ain't them." The gunnery sergeant looked around, and after a few moments skipped over to another tent. She soon rejoined Nadja and Greta on the trail with a large kerchief filled to bursting with greens.

They resumed their walk, gently sucking on the juicy greens as they did. The taste wasn't bad, and the shoots were remarkably refreshing. None spoke again until they reached the gate to the town.

"*Sit in the shade and finish eating,*" Greta told them. "*I need to find someone. Then I'll be back. Wait.*"

Their friend departed, and Gunny, apparently having understood the gist of Greta's words, immediately took a seat in the shadow of the tower on a smoothly carved block that might have been a bench. Nadja peered up and examined the enormous edifice before joining her. The heat of the day had arrived, but she couldn't resist standing a bit longer and pondering. It was an awe-inspiring citadel.

"Why did you name her Greta?" Nadja asked the NCO once she'd sat next to her, taking another green when she did. The day was dry, but so very hot.

"It was the closest thing to her name I could come up with." Gunny paused and gave a faint Mona Lisa smile. "There is definitely something feminine and almost maternal about her. I'm not sure if I saw that back then though."

Nadja sat for a few minutes brooding and groping for words. Gunny found them for her.

"I saw you getting a little misty back there," the Marine added. "I get that way sometimes too. These folks have had more than six months to get under my skin."

"I dunno," Nadja nearly stuttered. She usually wasn't comfortable with her feelings and words just came spewing forth. "I just … I never really had a great, um … with my … you know."

"I was never all that close to my own mom," the Marine confessed in a comforting way. "Her and dad were … are … bohemians and self-styled social activists. They always had time for everybody and everything else growing up. There was always some government office or corporation to protest, some underprivileged somebody that needed their help. Funny thing is … they actually don't seem to like anything or anyone. They always talked up the common man, getting back to the land and that kind of stuff, but when I fell in love and married a farmer, they about shit themselves."

"Oh, Jeez, Gunny…," Nadja was at least able to stifle a laugh. "How …?"

"The farm was too big … too commercial for their tastes. Or that's what they said. It was just bullshit. My folks are city dwellers, wouldn't know the first thing about 'getting back to the land.' They sure as hell couldn't give up their tech, and they'd lapse into coma if they ever got more than three city blocks from a gourmet coffeeshop."

This time, the two women did laugh, and loudly.

"No," Really Nice continued. "I swore to God I'd never be like that with my kids. They always came first with me. Course, maybe the pendulum swung too far. I think the kids were happy to get old mom into the Marine Corps and out of their hair."

"I don't believe that for a second."

"Nah, you're probably right. They seem eager to have me back home. Of course, the poor dears will have another century or more to get sick of having me around after I retire."

Nadja thought again of her own parents. "How about your folks now? Do you keep up with them?"

"Not much," Gunny admitted. "But they do have a good relationship with my kids … at least better than they had with me. I'm grateful for that."

She couldn't resist a moment or two of silent admiration for the gunnery sergeant. Gunny was remarkable—it was written all over the faces of those back on the platform when they'd spoken of her—but there was something Nadja couldn't shake. Maybe it really was some intoxicating something in the air, or maybe it was the Marine's candor. But Nadja unburdened now in a way she never had.

"I think my mom resents me," said Nadja calmly. She'd finally managed to step past her discomfort and say something she'd scarcely even admitted to herself.

"Ma'am?"

"Well, I mean … my mom looks great for a woman in her 80s, but she was too old for that last big thing in genetic engineering. I think she's like a lot of people: They want to live long lives, but they don't want to get old." Nadja shook her head. "I guess I can't blame her."

Human life expectancies had more than doubled since humanity first had travelled to the stars. With care and the benefits of genetic science, it wasn't uncommon for people to live 180 years or more. But the slow vagaries of time marked those same folks in all the usual ways. What use a long life if lived mired in successive levels of decrepitude?

Allele Stacking, which had emerged when Nadja was still a girl, promised something new: The same long life with all the whims and petulance of aging experienced only at the very, very end. People like Nadja and Gunny could expect to maintain their youthful appearance and great vigor for nearly two centuries before succumbing to sudden and overwhelming physical deterioration in the final months of their lives. That was a fair deal, wasn't it? Folks like Nadja's parents certainly thought so. But despite nearly 50 years of clamoring from people of their generation, certain hurdles in the process had yet to be overcome. Namely, the procedure, which most every child now underwent before age 2, was only effective if administered prior to the end of adolescence.

The treatment had been Nadja's 16th birthday present. The irked and ungrateful teen had wanted a new car, a fact, one of many, Nadja's mother never broached in their infrequent communications—Nilofer Bikram would never be so unrefined or boorish—but the unpleasant flavor of it was always there, concealed somewhere on the edge of a phrase.

How had people not foreseen the social and familial complexities arising from such a phenomenon? The envy and bitterness of the older generations who missed out on the procedure was the least of it. Future generations of young had their hands full. Easy enough to ignore grandparents, and great-grandparents, and great-great grandparents locked away in some retirement village in the country, but how does a person process or absorb ... well ... having a great-great grandfather or a grandmother standing next to him or her in a Marine rifle platoon? Looking more like a sister or a brother than an ancestor?

The very idea got Nadja to smiling again. She now was slightly embarrassed she'd raised the subject and hoped to change the topic. "Sorry, Gunny. I was just feeling sorry for myself. I've been doing that a lot lately and have no right. I'm a lucky, lucky woman."

The 60-year-old Marine flashed another of her girlish smiles before motioning to the natives around them. "I get what you're saying, ma'am. But as much as I'm gonna miss these knuckleheads when we're gone, I'll wait until we're back on the platform and out of danger before marking myself as lucky."

"That sounds like a fair call, Gunny. And I promise not to inflict my mommy issues on you until that day comes."

The Marine's only reply was to continue smiling.

The two spent the next hour awaiting Greta and discussing their possible next steps to extricate themselves from their current predicament. They hammered the problem from every angle, but came up with nothing new. After that time, Greta returned.

"*Let's go eat,*" said the medic when she arrived.

"*Where have you been?*"

"*I was with a friend of a friend. Someone I want you to meet tomorrow morning.*"

With that, the Lacertian gently steered the two women back in the direction of the band's pavilion.

16: The Scholar

Gaius was unlike any Lacertian Nadja so far had encountered. Three days before, Greta had taken her to meet the tall and patient black at his quarters high in the tower, and it was a meeting that was as confusing as it was eye opening.

The first and most obvious thing she'd noticed upon their meeting was the papers. There were documents, either paper or parchment, everywhere from floor to ceiling in his high and airy accommodations. Several writing surfaces were covered in them, and thick bundles of them polluted racks on his walls to the north, east, south, and west.

How could the linguistic and anthropological survey teams have missed such a thing?

Such a volume of writing could not imaginably be a one-off, a happening limited to this one tiny slice of Skiathos. Gaius told her as much. True, literacy was limited to a tiny stratum of the planet's society, but Nadja's new friend, a scholar of obvious breadth, knew of no fewer than five different writing systems used for numerous purposes in various corners of just that one region of the planet.

There was something terribly, terribly wrong with this planetary survey mission, and the more time she spent with Gaius the more she realized Dr. Gunter Wray was at the center of it all. Even before the attack that had killed the Marine commander and stranded Gunny and Spiros, Wray already had been the survey mission's senior civilian and lead social scientist, and as such he'd directed the pace and location of all research.

That fact could not be an accident. Despite the burdensome and tongue-twisting phonemes and often topsy-turvy syntax of the Lacertian language, it was a language, a spoken tongue that even a moderately qualified researcher should have been able to unravel in short order. And the decision to focus linguistic research on what they originally had imagined to be a cadet branch of a broader species had been the decision of one person: Gunter Wray.

She scarcely knew the man, having run across him several times at conferences and meetings, but his reputation was solid, his credentials first rate. True, there had been a small survey team on the planet before Wray's arrival, but it mostly had been dedicated to studying geology. The only linguists during that time had been a small team of naval specialists whose job was to record and document Lacertian speech for others to study.

She wondered. Wray had been a lead on the project from the outset, even before he'd arrived on planet to supervise personally. How much of the project's planning and research had he designed and directed from the beginning? She wasn't sure but remembered having seen his name frequently in correspondence and on documents.

"What the fuck is going on here?" she said aloud, not for the first time in recent days. She glanced up. The studious Gaius hadn't noticed her micro-outburst. But he wouldn't; Gaius also muttered to himself while pursuing his various projects.

If mothers are the same throughout the galaxy, she thought, *scholars must be too.*

She bent her head and went back to the maps Gaius had provided her. He had maps!!

They were rough charts, often beautifully sketched, but in that Lacertian way, wherein distance was a charming abstraction. But the one she'd studied throughout the day was a detailed draft of trade routes that moved to and from Madrid and other localities within the great Central Desert in which they were situated. At first, going had been slow. With Gaius's gentle help, though, she'd finally come to understand the frenetic chicken scrawl that locals used to mark such things. It was a mix of scholarly and commercial writing that, had Nadja not had the scholar's help and the use of her tablet, might have taken her months to decipher.

With that bit of help, things had sped along. The distances and proportions of the native maps were off, but she had access to Gunny's 3-D map in all its detail. All she'd needed to do was compare which landmark was where and, hopefully with Gaius's help, find a merchant caravan going in the general direction of the extraction point Gunny had identified.

She didn't want to depart Madrid without the support of Blacky and the band, but one way or the other she and the two Marines needed to get back to their own folk. And presuming the platform was still in orbit and Sgt. Lyn had requested naval support, as the young sergeant should have, Nadja would be able to come back later and patch things up with their friends in the band.

Their repatriation in recent days had come to feel much, much closer. It was now only a matter of when they got back, not if. She opted not to dwell on the possibility they might be the last humans on or near Skiathos. Instead, she glanced at the chronograph on her tablet. It was late, and Gunny would be along with dinner soon.

Really Nice had been a godsend, bringing food, greens, and water and running errands. Nadja had seldom left the broad workstation Gaius was allowing her to use, so she mostly had avoided the eat-till-you-puke culinary orgy taking place on the fields below. She had to admit though, the kine meat was best as Spiros and Gunny had described, fresh off the bone. And she was looking forward to the NCO's arrival.

As if on cue, the gunnery sergeant walked through the door. It took Nadja one look to know something was missing.

"Gunny, am I not getting dinner this evening?"

"You are, ma'am. But not until after the intervention."

"What vice do I need to forego this time?" asked Nadja with a smile.

"Nothing much. I couldn't make out the finer details, but Greta wants you back at the big tent. I'm guessing the band thinks you've been cooped up here too long."

"The games start tomorrow," Nadja said plainly. Both Gaius and Greta had mentioned the fact that morning. It obviously had been a hint.

"It's not gonna kill you to take a day off, ma'am. We can't leave Madrid until the gathering is over anyway. And I think Stig misses you."

Gunny again spoke the plain truth. It would be at least five or six days before caravans would begin to depart, and Nadja had more or less finished her survey of the maps. As much as she wanted to keep buried in Gaius's small library, there was always the chance the scholar might not be able or willing to help them find a caravan. Best to keep their options open and touch base with her friends in the band.

And to be perfectly honest, she missed seeing them. Greta had stopped by the office several times, but Nadja had caught only glimpses of the others when she'd gone back to the big tent at night to catch a few hours' sleep. And, yes, it would be nice to see Stig.

She leapt from her stool, went over to where Gaius sat reading a manuscript, and gave the scholar a warm hug. He hardly seemed to notice. "Let's go get something to eat, Gunny."

Slipping out the chamber door, Nadja bounded down the four flights of stone stairs like she wanted to be somewhere and soon found herself nearly skipping out the tower gate, Gunny hot on her tail. It was about a half hour before sunset, and much of the day's heat had dissipated. Gunny caught up, and they continued at a quick step.

The pair had walked only a short way, chatting about the events of the day, when a familiar form came into view. A hundred or so meters ahead, Stig stood near a group of other Lacertians, his hands on the reins of a kine, speaking in what appeared to be an amiable fashion. A minute later, Nadja was close enough to overhear. Her friend was negotiating a trade.

After a brief greeting, the two women took their place next to Stig, and as Nadja attempted to follow the conversation, Gunny was soon distracted by the products of a nearby stall.

The ebb and flow of their discussion was at first difficult for Nadja to follow, but as she caught the rhythm of their words, it was apparent Stig admired a dagger owned by one of the four warriors with whom he chatted and wished to obtain it in exchange for the animal.

The whole thing seemed a bit peculiar. Stig had numerous finely wrought and beautiful weapons. (He clearly was one of the wealthier members of the band.) And she'd learned enough of Lacertian ways to know the well-rounded animal Stig offered was of much greater value than the dagger, which seemed of only middling quality.

As the bargaining progressed, she was certain she was missing something. Stig appeared keen on obtaining the dagger, but the others looked to be driving up their own offer. Something was not right, a confusion she finally attributed to her own language skills and to the subtle accents of the four Lacertians.

In the end, her friend exchanged his plump kine for the dagger, a short recurve bow, and a bolt of dark blue cloth. Afterward, she and Stig recovered Gunny and headed to the big tent, which they reached only after pausing several times along the way to eat, drink, and puke.

At the band's tent, there was much less pressure to overindulge, and the humans spent the evening casually eating, drinking, and laughing with their friends. Greta, as always, was an absolute card and despite her calm and quiet demeanor had the entire tent in stitches for most of the evening.

"Did I ever tell you about the toe, ma'am?" Gunny asked after a time.

"The toe?"

"Yeah, so, about a month before you joined us, the band got in a tussle with some neighbors over a watering tank, and a few of the warriors were hurt pretty bad." The NCO glanced around the tent before settling her eyes on a Lacertian whose name was unknown to Nadja. "Anyway, from what I was able to puzzle out, when that bloke over there regained consciousness, Greta told him he'd lost a toe in the fight and that she'd lost track of the body parts in the chaos and accidently had sewn somebody else's toe back on him."

A surge of uncertainty hit Nadja. "Wait … can she really…?"

"No, ma'am. Me and Spiros were both there. Greta made the whole thing up. Guy didn't even lose a toe … but she swears up and down it's

90

true." Gunny began to laugh. "Every once in a while, I still see that poor dude looking down at his toe and giving it a little wiggle."

The story really wasn't all that funny. But such a ridiculous prank was so thoroughly and pathetically human that Nadja couldn't resist bursting into laughter.

17: A Desert Night

An hour later, it was time for their daily toilet. Before the gathering, finding a place to relieve themselves had required nothing more than taking a short stroll outside camp. Among the vast throngs of the gathering, finding a convenient place was often troublesome. At the tower, Gaius allowed Nadja a small pot in which to piss, which she'd taken to dumping surreptitiously in a drainage ditch on the outskirts of town—or not-so surreptitiously, given the sour looks she'd several times gotten from passersby.

For all its shortcomings, Lacertian food at least kept the three humans regular, which was something of a convenience, and since their arrival in Madrid, they'd taken to slipping off through the oasis pools to the sand dunes beyond for a short and satisfying squat.

That evening, having discovered their small ritual, Stig insisted on going with them.

"*It's not safe,*" he said quietly as they left the tent and turned toward the line of foliage that divided field from dune.

Nadja imagined what perils he might've meant and wondered if there might be some unknown something in the greenery that surrounded the pools. During the day, it was quite beautiful. There were all manner of bushes and flowers as well as long rows of what might have been palm trees if the person observing them chose to squint his or her eyes. The only real danger they'd encountered so far was stepping in a pile of vomit from the puke barrels that were emptied there, presumably as a form of fertilizer.

Gunny and Spiros were walking ahead, and Nadja looked up at Stig. "*Why isn't it safe? What dangers are there?*"

"*In the dunes. There are predators.*" Her companion then reeled off a list of names that were to her simply names. The only terror in them was the depth within Stig's throat from whence the words emanated. (She had no idea what a "*ghrr'g'g'g't*" was, but it sounded bloody menacing.)

"*But there are bands camping on the dunes,*" she countered. It was true, but only a few had set their tents there.

"*Only a few,*" he said, echoing her thought. "*And they post guards. The gathering is a time of great danger. Predators gather too.*"

It was another reminder of where the three humans found themselves. Most Human worlds were tame and well ordered. But here? Skiathos was a planet of prodigious violence and untold danger. It was more than just another world. *No wonder the members of the band cleave so closely to one another*, she thought intently.

It took them about 10 minutes to cross through the foliage line, and the two Marines immediately dropped trou when they reached their destination. There wasn't the least trace of modesty among their kind, and Nadja swiftly followed suit. The sparkle of watching humans poop, though, apparently had faded for Stig. For while they relieved themselves, he stood on a small hillock and peered into the gloom, as if carefully on watch.

The light of the planet's two tiny moons was paltry, but the thick canopy of stars in the Skiathos sky had provided ample illumination for their walk through the bush. As she wiped, stood, and buckled up, Nadja wondered what Stig could see through those two huge golden eyes.

Only a few minutes passed before all three finished their business and buried the evidence, and as a group they meandered to the rise where Stig stood vigil and, as they'd done on previous nights, flopped down on the sand to relax for a time before returning to the great tent. It took only moments for Stig to join them, after which they sat in silence, no one venturing a word lest they shatter the moment. The night was clear and calm and peaceful, and the great beauty of their surroundings, the heart-rending night vista before them, screamed that all was right in the universe and that creatures like the dreaded *"ghrr'g'g'g't"* simply could not exist. Not here.

What a strange place, she thought. At any other time, their surroundings would have been romantic. But there was none of that.

Still, after 20 or so minutes, Nadja found herself cozying up next to Stig for the warmth he provided against that cool desert night. For all the chill now, the heat of the Skiathos days was draining and exhausting, and glancing to her left, she noticed both Marines were stretched out and if not sleeping certainly were dosing. It reminded her that Gaius's offices were at least 10 degrees cooler than the 50 degrees centigrade of the normal day. She decided to let the Marines rest a while longer before heading back.

"Why did you need another dagger," she asked Stig quietly. The question came to her on an impulse.

"I didn't need another dagger."

"But you traded a big healthy animal for it."

"It was a big and plump animal," he agreed. *"And they gave me a good bow and a large blanket too. It was a fair trade."*

"But I don't understand. You have a huge bow and many blankets." For a scant moment, something in Stig's posture made her wonder if she'd not made him uncomfortable by her words, but when he spoke there was no hint of it.

"The band I traded with is from the north. They had a hard year."

Nadja wasn't sure whether it was her imagination, but thinking back, it occurred to her that the four with whom Stig had traded seemed a bit ragged. All were armed and armored, but none were draped in such finery as were the warriors of Blacky's band and others.

"What does it mean to have a hard year?" she asked.

"There are many bands in the north, and there is little pasture. And there are the Others. Only the strong survive."

The Others. Memory of her and Stig's conversation from days before returned to her. *"What is black rock?"* she asked, again on an impulse.

The answer, or part of it, came to her the moment she said those words. It was the first true epiphany she'd experienced since being on the planet. Blacky's true name was a series of light whispers she'd mastered while walking with Greta. It merely meant "Flower," hence, Black Flower—she'd even heard a few Lacertians from other bands refer to Blacky in that way, though the fact hadn't struck her until that very moment. Black Rock wasn't a "what." Black Rock was a "who."

"He's very bad," said Stig with what she thought was a hint of anxiety.

When they'd spoken last of Black Rock and "the Others," Stig's excitement had made the conversation difficult to follow. She wondered whether it was important at all, but before she could speak, Stig continued.

"It's nothing you need to worry about," her companion said in a hush. *"He's far away in the north and can't harm you here."*

Stig's last comments were ominous and prompted her to shift gears. If Black Rock was just another Lacertian warlord, as it sounded, then it wasn't all that important. She could always ask Gaius later, if her curiosity about the villain got the better of her. The Others though?

"Who are the Others?" she asked.

"They're not like us."

"Are they from another world?"

Stig glanced up toward the heavens. *"Like you are? ... I don't think so. Which of those are you from?"* he said, pointing skyward.

Was he trying to change the subject? The notion brought a smile to her face. *"You can't see my star from here."*

His eyes stayed on the heavens. *"Too bad. I wonder which star we come from."*

Those words took Nadja entirely by surprise. *"What?"*

"I wonder which star we come from," he repeated.

It took her several moments to sort her thoughts. *"Did you come from another planet?"*

"No." There was almost laughter in his voice. *"I came from the ground not far from here. But I heard once that the first of us came here from the stars."*

"Who told you that?"

"It was a storyteller at a gathering, an ancient black. I was young then, not much more than a cub."

"Do you think it's true?" she asked him.

This time, Stig did laugh. *"I did at the time. But I've heard lots of stories since then, all kinds of them."*

"What stories have you heard of the Others?" She wasn't sure why she asked. Unless she was missing something, the Others were a local group and unlikely to have the sufficient technology to attack Marine transports. So what concern was it of hers?

"Many, many stories."

Nadja sighed. She had to admit she was curious. *"What do they look like?"*

Her friend made some nonsensical sounds before speaking. *"They look a little like the animals we herd but smaller and ... they don't know right from wrong."*

"Do they speak?"

"Not like you and I do, not with their mouths."

"How do they speak?"

Stig gestured to the negative solemnly. *"I don't know. But they're not like us."*

"Then how do you know they talk?"

She felt his great arm wrap around her and give her a gentle squeeze. There were long moments of silence before he spoke.

"They say the Others once lived throughout the lands, but long, long ago there was much fighting between us and them. Over time, our people drove the Others from most places, and now they live only in the far-off mountains and other places where there is little pasture or food."

His enormous arm gave her yet another affectionate squeeze, and she knew there were more words to come.

"Many cycles passed. Then one day, long before even Black Flower was alive, there was one like us, but ... one who ... who didn't know the difference between right and wrong. And he was driven out, even by his

95

own band, and he went to live among the Others. For many cycles, he joined the Others in making war against us. Then, finally, there was a great gathering of the bands, and we went north and defeated them. The Others all dwell in the mountains again; and they only come down to kill and steal."

"*This one who didn't know right from wrong,*" she asked, "*is it Black Rock?*"

Her companion's gesture said it was so. "*He gathered more like us. I don't know how many. But they live among the Others still. They are all like Black Rock. They look like us on the outside, but they're like the Others on the inside.*"

She somehow sensed he'd completed his tale and wasn't sure whether she should press him further. But there was one thing about which she was certain she wanted to know.

"*Why did Black Rock's band drive him out?*" she asked. She right away felt a deep discomfort in Stig, an unease in him upon which she couldn't place a name.

Soon after, he huffed several times, and then, leaning closely, he breathed in her ear so quietly that it seemed as if he wanted to keep his words secret, to conceal them from all the world and from Heaven above.

"*He killed a cub,*" whispered Stig.

18: Finding a Place

A light rain hastened their return to the tent and maintained a gentle patter on the shelter throughout the night. It was barely more than a sprinkle, but it was the longest deluge they'd yet seen on Skiathos.

Nadja dozed fitfully, waking several times throughout the night. She'd concluded that Lacertians didn't sleep, at least not in the sense that humans knew it. There were periods of dormancy or torpor that came upon them for a few hours each day, usually at night, but even during those times some animal something within them remained alert, allowing them to engage in simple activities such as standing and walking or even tending the cooking fire, as she suspected some did throughout the night. It was like watching sleepwalkers, but sleepwalkers who could spring wide awake on a moment's notice.

The smell of roasting kine welcomed her to the morning, and as she stretched and smacked her lips, she took a careful look around. Stig was not to be seen, nor was Greta. Spiros likely was off on his morning piss, but she heard Gunny heckling the cooks out by the campfire in English and badly broken Lacertian. For reasons Nadja couldn't fully define, she again felt happy.

As she rose, she wondered who was present. Not all the band passed their nights in the big tent. Some went back to the band's camp past the dunes at night to check on the cubs or merely she suspected to enjoy the familiarity of their own tents.

After giving herself a shake and a few morning stretches, Nadja ambled over to the tent opening. The rain had passed for the moment, and the sun warmed the new day. She stood regarding the scene before her.

Outside, Stig sat on a saddle watching Gunny's one-sided wrestling match with one of the cooks. Over the next few minutes, her large friend tossed several tiny pebbles at a warrior Gunny had nicknamed Stuey—Nadja sometimes was at a loss to understand the Marine's naming scheme—and with each toss, Stuey, whose back was to the tent, would turn and look around suspiciously, before going back to his conversation. An innocent Stig would bide his time, pretending to regard Gunny's antics, before tossing the next pebble.

It was early, but the area was already in a bustle, and the kine seemed nearly ready for eating. As she watched, one of the cooks sampled a sliver of the meat before returning to the large handle that turned the spit. Three of his companions already were at a second fire preparing a newly skinned beast for consumption later in the day.

The band was wealthy and went through two or three animals per day, feeding all-comers. It was that thought that gave Nadja yet another epiphany. Food here was to be had aplenty, and none need go hungry during the gathering. Which was why Stig's lopsided trade the day before had so perplexed her. The warriors with whom he'd dealt had access to an abundancy of food. But now it dawned on her that what they lacked was meat to feed their guests. And Stig couldn't merely have given the warriors the beast; it wasn't how things were done.

A deep warmth for her friend and his openhandedness flooded her, a feeling tinged perhaps with a hint of shame. Life for the band was about more than raw strength and displays of power. That had been her earlier assessment, one she now sensed was not fully true. There was a great decency in these folks. Five days ago, Stig would have slain those warriors over a liter of water or a few shoots of greens. In five days hence, they yet again would be at swords' point. But now? Now they all came together as one, sharing the same affection and generosity of spirit with members of other bands as they did with their own.

She went over and sat next Stig on the saddle. He voiced an affectionate whirr when she did.

"*Will you compete in the games today?*" she asked.

"*No. That's not for me.*"

"*Who is it for?*" She found herself wishing she'd paid more attention to the subject during their earlier conversations.

"*Those who wish to test themselves, to show their strength. The young, the bold, those who wish to find a new place.*"

Nadja wasn't sure about that last category but suspected she knew what he meant. "*Those warriors with whom you traded yesterday, are they seeking a new place?*"

He made a gesture in the affirmative. "*I think so. They had some bad cycles and are fewer than 30 adults now. They won't survive another cycle.*"

"*How does that work?*" she asked. "*How does one find a new place?*"

"*Many ways. In a gathering, you compete to show your strength. If you're strong or swift, another band might take you.*" Stig's face took on that look it sometimes did when he was pondering something. "*That band of which we speak, I think their remaining fighters are strong. If they prove it in the games, I will ask Black Flower to bring them all into our band.*"

"Is that's all it takes?"

"Mostly. If they join us, we will be many. When next we make young, their seed and our seed will mix. Then we will be one band."

Stig reached into a bag on his saddle and retrieved a thick rag and a jar of what looked to be a white paste. Lifting his armor from where it leaned against his saddle, he began to polish and oil it with great diligence.

Nadja watched for a while and then sniffed loudly several times. Her nose and stomach told her it was time to eat.

After eating, Nadja was shanghaied briefly into turning the spit while others came and went, but the weather was still cool when Greta arrived and took her in hand. She and Stig, in their Sunday best, took the three humans to the carnival like two proud parents.

The rest of the day was a riot, an absolute carnival.

The violence they witnessed that morning at the broad amphitheater to the east of the town walls was shocking. There were no blunted weapons, no Marquis of Queensbury Rules—this was Skiathos—and the fighters in the pit went at one another hammer and tongs, in brutal, cold, and efficient silence. Fighting in this place was not an exercise in ritual or entertainment. There were no crowds cheering, no bloodthirsty fans. Warriors fought to prove their worth and perhaps to find a place, and spectators came to gauge the potential value of fighters to their bands. It took Nadja only a fleeting time to realize that most spectators had the black and dark amber cowls of older adults, leaders within their bands.

"Are your friends fighting today?" she asked Stig toward the end of the second bloody hour.

"No. They fight tomorrow and will win or lose as a band." He regarded her for a moment. *"Do you want to come then?"*

Nadja hesitated. In the past hour, she'd averted her eyes several times. Clearly her friend had noticed. She'd never thought of herself as squeamish, but …. *"Will they all live or die?"*

"Very few die," Greta interjected. *"It's usually only when two fighters are of equal skill that one is killed."*

Greta had explained everything at the beginning. The only real rule in these contests was that a fighter could not strike an opponent who was powerless to defend itself. Most bouts had ended quickly, with one or the other of the combatants delivering a devastating wound early on. Still, the carnage was ghastly.

She felt a gentle hand on her head. Stig.

"I've seen all I wish here today," he said. *"Let's get Gunny and Spiros and go watch the races. You'll enjoy those. I always do."*

It took them nearly an hour to reach the racecourse located on the dunes, picking their way through the press as they went. There were, of course, several stops to engorge and disgorge, and at one point a cheerful Greta stopped at a stall and obtained three brightly colored wraps, which she delivered to the protesting humans.

"I know this land is warm for you," she replied to their protests. *"It's also warm for us. These will help keep the sun away."*

It was extremely generous of her. Nadja wore fatigues almost like the uniforms the Marines were issued. These were hyper-durable and allegedly self-cleaning. In theory, they needed but one change of clothes, but it was delightful to have something to shield their heads from the sun beyond the thin uniform hoods. And the new garments were large enough to swath themselves from head to toe; it would be nice to have something else against their skin occasionally.

They spent the balance of the day sitting on a hillside, wrapped like mummies, and nibbling on greens, as they watched the spectacle of the flower of Lacertian youth racing one another and running their sleekest and fittest beasts across the dunes. The crowds were wild and loud and carefree, and the display was like every holiday should be, simply sublime.

Later in the evening, they capered over to the town's south walls and watched the most fantastic pageants of dancing, singing, juggling and tumbling, and storytelling. There was even a firebreather. The three humans were at a collective loss. In every possible nuance, the performances were completely different from any human gathering. The singing was … "interesting" was the only word to describe it. The dancing was difficult to describe at all. And the storytelling, which was an eclectic form of performance art, was hard even for Nadja to follow, let alone to explain to the others. But the skills of the jugglers and acrobats were breathtaking, beyond anything even the most highly trained humans could execute.

As different and alien as were those individual trees, the evening's entertainment was a forest that any human could have recognized. For the thousandth time, Nadja caught herself thinking how very much like, but how thoroughly different, their hosts were from humans.

19: Book of Gatherings

T he next few days sped by. They endured the melees, enjoyed the races, and reveled in the pageants and shows, which Greta helped her to understand. Nadja managed to slip away during the in-betweens and on a few occasions visited Gaius to peruse his maps and seek his guidance.

She had yet to mention the fact to their friends in the band, but Gaius had steered her toward several merchants who he knew were traveling in the direction the humans wanted to go and who he was confident would be willing to escort them most of the way. According to Gunny's map, the last leg of their trip, the portion wherein they would need to go it alone, was a stretch of only about 30 kilometers. The Marines were confident they could make the trip safely.

Nadja tried hard to avoid thinking that the journey would be a one-way trip, with no one there to meet them, and came up with numerous alternate scenarios. None of them were good. Either the platform was still intact, or it was not. If it were intact, the platform crew would detect their transponders once the three had gotten outside the EM interference that blanketed much of the planet. If there were no platform, they would know soon enough and would have to make plans accordingly. The ideal Plan B, if there were no recovery mission, would be to chart their way back to Madrid and, possibly, back to the band.

The only contingency she came up with was to write a detailed letter about their predicament and their plans and leave it with Gaius to give to any humans who might one day come looking for them. Perhaps a future search-and-rescue team would then find their well-picked bones in some animal's den in the wilderness.

She had no other ideas. Staying put simply was not an option. The planet was huge, and it might be decades before anyone found them, if they came at all.

To her great delight and vastly greater disappointment, Gaius was aware of the existence of alien races—it was, he'd told her, common knowledge among the learned—but neither he nor anyone within the local community at Madrid had direct experience with them. Worse yet, the scholar's modest library had nothing that addressed the subject. It was another dead end.

Her current visit with Gaius found her stopping in merely to say hello. It was the last night of the games and shows. Tomorrow, the gathering of leaders would begin, a three-day affair that marked the winding down of the entire holiday.

Nadja had mixed feelings about the whole matter, but Gaius was unusually voluble on this visit and managed to get her chatting about things upon which he'd been working. And, as always, he was full of questions about her world.

She had so far avoided asking the scholar about Black Rock and 'the Others.' There had not seemed to be a point, and as curious as she was, there were numerous other things with which to concern herself. But this time she had nothing else on her mind, and her interest in the mysterious characters got the better of her.

"What can you tell me about Black Rock?" she asked apropos to nothing but her own thoughts.

"The cub killer?" he asked. *"That's strange. Most don't talk of that creature."*

"Why not?"

"It frightens and upsets most of us."

"But not you?"

"No." There was a hint of laughter in his words. *"I'm very old and have seen much. Things don't upset me like they once did. Besides, we're outside all that."*

She'd come to realize the residents of the town, or at least some of them, were somehow outside the scope of normal Lacertian society, a stratum apart. Their nature wasn't thoroughly clear to her—she suspected they held some sort of sacred status—but it didn't matter at that point. *One thing at a time,* she thought.

"Such things don't alarm you?" she asked.

"Nadja, killing of cubs is much more common than any of us want to admit. In the city where I once lived, it happens every 40 or 50 cycles."

A city?

No! Focus, she scolded herself. Hell, the meaning of "40 or 50 cycles" had her at a loss. It irked her that she hadn't learned something so simple as how the locals calculated time. She knew a cycle to be a long period, their equivalent of a year, but she wasn't certain how long their years were, not exactly.

Before she could speak further, the old scholar rose and fetched a thick manuscript from the shelf nearest her.

"*I have something to do,*" he told her. "*Read through this. With the help of that little tool of yours, it should be easy.*"

"*What is it?*"

"*It's a story of the gatherings and of the bands that attended them, going back to before I was born. It will answer some of your questions. What you still want to know after, I will help you with.*"

"*Gaius,*" she called after as he stepped to the door. She cleared her throat. "*How long is a cycle?*"

He gave her a curious look that might have been pity. "*Nine days, by nine, by nine,*" was his reply. And then he departed.

The moment the scholar left; she was straight to work.

Gaius didn't lie. The chronology was remarkably easy to read, and it was just a chronology. There was little commentary and absolutely no analysis. And as such, she found herself moving to the end of the book and working her way backward, using the translation matrix from the tablet only when she needed it.

The most recent entry was for last cycle's gathering. There were lists of what bands had attended and who led those bands—she soon found Black Flower's name—things discussed at the gathering of leaders, and decisions that group had made.

Nothing seemed of towering importance, and she was disappointed as she ticked the cycles backward in time that it all seemed so perfunctory. The same words, names, and phrases came up over and over.

"Hmph," she said several times.

It took her only about 40 minutes to flip through the last 50 cycles, and with every changing cycle she found herself looking for things about the band and Black Flower. There wasn't much, the occasional comment at the gathering, a few mentions of mergers with other bands. But then something dawned on her. Nine times nine times nine.

She'd never been a math whiz but quickly calculated those numbers in her head. Seven-hundred twenty-nine days. She chuckled. That was almost exactly two standard years. Fifty cycles? A hundred years? *Black Flower looks good for his age*, she thought.

But, no. Days were 21 hours on Skiathos. Another round of calculations percolated through her head, followed by some number crunching on her tablet. No. It didn't make that much difference. Fifty cycles were still around 87 years.

Nadja buckled down and continued her perusal. The chronology was truly a summary, and each gathering was encapsulated in less than a page of the hefty codex. Backward she traveled. A hundred cycles, 200 cycles,

400 cycles. With each passing cycle, with each turn of the page, something slowly settled on Nadja, a feeling like none she'd ever before experienced. With each cycle there was a reference to Black Flower, a leader of one of the southern bands.

Five-hundred and twelve cycles ago, the scholar who recounted that cycle's gathering devoted 27 pages to the event. It was the cycle in which the gathering of leaders decided to form a great army and march northward to challenge the villain Black Rock.

One of the officers of that army was a leader of a southern band named Black Flower.

Nadja found herself shivering despite the warmth that remained in the evening air. There was no reason for such a reaction. All species on all worlds were different. But with Gunny's habit of naming them, and with an enormous boost from Nadja's own biases and imagination, she'd managed to anthropomorphize the Lacertians.

Her friends lived long lives. So what? Blacky was an oldie like her. Well, much older than her, more than 800 years older. But it was all relative.

It occurred to her that several hours had passed, Gaius hadn't returned, and she'd promised to meet Greta to watch the acrobats one last time. It took her only another 30 minutes to leaf through the last few hundred pages of the text she was reading, committing them to the memory of her tablet via a tiny detachable eyepiece camera, into a file holding a score or so of the scholar's other books she intended to read later.

She wrote a short and simple note to Gaius, who likely was lost in conversation somewhere, and dashed out the door.

It took her about 20 minutes to find Greta, where the medic sat amid a crowd watching a group of gigantic tumblers engage in a breathtaking display of subtle and gravity-defying leaps, spins, and vaults. Nadja was less graceful picking her way through the mostly seated crowd to where Greta leaned against a large stone. Her reward along the way was a ripple of irate squawks that were the local equivalent of "down in front."

Not seeing a space in which to squeeze herself when she reached her destination, Nadja slid into her friend's lap. Warm arms embraced her and pulled her close, but Greta's attention seemed not to stray from the spectacle on the platform before them. It was well Gunny was off with Spiros, Gwyneth, and some others taking advantage of the evening's cool breezes to race animals on the dunes. Despite herself, Nadja again was feeling misty eyed at the motherly embrace and wanted no humans present to bear witness to her shame.

The crowd was its normal raucous self, and the noise rose and fell in successive waves. Nadja sat silently watching the performance but sometimes slipped into reverie. For a time, she thought of the mission and the attacks against them, attempting to scry some pattern from it all. There was nothing. Attempts to figure out what Gunter Wray could have possibly been up to did little more than stoke her ire for the man.

For a time, she even found herself thinking of her teen years and what an ungrateful and shitty child she'd been. Devil only knows how such a thing came to mind; she seldom dwelt on the past.

She again spoke on impulse.

"How old are you?" she asked Greta.

"What?"

"How old are you? How many cycles have you lived?"

"I don't know." Greta broke into the deep trill that was her laughter. *"You ask the strangest questions."*

A peculiar sensation swept over Nadja, a growing awareness of just how different her friends were. *"How long do your people live for?"*

The laughter had ended, but Greta canted her head, her many eyelids flicking affectionately, and regarded Nadja. *"We live until we die. Don't worry, darling. I won't let anyone hurt you."*

"No," she insisted. *"How old are you when you die of old age?"*

The laughter returned. *"Nadja, what are you talking about? Age doesn't kill someone. It's just the opposite. The longer you live, the more life you have."*

Not for the first time since she'd arrived on this planet, Nadja was speechless. Was it possible? Were the Lacertians a people who knew no natural death? Through her chats with Greta and others, Nadja slowly had come to realize Gunny was right: no diseases afflicted this people. There was no such thing as sickness on this world, at least none discernable to the human eye.

And they appeared to live forever, absent some violent death. It was a wonder then that they lived the way they did, always on the precarious edge of a sword. Violence was part of the warp and woof of their society. But perhaps there was a reason for that. Would eternity be too unbearable otherwise?

Nadja shook her head and did her very best to concentrate on the display of tumbling before her. It simply wasn't possible for her to digest all this in one swallow. She needed time to think. She'd never been one for prayer, wasn't even sure she believed in such things, but she conjured up an old mantra taught her by a former girlfriend and through mere force

105

of will steadied herself. The effort took the better part of an hour, by which time the presentation was coming to a climactic end.

After the performance, the two meandered toward a nearby tent for a bit of eat-and-puke, jostling and teasing one another all the while. Well, Greta did most of the teasing. The surgeon announced to Nadja at one point that she was going to name her longbow 'Old Age' in fulfillment of Nadja's words.

Gunny and Spiros often boasted of Greta's prowess with the weapon, and on three separate occasions during the recent fight at the water tank, Nadja had witnessed her friend bound gracefully and fully armored from the medical tent to spring foot-first onto the back of a two-meter high riding beast and thereon, balanced on but two toes, one leg hiked to maintain her balance on the shifting animal, deliver an unerring flight of arrows into small groups of enemy scouts that had strayed too close to the camp. With all her gentleness, it was easy to forget Greta was a seasoned and bloodied warrior like the rest.

Despite Nadja's confusion and anxiety of just minutes before, the notion that her queries had inspired Greta to name the enormous weapon to such a comical effect set the human to laughing. The surgeon/warrior was infectious, and by the time they reached the band's great pavilion many hours later, after much eating, laughing, and cavorting, Nadja again was happy.

20: Gathering's End

The humans saw little of their friends over the next day and night. It was an odd affair according to the younger adult Lacertians with whom they now kept company. The gathering of leaders was usually a lazy affair with the typical political huffing and puffing, but little real work.

This time, Black Flower had been off in town with all the senior members of the band conferring with the other band leaders for 25 hours straight. There was something afoot, and Nadja hoped it had nothing to do with her and the Marines, at least nothing that would delay their departure.

For better or worse, the distractions experienced by those members of the band closest to her had enabled Nadja to get much done. She read more of Gaius's chronology and made her first attempts to understand the manuscript she and Gunny had obtained from Trixie.

The chronology largely had been more of the same. Its last reference to Black Flower was recorded nearly 800 cycles before. But references to Black Rock went back even further, to the first cycle recorded in the volume, nearly 1,200 cycles in the past. There were earlier volumes, according to Gaius, but Nadja felt she had learned enough for the time.

The manuscript was different.

Her scholarly friend hadn't recognized the language that made up the main text of Trixie's manuscript. In fact, it was unlike anything he'd ever before seen, fueling Nadja's suspicion that it was not a language native to Skiathos. But Gaius did recognize the material on which the text was written, pronouncing it to be animal skin of the very finest quality and best manufacture. Even more, the marginal writing on the manuscript was an older scholarly script, a combined alphabet and syllabary with which Gaius was intimately familiar. With his help, it took Nadja only about four hours to program the script into her tablet's language matrix, an effort that hopefully would shed light on the meanings of the main text.

Gaius also had spent an hour taking her and Gunny to meet a merchant who two days hence would lead a caravan in the direction the humans wanted to travel. The scholar had known the merchant, who Gunny immediately had christened Fatima, for many cycles and spoke well of her, and the merchant, for her part, was happy and curious to shelter the three strange cubs for the necessary part of the trip.

That encounter had been the evening before.

It was now noon on the second day of the gathering of leaders, and Nadja and Gunny had spent most of the previous evening and all the morning planning and re-planning their exit from Madrid, as well as discussing how best to explain the situation to the Lacertians to whom they'd become so close.

"I should have spent more time laying the groundwork with them," Nadja told the Marine. "I don't want to sneak off, but I also don't want to get in a tussle with them."

"Ma'am, you know how protective our friends are. This was never going to be easy. My best advice: tell 'em straight up. They're smart, and they understand loyalty. We have to get back to our band."

"Yeah, I ...," she flashed the NCO a smile. "I guess I let these guys get under my skin too."

"Impossible not to do, ma'am."

"Hey ... is Spiros thinking about desertion?"

The young lance corporal was having a heavenly time at the gathering and despite the heat was, even now, again in the dunes racing mounts with some of the younger adults.

The NCO laughed. "No, ma'am, he's a good Marine. He likes it here, but he's as eager to get back as you and I."

Gunny was wonderful, a splendid person and top-notch combat leader. For just a moment, Nadja pondered again unburdening herself on Really Nice, but instantly rejected the idea. Nadja always had been strong and disciplined, at least she had been since her naval days, and didn't like people seeing weakness in her.

But the previous morning, before Greta had departed for the leaders' gathering, the medic had stopped Nadja outside the tent and, as she so often did, had asked her some shy questions about humanity. This round of questions—or, rather this question, singular—had returned to the conversation Nadja had started the night before.

"*Nadja,*" her friend had asked with great hesitation, "*do humans die of old age?*"

Nadja at first hadn't known what to say. Her companion had pitched the question in such a way that the truth could only pain them both. But Nadja couldn't lie to her, not to Greta, so she'd answered as gently and honestly as she'd been able.

"*Is there no way to defend yourself,*" her friend nearly had pleaded in response, "*no way you can fight back?*"

She'd assured Greta that humans lived long and healthy lives and that their lot was a perfectly normal thing that all humans accepted. But was that true? Weren't most of the social complaints of people like her parents, like people of all ages, demands that they all live longer and healthier lives?

No. Nadja had been forced to set that burdensome thought aside. She'd instead done her very best to reassure Greta there was nothing about which she needed to worry, but several times during that talk the doctor had made faint sounds of pain and worry, the kind of heartrending keens Nadja herself had observed band members make upon the battle deaths of their friends. For the briefest of moments, Greta had seemed as if she was on the brink of slipping into mourning but somehow had recovered herself.

It was the only time Nadja had ever seen her friend in such anguish, and it was a sight she hoped never to see again.

Despite that single sad episode, events otherwise had gone on as they had since the band's arrival at Madrid. After lunch, the two women joined Spiros and some of the youth at a pool and bathed and frolicked about in the water. The Lacertians at first were wary of the pool but soon joined in the horseplay, and the soggy crew didn't return to the band's pavilion until the dinner hour approached.

They found Stig sitting on his saddle by the cooking fire when they did.

"*Is the gathering of leaders over,*" she called out affectionately, as she and the small group approached the fire.

"*No. There's much to do yet.*"

"*Are you sure? I think you're in town eating and dancing and playing games. And you just don't want us to know.*"

He gave his Lacertian laugh. "*It's usually like that. But this cycle we're discussing something very important.*"

"*And what's that?*"

"*Black Rock.*"

That name again. Nadja took a seat on the saddle next to her friend. Gunny joined them, taking a place on the ground at Stig's knee. The Marine's language skills were scarcely strong enough to follow the conversation, but she often made the attempt.

"*What about Black Rock?*"

Stig lay his hand affectionately on Gunny's head and turned to regard Nadja. "*There was another gathering at a small village north of here. He and his creatures attacked there and stole some cubs.*"

The tone of Stig's voice alone told Nadja that such an act was one of great villainy, something nearly unspeakable to their kind. But this wasn't her fight; it wasn't the Marines' fight. The caravan with which they were to travel was set to depart late the following day. Given the crisis over Black Rock, this might be her last chance to inform Stig of their departure.

She steeled herself. *"I'm sorry for the lost cubs, but Gunny, Spiros, and I need to get back to our band."*

"I know you do," he said quietly and to her great relief. *"But I thought you would want to know about Black Rock."*

"I don't understand."

"One of the stolen cubs was different. A smelly mess sometimes came from its backside."

"Gunter Wray," she said aloud.

———

There was always the possibility the stolen 'cub' might be someone other than Wray. That was the first thing that Gunny had pointed out after Stig left them and returned to the leaders.

The NCO was right yet again. The only glimmer of hope to which Nadja had clung regarding the fate of the other Marines on her team was the fact the band knew of no downed aircraft within their territory. Of course, the skiffs and troop transports they'd used were fast and had impressive range. Even 10 or 15 minutes flight-time under combat conditions might have found the vehicles many hundreds of kilometers from where Nadja had toppled from her skiff, and a crashed aircraft may have had survivors.

But that made it more pressing that they find this person. Gunter Wray was an ass who had chosen his own fate, and Nadja wouldn't grieve overly much if he ended his days as a steaming pile of *'ghrr'g'g'g't'* shit—if that species even produced such an excretion. But she wasn't going to leave anyone behind who was still alive, not even Wray. Whoever this person was, she was going to find them.

So Nadja and the Marines spent the evening and most of the following morning plotting, scheming, and revising their plans. Naturally, what they would do balanced on what the band did. Stig had informed them before departing that the gathering of leaders nearly had decided to launch another great effort and again wage war against Black Rock and his monsters. If that were the case, going with them seemed the only option to finding the other stray human.

For a Fleeting moment, Nadja toyed with the idea of going it alone and sending Gunny and Spiros on to the extraction site. She dismissed the idea out of hand. There was no guarantee anyone from the platform would come to extract the two, and Nadja had no intention of herding geese the width and breadth of Skiathos. No, the three would stay together. They just needed to convince the Lacertians to take them along on whatever rescue mission or war party they decided upon.

After a little more thought on the subject, Nadja finally broke down and shared with Gunny her doubts about Wray and the mission.

"I didn't realize it until you and Spiros introduced me to the band," she told the Marine, "but there is just something terribly off about this survey mission. This planet should have been easy to crack. Missing the fact that the linguists were trying to communicate with a bunch of pre-vocal children was a howler, but those kinds of things happen. I might overlook that single issue as a screw-up. But how does one miss the ubiquity of writing systems, of sophisticated trade networks, and such highly advanced skills in metallurgy? And no botanical research at all? Really? There were no out-and-out lies, but everything Wray was putting out to the off-world members of the research team appears to have been hedged or shaded in some way. And there was only one person who could do all that."

"He is an odd duck, ma'am. And, you know what, I got the sense the last week or two before we got shot down that Dr. Downey and him were having some sort of dust-up. I got the distinct feeling that he didn't want her researching on this part of the planet."

"Really? I was under the impression it was his idea."

"Nah, ma'am. He said there were plenty of places closer to the platform. But she seemed keen on this area … something about commerce and population density. I really wasn't much in the know."

Gunny's words made a certain amount of sense. For all its apparent scarcity, the area the band inhabited was one of the richer and more fecund regions of Skiathos. Many of the world's deserts, especially those immediately astride the equator, were simply too harsh for even the Lacertians to thrive in large numbers.

"Hey, ma'am," said the NCO, "here comes Stig again."

Their friend was making his way evenly and alone through the crowd of people assembled near the pavilion for dinner. It was only then that Nadja recalled she and Gunny were sitting on Stig's saddle. She moved to rise before she caught his affectionate look.

He stopped and squatted next to them.

She spoke first, hastily and without preamble. *"Gunny, Spiros, and I want to go with you."*

"OK," he replied.

"What?"

"I said 'yes.'"

"We can go with you? …. You're marching to war against Black Rock?"

"We are. That was never in any doubt. We merely needed to determine how many warriors the land could support."

"The land could …," she began. *"Stig, I don't understand."*

"The pastures are frail and weak in the north," he said. *"We can't all go to war there. Our mounts would starve … then we would starve. We decided that each of the larger bands would send 18 warriors and each of the smaller bands nine."*

"How many will go to war in total?"

"Counting warriors from the other gatherings? We will be 3,000. We will go north, scour this evil from the land, and return home."

"And Gunny, Spiros, and I will join you?"

"Yes. You will join us."

"OK."

———

The great gathering dissipated swiftly. In no time at all, the pavilion of Black Flower's band was struck and packed away aboard a beast of burden. Only 18 of the band would go with them. Stig and 17 younger warriors would form the band's contribution to the war party. The rest of the band would go back to their southern pastures, to the even, calm, and steady rhythms, interspersed with great and bloody skirmishes, that formed the bulk of life in that scorched land.

The only things that were difficult, the only thing that mattered at that moment, were the goodbyes.

Their friends were loving, but swift, in their adieus. The three humans were passed around the assembled band-members like beloved tokens, with strong embraces, affectionate fondling, and loving Lacertian kisses for each. Of all the band members, Greta lingered the longest. Taking one long and final embrace of Nadja, the medic knelt beside her and held her close. There was one sweet whisper only. *"Be safe, my little darling. I'll find some way to keep death from you. I promise."*

And then she was gone.

The remaining war party was 30 souls. In addition to Stig and his 17 fighters, the northern band whose cause Stig had championed, and whose members Black Flower had decided to add to their band, had provided an additional nine warriors to the effort. It was a third of that small band's

112

remaining fighters, a token of their devotion to the cause and their last hurrah at independence.

"They know the north well," Stig said in reply to Nadja's query as they packed their animals for the march north. *"And they will help us find water and pasture before we rejoin the rest of the army."*

"What do you mean 'rejoin'?"

"I told you, Nadja, pastures are thin and fragile in the north, and water scarce, especially near the mountains to which we're travelling. We will travel most of the way as separate parties before rejoining near Black Rock's fortress."

"How long will the trip take?"

"Oh, it's difficult to say. If we find ample pasture and water, 12 to 15 days. It likely will be longer. We either will have to take time to find fodder for the animals or allow them to rest so they can take nourishment from their tails. It will be harsh."

It took the war party less than an hour to prepare and to set off north from Madrid. As they left the place, a slight something tugged at Nadja's heart. She would miss their holiday.

The war party travelled light. Nadja rode with Gunny, but there were several spare riding mounts—she would have to learn to manage her own reins in the days to come. There otherwise were several beasts of burden hauling supplies. The only thing out of the ordinary was a large blue banner flying from a spear stuck in the saddle of one of the animals. It was the sign for all passing tribesmen that Stig's war party couldn't come and play. They were part of the great war effort and hence were exempt from the normal cycle of attack and retribution practiced by the locals.

Still, the war party wouldn't tarry longer than necessary and wouldn't take more from the land than they needed.

Gunny had her 10 mm semi-automatic back on a holster to her side. "Stig said that rain we got this morning will be the last for a while."

"How does he know?"

"I dunno, ma'am. I didn't get that part of the conversation. He always just seems to know."

"Lots of experience."

The Marine glanced back to where Nadja sat the saddle behind her. "How old do you think he is?"

Nadja had shared with the Marines her observations on Lacertian longevity. Both had accepted the news with characteristic equanimity. "I couldn't guess, Gunny. But older than us. And you and I are a couple of old birds."

"I dunno, ma'am. I've seen Vivian checking you out a few times."

"Well, we *are* stranded on the galactic equivalent of a desert island."

"Oh ... well said," the Marine observed with a laugh. "So, ma'am, we haven't talked about our next step. We cross a scorching desert, assail an impregnable castle, and rescue the fair dimwit. What do we do after that?"

"I dunno, Gunny. Things have moved fast. If we get through all this alive and rescue Wray, or whoever's there, then I plan on badgering Stig to take us to the extraction point, every centimeter of the way back if necessary."

"As long as we're up here, ma'am, why not? According to the map, we'll pass within a hundred and fifty klicks or so of the place on the way north."

"Yes, that would be too perfect. Are there other EM free zones in this part of the region?"

"None that I know, ma'am. Dr. Sokay said they were scattered throughout the planet, but she couldn't see a pattern."

"Shit. And we have absolutely zero equipment to monitor for such things."

"Well, one thing at a time, ma'am. I think you've done a lot better job of softening up Stig than you imagine. At this point, I reckon he'd do just about anything we asked."

"Within reason, yeah." Nadja felt another knot rise in her throat but knew she had to tell this story. "I was talking to him this morning, and ... um ... you know, I asked him why they were doing this. Black Rock was far away in the north, and the band's pastures were far to the south. He looked at me like I had a dick glued on my forehead and said, 'it's the duty of the strong to protect the weak.' Fuck ... I about started bawling."

"He is something, ain't he?" The gunnery sergeant began laughing.

The whole thing was just too funny and too beautiful for words. "Hey, Gunny, after our next break, why don't you let me ride up front for a while. Stig's given me a few lessons, but I need to figure out how to steer one of these things."

"Will do, ma'am."

21: A Desert Journey

T
he days stretched out and blended together like some fevered dream. For it was hot, hotter than it had been since they'd been on the planet, and Stig had announced several days before that it only would get worse. On the good side, they'd had little trouble finding pasture despite the rapidly drying desert, and the beasts seemed to draw all the moisture they needed from a few hours grazing at night. The riders, both human and Lacertian, were uncomfortable but endured.

It was late on their sixth day in the saddle when Stig rode up beside them. Nadja was just out of training wheels, with Gunny behind her still giving the occasional bit of advice.

"The way ahead is dry, and there will be danger," he said.

"What type of danger?" she asked.

"The normal ones, but Festus says there is a type of large predator that lives in the hills to the west. When days grow warm and dry, they often come down to the plains and hunt in groups. It is especially dangerous at night."

Festus, as Gunny had christened him, was the senior warrior among the northern recruits, all of whom had received fresh and often humorous handles from the gunnery sergeant.

"We won't stray," Nadja said before conveying his words to Gunny.

"Describe the predators," Gunny asked Stig in serviceable Lacertian.

Stig did so in just a few minutes and then rode ahead to meet a returning scout. Nadja summarized Stig's points that she thought the Marine might've missed.

"I recognize that one from your database, ma'am."

Nadja slipped the tablet from her pocket and flipped through some files. Much of the zoological research Wray's team had gathered was loaded on the device, but she'd only begun systematically reviewing the files and comparing them to the local knowledge held by Stig and the others since they'd departed Madrid.

It was useful and interesting. Part of the utility came from another observation made by Gunny. Most of the animals examined by Wray's team had been predators. That fact had seemed odd. Planetary survey teams had protocols to follow, and though Nadja didn't know what the protocol on such a subject would be, it didn't seem a survey devoted largely to predators was terribly systematic or scientific. It was more like the thing a 12-year-old schoolboy would do, or so Really Nice had observed.

Nadja shrugged mentally. It certainly was useful for them now. "What do you want to name this one, Gunny?" The survey team had assigned only serial numbers to each species.

"Lemme have a look at the pictures again … umm … how 'bout 'snaggletooth'?"

Nadja looked again. There was something vaguely canid about the species, and its teeth were a mess. "Snaggletooth it is."

Gunny reached forward. "Here, eat a green, ma'am."

Hydration and protection from heat injury was an understandable obsession of the NCO, and she spent a great deal of time badgering Nadja and Spiros about nibbling on greens and minding the sun. The small shoots were far better and more hygienic than drinking water, which they bottled after passing it through survival filters built into their uniforms, and the greens didn't seem to shrivel after having been picked. The war party carried copious amounts of them in the ample panniers on their mounts, and the humans had taken to swathing themselves in Greta's colorful gifts as proof against the sun's bite.

The two lapsed into silence.

It was hot.

It was so hot that it was sometimes hard to think straight. Nadja fumbled for ways to exercise her mind, but instead she bit harder than was advisable into the green she was sucking. As she hoped, the minor shock cleared her head. There was something she tried to remember from earlier.

Had Stig seemed more concerned about the snaggleteeth than the usual threats they faced? He may have.

"Gunny, how much of the 'good stuff' do we have?"

"Those five liters, ma'am. And we have another five kilos of the roots ground down." The Marines had become quite adept at sewing broken Lacertians back together, so the humans formed the war party's medical corps. A concerned Greta had loaded them down with roots, salves, and various implements of the healing arts.

"Is that enough?"

"For a pitched battle? I don't know. But it's about what Greta usually kept on hand for the entire band. I think we're ready for any fight." The NCO shifted to get a better look at Nadja. "You expecting something?"

"I don't know. Stig seemed a little more concerned than usual."

Gunny nodded. "He may have done, ma'am. Here, have another green."

22: Rite of Passage

I t wasn't speed or great strength that kept Nadja alive during the fight at their camp two nights later. It was great fortune, that and nothing more.

Since Stig's warning, there hadn't been so much as a single trace of snaggleteeth, or any predators for that matter, and she'd begun to think the threats overblown. What creature would challenge an armed and armored Lacertian warrior, let alone a war party of nearly 30 of them?

Their big worry and the focus of most of the war party's attention that evening had been a group of riders that had been pacing them at a distance for most of the day. Stig thought it possible the group merely might have been moving in the same direction as their party, but Festus was skeptical. The band from which their new friends hailed had fought the warriors of Black Rock many times, and just two or three cycles before, it would have been unheard of to encounter their great enemy this far south. Now?

Festus urged caution, and Stig took him at his word. They chose a camp that promised easy defense from outside attack, doubled their guards, and pushed those guards out farther than they ordinarily would to give them ample opportunity to alert their fellows, should their shadows in fact be enemies. And they rested throughout the dark.

Nadja had come to depend on the senses of the others, the warriors and Marines, and it nearly cost her everything. Their large friends had phenomenal eyesight, better even than the enhanced vision of the Marines, and seldom set campfires. At the very most, they sometimes kept tiny oil lamps by which to see after dark, but prudence had demanded they dispense even with those in recent nights.

After a meeting with Stig and his officers that evening, Nadja began the short 20-meter walk back to the tiny shelter she shared with the Marines. She was paying scant attention to anything but her footfalls, and after several dozen strides in the gloom was forced to stop and reorient herself. It was at that very moment that she began to laugh. Out of nowhere, a familiar and pungent smell assaulted her senses. It was as if someone had just opened a fresh jar of pickles under her nose. Her senses did a summersault, and then she stopped laughing. Because that's when she saw it and remembered.

The thing didn't quite slither toward her but slunk toward her rapidly as a low-slung housecat might stalk toward a toy mouse. Except this was no housecat, and though just visible in the gloom, it was large enough to be frightening.

She'd taken to carrying Gunny's enormous double-edged dagger on a baldric over her shoulder, and she later liked to think she pulled the dagger before she began to scream (rather hysterically) for help. But, in the end, she did both.

Even with a couple of backpedals, she found the creature was on her in a few heartbeats, snapping at her legs and making a hungry and guttural snarl. Reflex allowed her to swing the enormous dagger like a sword and clip the top of the creature, which up close seemed even more catlike. The blow was feeble, barely slowing the thing, and she almost lost heart until an enormous form sprang to life beside her. She thought it was Festus but wasn't sure. Whoever it was pinned the monster to the ground with a spear and a deafening roar.

Then the creatures were everywhere, dozens of them, hundreds perhaps. Each was about the size of a hound, but they were so many!

More Lacertians sprung up around her, hacking, stabbing, and screaming, their war-cries so loud as to deafen. And their voices were like madness, sucking her in. Nadja found herself hewing and stabbing at anything that appeared before her. She swung and screamed until her arms were heavy and her voice was raw.

And the creatures kept coming, files of them and then piles of them stacked before the party.

It may have gone on for hours, it may have gone on longer, but after a time her mind cleared enough to worry for Gunny and Spiros, and shouts of their names replaced her feral screams. And still it did not relent.

At a point she couldn't identify, the chaos slowed and stopped. From a crouch she didn't recall having taken, her exhausted and trembling body fumbled to an awkward seat on the ground, her long knife still at the ready and her eyes still darting about for potential adversaries.

The voice spoke several times before she recognized it.

"Hey, ma'am," said the gunnery sergeant.

The moist spout of a water flask found Nadja's lips. It was like nectar.

"You with me, ma'am?"

Pulling her lips from the liquid, Nadja nodded. "Where have you been?" Sounds of fighting continued nearby, but the tumult of earlier had passed. She could just make out the profile of the gunnery sergeant in the umber.

"I've been right next to you for the last few hours. You alright? You hurt?"

"No. Just more water." The flask returned.

"Good. It'll be daylight soon, and the troops have about got this under control. But some of 'em got tore up pretty good, so Spiros is setting things up at the hooch. I need you back in the game."

"Yeah, Gunny, roger that." Strong hands helped Nadja to her feet. After she fumbled the dagger into its sheath, they began to move.

"Drink water while we're walking, ma'am."

Back at the hooch, three small lamps cast a remarkable amount of light, illuminating a blanket on which reclined one of Stig's soldiers. Nadja thought it was the one Gunny had named Milos. The warrior had a badly lacerated left leg and a left arm that looked like it had gone through a meatgrinder. Spiros, who was busy threading a needle, had slathered ground root paste on the worst of it, and gunny prepared to dose the patient with the "good stuff."

Nadja snatched up a fourth lamp from a bag, lit it, and began to examine the others who had arrived. The wounds were dreadful, and even the strongest warriors couldn't contain faint rumbles of pain. Taking each in hand by turn, she organized them from worst to least injured. In doing so, she nearly stumbled over a warrior with injuries so overwhelming that she nearly cried out. He obviously had been pulled to the ground and mauled by a pack of their attackers. Placing herself under the Lacertian's left arm, she half-lifted, half-guided him to the front of the line.

"Oh, Gaspar!" was Gunny's husky whisper. "Ma'am, put him on the blanket over here."

The Marine was a wonder. Nadja sometimes had trouble distinguishing some of their companions in broad daylight, but Gunny could make them out covered in blood in the dead of night. The NCO had a deep empathy for this folk.

The surgery was open throughout the night and into the morning. For all the injuries—fully half of the party had suffered some sort of serious wound—none had died. Two, including Gaspar, were so badly off that it would be a day or more before they traveled, even with the help of the "good stuff."

"You did good, ma'am," said Gunny as they lay their last patient on a blanket near the hooch.

"I'm not the doctor you are. I just followed orders."

"Not that. You came through your first fight OK."

Nadja felt a slight blush coming on. "I was out of control, lost track of where I was and who was near me, Gunny."

"Tunnel vision. It's a natural body reaction. Keeps you safe. After your first few fights, your situational awareness will improve."

Her friend's words were both flattering and irksome. Nadja had been in fights, a few fistfights and some minor naval engagements. But, yes, Gunny was right, even counting their previous skirmish at the water tank, this was her first real combat. And she was alive to tell of it. "How many fights you been in Gunny?"

The NCO coughed. "Been in the Marines 14 years, ma'am, going on 15. Ain't never been in a real war, but out here on the frontier I've been in more shooting scrapes, firefights, and skirmishes than I can count. You get used to it."

"You ever afraid? Freeze up?"

"My first couple of shootouts took me aback a little, but I'd had six kids by then, including two at once. Childbirth and mothering were the highwater mark of terror for me; everything since has been a smooth downhill ride. Hey, Spiros, flip me a few of those roots and a grinder."

"Wait … I didn't hear you fire your pistol?"

"Tunnel vision. I was right next to you … but only got off a dozen rounds in the chaos. Didn't want to hit one of our friends."

"Tunnel vision," Nadja murmured. She had just finished rinsing out some bandages. "I'll go find Stig and see if we're moving today. I don't think so."

Nadja found Stig speaking with Festus and a few others 50 paces or so down the trail. Their discussion seemed friendly but animated. It ceased as she arrived and received the smiles and friendly greeting of the warriors.

"*I don't mean to interrupt,*" she said, "*but two of the warriors are hurt badly. They shouldn't move for a day.*"

"*That decides it,*" said Stig.

"*Decides what?*"

"*Festus says it is safe to stay for a day and rest the animals.*"

The other warrior spoke next. "*The ch'brr't are creatures that dig holes and lie in wait for animals to come to them. They consume prey and predator both. It's why we haven't seen other animals for the past day.*" He gave Stig what she could only imagine was an apologetic look. "*I should have guessed that. But I've never seen such a large nest. They usually are far fewer.*"

"*Are they all dead?*" she asked.

"*All of them,*" Festus replied. "*I have warriors searching for more burrows, just in case. They would have consumed other predators nearby as well, so it should be safe here for a brief time.*"

120

Boris L. Slocum

As they spoke, Stig walked over and recovered one of the creatures. It was her first look in daylight, and save for the shape of the creature's skull and arch of its back, it looked nothing at all like a feline. The beast obviously wasn't the snaggletooth they'd feared from days before, but it strongly resembled another animal from the survey team's files, one which the entry indicated exuded a strong smell somewhat like vinegar.

Festus squatted next to the animal and with a single claw drew a line down the creature's back and peeled back the flesh. *"They have a thing here that gives a black oil that makes it impossible for our people to smell them. They are hard for us to detect."*

"I smelled something last night," said Nadja. *"It was familiar."*

"You saved our lives," said Stig kindly. *"Some types of animal can smell them. It's how the ch'brr't attract its prey, by giving off a smell of food and then lying in wait."*

Festus continued cutting away at the dead animal. *"The warriors of the fiend Black Rock collect these black organs and use the liquid to disguise their scent when they attack our camps and villages. We should gather and bury them if we are to stay longer."*

Stig agreed. *"We will wait and leave here tomorrow morning. And Nadja, go rest. Even we can see you're exhausted."*

When she returned to the hooch, Spiros was already stretched out asleep and Gunny was sitting cross legged and unconscious with the stub of a root in one hand and a grinder in the other. Nadja checked her work. All the ingredients had been properly restocked.

She rolled Gunny over onto a blanket near Spiros, finished putting away the mixings and raw material, and did a swift cleaning of their work/living space. She spent another 30 minutes examining their remaining patients, checking their wounds and sutures, reapplying root paste, and dosing two of them with yet more of the "good stuff." When all was well, she dropped insentient onto a blanket between the two Marines.

23: The Northerners

It was the heat that finally roused her. Several times throughout the morning, Nadja had rolled awake, stumbled over to check on their patients, and then taken her bleary eyes back to sleep.

The heat no longer would allow that.

It must have been some hours after noon, but there still was a bit of shade on their hooch cast by the cliffside above. All but three of the injured warriors had departed, presumably under their own power, the roots having done their duty. Spiros was attempting to give a dose either of water or the "good stuff" to Gaspar. Gunny was still asleep. It was the first time Nadja had woken before the woman.

Rising, Nadja went over to assist Spiros. Her throat was raw from screaming, and her every muscle ached. "How's Gaspar doing?"

"Dodgy, ma'am. I've seen them not pull through when they're this bad … but the stuff does wonders."

Gaspar made a low groan and cracked a hazy eye but once. Nadja took a damp rag and patted his muzzle and head.

"How did Gunny come up with that name?" Most Gunny-brand names were approximations. (Stig's true name was 'eessssti'k'k'k'k', the final phonemes of which were a glottal staccato the duration of which varied depending on how much the speaker wanted to catch Stig's attention. Often the name was stretched out over many, many seconds.) But other faux names the NCO had conjured were in no way an approximation.

Spiros clearly knew what Nadja meant. "Anybody's guess, ma'am. Some of these guys remind her of people she's known. Sometimes I think the names just tickle her."

"Like Festus?"

The lance corporal laughed.

"Is she like that with the Marines too?" Nadja asked.

"Oh, no, ma'am. I wasn't kidding about Gunny being a hard-ass. She is, trust me. And she's loyal, freaky loyal … but, maybe … I think she'd like to be a little more easygoing."

"Like she is with these folks?" said Nadja as she motioned to the sleeping Gaspar.

"When I first got to the platoon, I never thought I'd see her goofing around the way she does with these guys." The young man seemed to hesitate. "I gotta admit. There is something nice about being stuck with the big oafs. It can be … well. It's nice not to have responsibilities. But I'm dying to get back."

"You and me both, brother." She gave the lad a pat on the shoulder and rose. "You good here?"

"I'm good, ma'am."

"Good. Let Gunny sleep. I'm gonna find Stig and see if he's figured out what's gonna eat us today."

Festus was with several others hunkered by a fire near where she'd last seen him, grilling what looked to be legs. Their hosts ate most of their food either raw or dried and heavily spiced. Only rare delicacies were cooked.

"Is that one of the ch'brr't?" she asked. The reward for her enquiry was a long drumstick that looked a little like an overgrown turkey leg. It smelled delicious. Never having been finicky, she sunk her teeth in. It was not quite as the scent had promised, but still very good.

"Only the legs are good to eat," said one of Festus's companions.

"It is very good," she admitted. *"Better to eat them before they eat you."*

The Lacertians laughed.

"Where is Stig?" she asked.

"Up ahead," said Festus with a toss of his head. *"He talks with the scouts. There might be trouble ahead."*

"What type of trouble?" she asked.

The warrior nibbled at a piece of leg. *"If we want to stay hidden, we must move through some narrow points. That's dangerous, a good opportunity for predators or enemies to attack. Otherwise, we have to move out into the open of the plain."*

"Why is that bad?"

"Our enemies will see us coming from farther away in the open. Greater chance of attack farther ahead."

"So, we have a choice," she asked, *"a greater risk now, or a greater risk later?"*

Festus gestured in the affirmative. *"I think the danger is greater now. We should move into the open. Stig looks to see if we can join other war parties to increase our numbers."*

"Why more warriors? Won't it make it harder to find pasture?"

More affirmative gestures. *"It will. But the farther we go north, the more likely we are to face enemies instead of just predators. And the enemies there will be in larger numbers."*

"Is the enemy looking for us?" Jeez. What was she asking? Stig, Festus, and the warriors had this down pat. She needed to remind herself the Stig and Festus did this for a living and that she was just cargo.

Oddly, Festus addressed Nadja's own self-doubt. "*I know you're not a cub, but you are very clever for one so small. I think our enemies are looking for us. If the warriors of Black Rock can ambush our small war parties now, there will be fewer of us to fight in the north.*"

It dawned on Nadja what a logistical nightmare war would be in a land of such profound scarcity. Moving and massing troops would be a nigh on impossible task under such circumstances. Marching 3,000 warriors many hundreds of kilometers across a virtual waste to do battle against a well-entrenched and ruthless enemy? What boldness. What audacity. What solid brass.

These were a people of untold daring and indescribable resolution, the type that on Nadja Bikram's world lived only in the pages of childhood picture books and on the screens of popular holographic motion pictures.

"*How large should the war party be from this point forward?*" she asked.

"*Stig thinks four or five times our current number, but it might take a day or two for our scouts to gather that many as other war parties move north. And it will slow our march in the future.*"

She shook her head. "*The delay is unfortunate, but it will give the injured time to heal.*"

The warrior gave a sweet Lacertian smile. "*We are all grateful for your joining this great effort, and for the healing you provide. Our healer was killed this past cycle.*"

Had she heard something else in his alien tongue? There seemed to be something Festus wanted to say, but as his folk sometimes did, he was being shy. "*Is there something you wanted to ask me?*"

All four Lacertians smiled as one. Festus spoke. "*Stig says you fell from the sky.*"

"*It's true, and he found me, and his people healed me.*"

"*Where do you come from?*"

The ways of these beings were a wonder. It was obvious that the candor-gate had been flung wide open, and now all manner of questions would follow. Something occurred to her. "*I come from far away, another world. Have you seen beings like me before?*"

"*No,*" said one of the warriors. "*But we've all heard stories.*"

"*Stories that are hard to believe,*" said another in a skeptical tone, before looking to Festus.

"*In the north,*" Festus began, "*we hear all manner of stories about Black Rock and his monsters. Some believe them, some don't. We all know he fights for the Others ... or they fight for him. There are so many stories.*"

I've even heard tell that Black Rock has power over the predators and sends them against us."

"*Like last night? ... But you don't believe that.*"

Festus made a noncommittal gesture. "*We all hear many things. Not all can be true. But ... I've heard stories of cubs who are not cubs.*"

"*Like me?*"

He gestured energetically to the contrary. "*I've never seen them. It's always someone heard from someone else. When you ask someone how they heard such a story, they point you to someone else. And if you ask that person, they point you to someone else. And sometimes that next person will point you back to the person who first told you the story. It's all a big circle.*"

The warriors all began to laugh.

"*Until you met my friends and me?*" she asked.

"*Maybe,*" said Festus. "*Maybe.*"

"*You are far too nice to work with the Others,*" joked another warrior to the further laughter of all.

Despite their faint accents, the warriors were all as friendly and goofy as the members of Black Flower's band, and she spent another 20 minutes yakking and joking with them before returning to the hooch with a heaping platterful of delicious critter legs—Gunny would have to come up with a name for the nasty little buggers. But the warriors had given her much to ponder. The tales were little more than a few stories describing small cubs that weren't cubs. It could mean something or nothing at all. They'd find out when they got to Black Rock's fortress.

———

"Mmm ... wild boar, ma'am." The Marine NCO smacked her lips.

"What's that?"

"Spiros said they taste a little like pork, but I say wild boar. They have a lot of those on Nuevo California."

"Really?"

"No, ma'am. I lie not. They've kept about a third of the planet completely wild. You wouldn't believe the big game animals they brought in after terraforming."

"You a hunter, Gunny?"

"Nah, but Javeed would bring in a duck or a goose a few times a year. The only wild boar we'd get was at those school fundraisers. It was mighty tasty."

"I like these new friends of Stig's," Spiros opined. "You think Gaspar and what's-his-name there will be ready for solid food when they wake up?"

"We'll ask 'em when they wake," replied Gunny around a mouthful of faux-boar. "The grub'll all go bad if somebody doesn't eat it."

"What do you think Wray was up to?" Nadja had sat listening with half an ear. She'd already told the two Marines about the confusing tidbit she'd gathered from Festus and the other about "cubs that were not cubs."

"What do you mean, ma'am?" asked the gunnery sergeant.

"I mean … we talked about this. What was Gunter Wray up to?"

Gunny licked a finger and sat up. "Ma'am, just spit it out."

"What?"

"What you haven't said, what you've been thinking. Just spit it out."

For a moment, Nadja was at a loss. And then she spoke. "He was sabotaging the survey mission." Why had it taken her so long to say that aloud? It long had become obvious.

"Why would he do that, ma'am?"

"Oh, shit, Gunny. I don't know."

"Nibble on some greens, ma'am." In emphasis, the NCO got up and fetched a few from a saddle bag.

Nadja took the offered plants. "Am I not thinking straight?" she asked meekly.

"Ma'am, the heat is sucking the living shit out of all of us. It makes it hard to concentrate sometimes. All you need to do is stay hydrated, relax, and focus."

Nadja put the shoot to her lips and began to nibble gently. "OK," she said after a time, "why would he do that?"

"Perfect question, ma'am. Me and Spiros got nothing. Why don't you tell us?"

"What's on this planet?" Nadja asked.

"Not shit," said Spiros.

"Agreed," confirmed the NCO.

"Natural resources?"

"Dr. Sokay said there are plenty of minerals, but the same minerals can be mined on any uninhabited world or any asteroid belt for a fraction of the trouble and cost."

"Well, she'd know," said Nadja absently.

"Yes, ma'am. In fact…," the NCO hesitated. "I think … I think Dr. Sokay is fascinated by this place, but I remember her saying a time or two that all the work she did here could just as easily have been done by the AI."

"I thought it was these guys," said Spiros, motioning around. "I thought the reason we were here is because these goofy cusses are so much like us."

"That's a large part of it," said Nadja. "It's certainly the reason I got involved in the program. But … you know what, the government likely would have abandoned the whole thing if Wray hadn't found those alien artefacts after he got here."

Gunny again sat up. "What are you talking about, ma'am?"

"Gunter discovered traces of alien influence on the planet."

"That's not how I remember it, ma'am. The anthropology team started bringing up tiny bits of alien tech not long after me and the Marines got here. But it didn't have anything to do with Dr. Wray. In fact … he put…," she hesitated, as if again lost in thought.

"What?" asked Nadja.

Gunny took a moment to answer. "Well, as I remember it … Wray put the kibosh on releasing any information about alien tech from the moment it showed up."

"How'd word get out, then?" asked Nadja.

"I reckon somebody mentioned something about it in a personal data-pack home. One day, we got a Pinpoint from State Department enquiring about the stuff, and not long after that Wray just started harping about how great his finds were. I mean … the captain and I just rolled our eyes. Wray was that kind of self-aggrandizing prick."

"Motherfucker," Nadja hissed under her breath. It was true. Despite everything, Gunter Wray had done all he could in his not-so limited power to subtly undermine this mission. What was the goal? To get the government presence off the planet? Maybe. Without the incentive to find further spacefaring species—or some valuable or unique natural resource—the government likely would have sidestepped a tiny little dustbowl like Skiathos. There simply was nothing tangible there to recommend it for further interest.

True, it was a fascinating place from a linguistic and anthropological standpoint, intensely so. And having State and the military there facilitated the academic work in which they had been engaged. But absent that, absent government credentials or administrative support, even a highly accredited scholar would have needed to ply through endless red tape and to have waited many years for an opportunity to do such on-planet research. Those were the rules.

But was that what it was? Did Wray want the planet to himself, for his own research? Was he trying to game the system in some way? Nadja knew academic politics was petty and vicious, but that idea seemed ridiculous even by those standards. Worse, it just didn't seem right. The cost alone of mounting research on such an isolated planet, absent government funding? The only reason ships like the *Mathilde* ventured in this direction twice per year was because of government money.

"Motherfucker," she again hissed. What the hell else could be going on? "Motherfucker."

"That tears it, Spiros, this is officially a three-motherfucker day."

"That's a bad sign, Gunny," replied the young Marine.

Nadja turned to the Marines. Seeing them pulled her back in the general direction of reality. No. It had to be more than academic nastiness. Scholars generally didn't go around attacking Marine patrols. That had happened twice—twice so far. There had to be something else at work, some other players. Some other agenda. But who? What?

Cubs that aren't cubs, came a whisper from her mind. There was something there, just out of reach. If she could just touch it.

God, it was hot.

24: A Plan

They were up early the next morning and spent the next two days in the saddle with little sleep. Gunny at first rode with Gaspar. It was almost comical watching the Marine guide the giant animal while supporting the great bulk of the warrior. But it was also touching, and by the end of the first day, despite their increased pace and the onerous heat, the "good stuff" seemed to have woven its magic. Gaspar was again at the reins of his own mount and, after a short break in the evening, seemed more or less himself.

The same could not be said for the humans. The course of the war party was hot and tiring, and Nadja suspected the warriors sometimes rode in their sleep that was not full sleep, an option not quite feasible for her and the Marines.

Their party rode throughout the night and now numbered nearly 100. But it was hard to keep tally with the constant coming and going of scouts. Several times on the second day, smaller parties wordlessly merged with theirs, and on two separate occasions they took short breaks in the shade of nearby outcroppings to watch and listen and plan.

Their course took them inexorably northward. To the west they skirted a long series of hills and ridgelines. Eastward the great sweep of the Central Desert was spread before them. Despite the shimmers of heat, they could see clearly for what Gunny Nice estimated to be 100 or more kilometers. Throughout the day, Nadja spied lines of riders through the shimmers. Most charted a northward course. Some raced, some paced steadily, and other still moved in measured bursts.

After several hurried talks with Stig and Festus, it dawned on her how much of this was organized chaos. There was a design to this madness that Stig revealed when the war party rested for a few hours before daybreak on the third day.

"*The scouts are our eyes and ears,*" he explained patiently to the sleepy and exhausted woman. "*They see the enemy, and they allow us to communicate from war party to war party.*"

"*Is that why we are massing now?*" she asked. Their party had swollen to more than 200 warriors, and the parties in the distance seemed to be merging into larger groups as well.

"*You are clever,*" was his kind response. "*The enemy has pushed south with much of its force to attack us while we are still in small and isolated*

129

parties. But they made a mistake. There is one regular water source in this part of the north, and our scouts say it is but lightly guarded. Our party will race far ahead of the others, around the ranks of the enemy, and seize their tank."

"How far is it?"

"Ordinarily, a five- or six-day ride, but we will race a day and a night and another day. That will bring us there."

Nadja felt a sudden alarm. *"But it's a long way. When the enemy discovers we've seized the waterhole, won't they return and try to retake it?"*

"Yes, I hope so. It's part of the plan." The warrior's words were patient, but a little amused. And it appeared he'd come to read a human face, for he seemed to sense Nadja's worry and confusion. He continued. *"Our kind are hardy, but even we need water, Nadja. If we seize their only tank, they will almost certainly rally their forces to return and attack our single war party...."*

"And if the enemy is attacking us at the waterhole, then they can't attack your war parties as they move up from the south."

He gave his Lacertian smile. *"You are learning our way of war."*

"But it's dangerous. How many enemy warriors will there be?"

"They will be many, and we will be few," he said patiently. *"But worry about that later and rest now. The race to the water tank will be long and hot. Some will not make it."*

She nodded, hoping that he couldn't read the further worry on her face, and then went to brief Gunny on their plans.

"It's a bold move, ma'am. Like I've always told you...."

"These guys do not bullshit when it comes to war."

"Damn skippy, ma'am." The Marine laughed and pulled out her map. "You need to hydrate and grab a few minutes sleep. If I'm reading this map right, the water tank we're heading to is a ways off. And there have been a few days recently it's been upward of 55 degrees at midday. We're gonna be riding some animals to death come tomorrow afternoon."

Nadja understood. It was life or death, and everyone here knew it, everyone including her. She reached into the saddlebag and pulled out a handful of greens. Hydrate now—she could always tie herself into the saddle later. And she mentally braced herself for what was to come.

25: The Sun

The first day of their race to the northern tank was nothing short of hellish. They left the small outcropping where they'd rested at about 20 minutes before the first rays of light cracked the horizon. The pace of the main body was a steady trot, but a continual flow of scouts and outriders raced hither and yon, often ducking in only to relay a short message or jump on one of the spare animals and depart without so much as a saddle change.

Compared to the normal and sedate pace of the band, the war party's rate of speed was breakneck. But Stig and the others had assured her the mounts were sturdy. They could race with great speed, and they could run all day. Only the next day would show the true limits of their endurance.

Nadja did indeed tie herself into the saddle. She'd been riding solo for the last three days, a period of time that seemed like an eternity in the vast and timeless wastes of Skiathos. She felt like an old and hardened hand now. It was far more likely she might fall asleep than that her trusty steed might buck and throw her, so a single hitch across her waist and thighs would keep her in place and enable her to leap free if something urgent transpired.

As was the usual, the heat of the day began to pound them like a hammer on an anvil at just before mid-morning. By that time, the humans already had deployed their large and colorful cloaks. The sun was like a physical force sitting upon Nadja's shoulders, and it was the only thing that kept her from falling asleep as they rode. But the rhythm of the beast was like swaying in a hammock, the exhaustion of the three days in the saddle a soporific, and her inability to doze left her something like an inanimate husk, in no way asleep, but not discernably awake.

After she knew not how long—it may have been hours—a sharp poke roused her from her quasi-catalepsy, and glancing listlessly over, she saw a keen set of eyes peering at her through a slit in a veil.

Gunny's hand was extended, her voice crisp and clipped. "Ma'am, this is not a joke. If you don't keep your electrolytes up, you are going to die."

What had happened?

Something in Nadja's lizard mind knew the woman was right. If she didn't drink fluids, she would die of heat stroke. That meant a constant flow of fluids, which meant staying awake. What had she been thinking? Had she been thinking? For all her weariness, there could be no sleeping

131

in the saddle, even half sleeping. A moment of panic hit her. They barely had begun their sprint and she already was flagging. She needed to focus, but felt for a moment helpless.

Gunny Nice seemed to know her thoughts. "You can sleep in the saddle tonight ma'am. You have to hydrate. Drink water or chew greens. It will help you stay alert." The last words were more than the Marine's usual friendly admonishment. It was an order. She raised a handful of greens in Nadja's direction as a further emphasis.

Nadja raised a hand and after several drunken misses took the proffered succulents and bit into one. The surge of electricity did little to rouse her, and though the sweet moisture of the green shoot was delightful, it filled her with a scant hint of panic that the wonderful taste might lead her to want a nap after. But she took another green, then a third. With each successive green she felt more awake, but became more aware of the way her head throbbed and her stomach pitched. She recognized the signs of heat exhaustion—that small clarity of thought was a victory in itself—and continued to bite and swallow greens.

Gunny was still to her right, and her still groggy mind noticed that Spiros's mount had pulled up to her left. Feeling something at her left shoulder, she grasped the flask she was offered and took an enormous gulp—her body was so wracked by coughs and choking by the contents that she nearly dropped the flask. It was the bitter and slightly sweet tang of the "good stuff."

"It couldn't hurt," she heard him utter, probably to Gunny, and she could almost hear the young man shrug. She felt the lance corporal lean across the gap between their mounts. A gentle hand touched her back and another relieved her of the flask. She immediately felt the lip of the container against her lips.

"Just one more, ma'am," the young man whispered.

Nadja complied. This second round wasn't quite so gagging, prepared as she was for it. She reached down reflexively for another handful of greens after she did. The first helped clean her palate. She blinked and looked around, first to Spiros and then to Gunny. It dawned on her that her vision had become indistinct and shadowy and was just coming back around to normal.

She was used to being the strong one, the one in charge, and a cold hand wrapped itself around her heart. She really had become cargo. "I'm not used to people needing to baby me." The laugh she gave sounded forced even to her.

Spiros smiled. "Welcome to the Marines, ma'am. We all baby each other every day. We never let our fellows fall, always help back them up, and never leave them behind. We check our egos at the door."

The optimism and cheerfulness in the lad's words were a wonder to her, and a minor tonic. Both Marines were as hot and as bone-dead fatigued as she was, but Gunnery Sergeant Nice was so strong that it was easy to forget how stout and resilient Spiros was, despite an injury that clearly still caused him pain. Though he was nearly dead when he first was stranded here, this haunting and grinding planet had not rendered Vivian Spiros to dust. Nadja didn't need to know him from before to realize the youth was all the man now that he was then, that and more.

Gunny's mount sidled up even closer. "Ma'am, I want you to keep nibbling on greens, as many as you can stomach, until you have a good healthy piss." The Marine continued talking to forestall any complaint. "Just wiggle out your britches and hang it over the side when you're ready. I know the 'good stuff' sometimes makes passing water harder, but you need to pee, or your body might start shutting down."

Nadja nodded and chewed. After an hour had passed, she was still tired, and her head pounded, but the overwhelming urge to sleep and intense nausea had left her.

Now her ass began to hurt and throb, and her back and thighs cramped painfully. Her hands and feet were swollen, and her shoulders and arms were numb. She wasn't going to complain. She refused. The animals jogged at a healthy gait—they were doing all the work she scolded herself—and from time to time one or the other of the Marines would stand, their feet in what passed for stirrups, and stretched and twisted slightly. The three had never spent this much time in the saddle without break before.

She mimicked her comrades and chomped on the greens until she felt bloated. The saddles were designed for a much different physique, so she found it more comfortable to pull up a leg and ride with it half-crossed in front of her, careful to rope herself tightly when she did. It was hard and onerous, but shifting around on the ever-rolling and swaying mount kept the worst of the discomfort at bay.

It was another three hours before the sun lifted its jackbooted foot from her neck, and Nadja began to feel that she might survive the day. It was still sizzling, but tolerable, when some minutes later she did as she'd been ordered and, snaking one leg from her britches and balancing precariously on the right side of her saddle with Spiros's strong hand for support, had the most delicious piss of her life. It was almost worth the agony that had come before.

"You feeling a little better, ma'am?" Gunny called up from about five meters back.

Nadja struggled to get her pants back on. "I do."

"Excellent. Your flow was a little brown, so keep drinking. And brace yourself. If I know Stig, he's gonna pick up the pace now that the worst of the heat has passed. The night is not going to be pleasant."

As Gunny had predicted, the pace soon increased, and after needing to take yet another pee from the saddle, Nadja clumsily shoved her britches in a saddlebag and swathed herself from waist down in the green cloak Greta had gifted her. Her boots though returned to her feet, put there by swollen hands that felt like 10 thumbs.

After her head had cleared, she'd noticed more comings and goings in the war party, sometimes eight to 10 warriors at a time. Overall, though, the number in their party seemed to have grown. They appeared now to be more than 200. She asked Gunny about them when the NCO next pulled abreast of her.

"My guess, ma'am, is the enemy either has figured what we're up to and those guys departing are trying to run interference for the war party, or Stig is sending out little squadrons to hunt and kill the other side's scouts."

Nadja chose not to scold her own earlier inattentiveness, but decided to engage herself more carefully in the future. "What does that tell you?"

"Tough to say, ma'am. This was never going to be totally secret. The whole idea was to get the enemy's attention. But from the direction our patrols have been departing, I think the main enemy force is off in that direction." She turned slightly and pointed to her right rear, the southeast. "And if they're not ambushing enemy scouts and patrols, Stig's guys might be attacking the main enemy's rear, to scare them and maybe get their attention."

"So, they'll follow us north?" It made sense, even to a former naval officer.

"You're the one who talked to Stig, ma'am, but I think that's the plan."

"How long before dark, Gunny?"

"Another two and a half or three hours. That's when the fun will begin." The Marine kneed her mount and brought the animal closer to Nadja's and, in one smooth move, lifted herself to her saddle seat and stepped lightly across the gap and took a seat behind Nadja. She knotted the reins of her erstwhile mount to a ring on Nadja's saddle.

Nadja made a confused sound.

"Flip your right leg over, ma'am."

"What?"

"Flip your right leg over and lean into me." The NCO had begun to undo her own sun cloak. "You're not getting any sleep in the saddle tonight. As soon as it gets dark, Stig is going to have us ball busting as fast as these critters can run. I need you to get an hour or two's sleep before then."

Swallowing her feelings of embarrassment, Nadja complied, and she was soon swathed across Really Nice's lap like an overgrown infant, the cloak knotting them tightly together. The day was still uncomfortably hot, but now exhaustion outweighed any other discomfort. She lay her head on her friend's shoulder and closed her eyes.

"Sleep as best you can, ma'am. I'll wake you in an hour or three, when the pace picks up again."

"What about you Gunny?" Nadja could feel the Marine's laughter rather than hear it.

"I can go days and days without sleep, ma'am. Remember … I'm a gunnery sergeant."

26: The Heat

The night's ride, as Gunny had predicted, was again hellish. But as sunrise approached and they took the first and last breather of their mad dash north, Nadja felt for the first time that she would make it. She was physically exhausted, worn to her marrow, but that no longer mattered.

The two hours' sleep she'd gotten in Gunny's arms the evening before had been more rest than she'd had since leaving their last camp four days before. It had made her into a new woman. But the night that followed had been a breakneck run across the open country, one in which Nadja never fully knew what was going on. Warriors had come and gone she was certain, and on at least three occasions, the sound of clashing weapons had informed her that they'd encountered enemy squadrons or patrols in the night.

But the main war party had pressed ever onward, never slackening their brutal pace. On two separate occasions, her mount had stumbled or ran upon another animal and, but for the rope that held her tight, very nearly pitched her from the saddle. The beasts no longer had lumbered gently or jogged along. Their new gait had required her to bend her every muscle to maintain a seat in a saddle not designed for a human bottom and thighs.

By the time the first light came, and they began their short rest, Nadja was hot, sweating, and trembling from the exertion. Her first act was to wolf three bitter pieces of pemmican and down as many of the greens as she could.

As Nadja did, Gunny walked her beast up, with Spiros immediately behind. Both Marines looked exhausted and ill-used.

"You two look how I feel," she said around a mouthful of pulpy greens.

"We're tougher than we look, ma'am." Gunny mustered a convincing smile.

"And this still isn't as bad as Marine basic training … doesn't even touch recon survival school," added Spiros.

The NCO nodded her agreement. "Don't fret, ma'am. We got each other's backs, and I wasn't joking back there. Part of the Marine Corps genetics package: we can go days without sleep when we have to."

"I wondered why you were always up before me," Nadja replied with a laugh. She knew Marines received good augmentations, some of the best, but still wasn't sure whether Gunny was pulling her leg.

"We don't like people knowing we stack the deck when we play cards either," added Spiros. "So, keep that under your hat."

The three began laughing giddily, and despite knowing to the contrary, Nadja felt the worst was behind them. It was how folks in the military always dealt with stress, careful planning and inappropriate humor.

She glanced around. "How many are we now?"

"I couldn't guess, ma'am. But I'm sure we picked up a few last night." Gunny stood in her saddle and looked about in the morning's half-light. "It looks like we're starting to roll again. I see Stig and … um, there's Festus. Hold on … nope. I don't see any of the others we started with, but some of them must be in this mob somewhere."

She heard Stig's voice, and the party again began to move. Hearing their friend gave Nadja heart. "OK," she said to the Marines. "I don't know how this is going to play out, but stick together. We're smaller than these guys, and if we lose a mount, we can double … or even triple up."

"Good thinking, ma'am," said Gunny as she gave a few last-minute stretches, like an athlete preparing for a great race. Spiros twisted his neck several separate ways and mouthed a few greens. It was time, and they were off.

The pace wasn't as fast as it had been just minutes before their break, but it was a steady run. Nadja guided her beast over toward Gunny, a task that she now found easy.

"How long will we keep this pace?"

"I don't know, ma'am. We're still a ways away from the objective. I would think they'd take advantage of the cool air to run the beasts harder, like they did last night. But these guys are built different than us. Stig might be resting them for a sprint ahead, or maybe letting them stay cool for the heat of the day. I'm just guessing."

"Or maybe the animals are on their last legs?"

The NCO nodded. "I've never seen them run this hard and don't know the signs. That might be true."

"How far is 'a ways away'?"

"If I've got the right objective, ma'am, I'd say about 200 klicks, maybe a little less. We're moving about 30 klicks an hour now, and it's another three hours till the heat starts to really beat our ass."

"That means another hundred kilometers during the worst of the day?"

"Yup," said the NCO succinctly.

"OK," said Nadja with a shy smile, "eat greens." She had no intention of allowing herself again to become so dehydrated. Nadja was certain a second time would kill her.

There was something more, though. Perhaps it was the dose of the good stuff Spiros had given her, but as exhausted as she was, she felt far better than she had any right. She'd had minor bouts of heat illness in her life, usually when working out or hiking and climbing with friends, but there was no headache or general sense of unwellness now that she'd had on those previous occasions. And much of the swelling in her extremities had abated.

All the same, she reached for more greens from the deep pannier to her side and began to nibble as they rode. From time to time, she'd shift or stand or stretch to keep out the cramps and kinks, and before long she'd established what she thought was the proper rhythm to get her through the morning's ride.

It was less than an hour after she dropped into her silence with Gunny that the three humans crested a slight rise and saw the arch of the desert below. It was magnificent, and to the north and east the sun painted the entire desert an ethereal gold and yellow. It was like something from a life-sized Renaissance painting, so clear and crisp it took her breath away. For the first time, she saw high mountains to the north and east and thought to ask Gunny their distance. She felt a tap on her shoulder instead.

"Down there, ma'am." The NCO pointed to the southeast.

It took Nadja a moment on the swaying mount to make out what drew Gunny's attention, and when she did it was faint, barely visible. But a body of mounted warriors evidently was headed in their general direction, and it was too far north to be friendly riders. It was her first sighting of the enemy.

"If we weren't on this rise and there weren't so many, we wouldn't be able to see them," said Gunny.

"How many are there?"

"I'm guesstimating, ma'am. A hundred or more? And I'd say about … oh, 50 or 75 klicks away."

"Enough warriors to pose a threat?" Nadja sucked on a green as she turned in the saddle to face the enemy force. Her balance on the still-running mount had improved.

"Nah, I don't think so. But look behind."

Nadja craned her neck further. "I don't see anything."

"That haze of dust, ma'am."

"Oh, I see it. More troops?"

"I'm pretty certain they are, but I can't tell how far. Maybe another 25 or 50 klicks … maybe farther. From the amount of dust, I'd say a lot of them."

"So, they took the bait. Should we tell Stig?"

"Nah, ma'am. He sees them. That's why I started looking in that direction."

"And we haven't picked up the pace."

"No, ma'am. I reckon Stig thinks we've got enough of a lead." The NCO raised slightly in the stirrups, looking around carefully, and after a few minutes spoke. "And I'm guessing we've got about 300 warriors in the party now."

"So, this end-run is working?"

Gunny gave one of her girlish laughs, her first in many days. "Ma'am, such things don't work until they've worked. Ask me again when we're in an air-conditioned mess hall back on the platform."

The two laughed as they rode, and when Spiros galloped closer, they briefed him on the approaching force.

"He's sparing the animals, ma'am," said the young man. "I just came up from the rear. A few mounts have keeled over, and we have a few stragglers."

Nadja knew this wasn't her war, but as time passed she'd become more and more invested in the welfare of their friends and allies. It was now about more than just rescuing that peckerwood Wray. She had in several different ways tried to justify it to herself, but finally had stopped trying.

"How many spare mounts does the party have?" she asked.

Gunny raised her head and looked back. "Two dozen maybe, but I've seen them ride kine and cargo animals before. They're not as fast, but there are 10 or 15 of those."

"Let's not let it get to that," said Nadja. "Once they run out of spare animals, we go double or triple. I know it ain't comfortable, but the three of us don't weigh as much as one of our hosts."

Both Marines nodded enthusiastically.

"Hey, they're picking up the pace a little, ma'am."

At the precise moment Gunny spoke, the sounds of shouting and weapons rang out ahead, and two dozen warriors split off from the right of their loose column and bolted ahead. The humans pushed their mounts forward to keep up with the party.

The skirmish was short, and the war party returned to its previous pace, but other clashes followed, many others. Invariably the attackers were small enemy patrols whose goal seemed to be to slow the war party or inflict as many casualties as possible. On two occasions, the attacks consisted merely of enemy riders dashing parallel to the party flinging arrows as they went.

All the attacks were either brushed aside swiftly or dealt with by smaller parties, while the rest slipped through and continued their juggernaut course for the northern tank. Nadja saw no serious injuries that required their immediate treatment, but doubted she would. Speed was their friend and their only chance at victory. For all their many, many virtues, their Lacertian allies were not Marines and would, if necessary, leave fallen comrades behind to keep the band or the war party safe. It was their way of war.

It was hard to keep focused on such things, but Nadja forced herself to keep hydrated, and several hours before noon again had herself wrapped mummy-like against the sun. She kept a careful eye on the Marines, and despite the invariable fog that settled on her thoughts when the sun hit its zenith and the temperature again cracked 55 degrees, she attempted to keep an eye on Stig and the small coterie of warriors she'd assumed to be his lieutenants. What was the phrase Gunny had used? "Situational awareness." She had no intention of being cargo anymore and strove to keep focused on what transpired.

By some great miracle or by mere happenstance, the frequency of the enemy attacks faded as the heat increased. Her thoughts were clear enough to realize that they must have left most of the enemy fighters behind them as Stig had planned. He'd mentioned something about a small garrison at the tank. Was that all that now stood between them and their objective?

It was past noon when she tugged on Gunny's sleeve.

"How far do you think?" She popped another green in her mouth to quiet the frog she'd heard there when she spoke. She was determined simply to ignore the heat. It made her feel slightly better that the NCO had to clear her voice several times to reply.

"See that reddish peak up to the left, ma'am?"

Nadja squinted. "Yeah."

"If that's what I think it is, we have less than 50 klicks to our objective."

Nadja remembered her tablet and chronometer were packed away. "What time is it?"

"About three hours past noon, ma'am."

"Hey, Gunny, double up."

Nadja glanced back toward where Spiros dismounted to pass his reins to one of the warriors and was disheartened to see how the war party's ranks now straggled. Ahead, the party remained nicely bunched, but behind them the warriors were spread in a ragged line at least a half kilometer long. Many animals obviously labored, and some of the fleeter warriors ran alongside to spell their mounts.

On an impulse, Nadja turned her mount and rode it to the rear at a trot. When she reached the last rider, another movement caught her eye. About 200 meters back, a lone and still-armored warrior jogged at a steady pace. In this furnace, the feat would be difficult even for the strongest Lacertians. She urged her beast toward the warrior, and as she approached, she realized it was Gaspar.

"This is a bad day for animals," she hollered.

"And for someone on foot."

She reached him and wheeled the animal about. It was only then she realized how exposed they were. None were about, but there were several boulders and hillocks nearby behind which an enemy might lurk. They best hurry. *"Can I give you a lift?"*

"I don't want to impose," the warrior had the nerve to reply.

Fucking Lacertians, she nearly said aloud. The poor bloke obviously was on his last leg—even these mighty warriors had their limits—but before she could formulate a polite comeback, a thunder of battle screams erupted in the direction of the war party. Looking up, she saw a large enemy force appear to the north. An attack was in progress.

"I don't want to be rude, but get on!" she snapped at Gaspar.

The warrior vaulted onto the mount behind her, and Nadja goaded the beast to as great a speed as she thought the beleaguered animal could muster. The two were more than half a kilometer behind Stig and the main party, but to her surprise, they caught up in no time. Stig had chosen to fall back to the rear of the column in order to rally the entire war party. The enemy was less than a kilometer distant and already charging, but Stig stood in the saddle and began to address his troops.

Nadja was proud of her swift mastery of the Lacertian language, but the truth was that she understood most of what was said to her because her companions spoke slowly and patiently with her. Even then, there was much that escaped her, the subtle nuance that every language kept locked away, to which only time and patience gave a key.

Stig showed her that now. His words were short and impassioned, and in but a few phrases he pressed a fire and steel into his warriors that heat and exhaustion might have checked. The only words she understood that mattered were simple: *"Don't stop, fight your way through. Victory lies beyond."*

The war party moved as one and met the enemy's riders with a sudden clash. Nadja had found the Marines, now on a single mount, and the three fell in behind Stig and a small knot of others. She knew full well the rules for the enemy were different: They would not hesitate to kill a cub. So, she kept her head down and ran her mount as fast as she was able.

Seconds after first contact, Gaspar was out of the saddle, vaulting upon a mounted enemy warrior with his sword in one hand and a dagger in the other. She didn't wait around to see the result of the combat, but pressed onward. To her great surprise, she was soon riding beside a laughing and shrieking Spiros and Gunny. On their other side, Stig howled. The war whoops and victory cries confused her.

She looked over to Gunny and expressed her confusion.

"That was the garrison, ma'am. And they were fewer than a hundred," the exhausted and parched NCO hooted. "The objective is only 40 or 50 klicks ahead, and there's nothing in our way."

Glancing back, Nadja realized the fighting behind them already was all but over. The war band's members raced at their best speed north, and she saw a screaming and hooting Gaspar gallop by on a newly captured enemy mount.

Nadja began to scream and hoot and cry like a victorious Lacertian warrior, and the Marines soon joined her.

27: Better Angels

T hey kept the surgery at the northern tank open only briefly. Mostly, the members of the war party needed only rest and rehydration. There were a few arrow wounds and some wicked sword and dagger cuts, but those were simple procedures for the Marines.

As frightening as it had seemed at the moment, their fight with the tank's former garrison hadn't been long or costly. During the short engagement, they had lost a few mounts, stolen some more, and even managed to pinch a bit of war booty from the bodies of the tank's former defenders. Afterward, it had taken about two hours for the last of the war party to come straggling into the ample watering hole.

In all, the two-day forced march was far more successful than Stig had envisioned. Throughout the last two days, they'd lost around 50 warriors and half again as many mounts, offset only slightly by the animals they'd captured. Nadja didn't want to think of those wounded who may have been left behind. And in the hours following their arrival at the objective, another two small war parties fought their way through.

Nadja wanted to spend some time with Stig and get his estimation of what likely would next transpire, but he soon was off with his officers, and, frankly, Nadja was beat, completely and totally gutted. She settled instead for discussing the issue by the water tank with Gunny while lines of warriors watered their exhausted mounts nearby. The Marine's assessment of events had proven uncanny many times before.

"Ma'am, I'm guessing with those two new war parties that followed us here that Stig's troops number close to 400 now."

"So, even better than he envisioned."

Gunny recovered a rag from the tank and wrung water over her head. "I don't know, ma'am. It might be he was just being cautious in his early estimates, but it was a ballsy move." She looked around and pointed to the various outcroppings and cliffs nearby. "This place is wicked easy to defend, it's the only dependable water for hundreds of kilometers, and the garrison was stupid for coming out to face such a large party. There were more of them than Stig's scouts thought, and if they would've stayed put, they could have bled Stig and his boys and maybe held them off long enough for Black Rock's reinforcements to arrive."

"How long before those assholes get here?"

"The ones we saw this morning should be here anytime. The ones behind them? I dunno. If not later today, then sometime tonight."

Nadja smiled. "And they'll be tuckered out and parched just like Stig's people, except they won't have access to water."

"Yup." Gunny smiled back. "They may be carrying water and other supplies, but they'll be in a bad way. And their mounts will be exhausted and parched. See up above us in that draw? Festus said that and the fields beyond are the only grazing for several days in any direction. The enemy will have to get past the tank to get to it."

"Did Stig plan it that way? Is that why he timed the march the way he did, so it would force the enemy to race all day in the heat?"

Gunny shrugged. "If not, Stig is one lucky cuss. I think he's a really smart and cunning soldier."

"So," said Nadja, "Black Rock's forces get here later today?"

"Yes, ma'am"

"They'll outnumber Stig's party?"

"Almost certainly."

"How long before the rest of the southern army shows up?"

"It's another guess, ma'am, but I'd say they should start trickling in any time. But they won't get here in any numbers until probably late tomorrow. They'll want to husband their strength and be fit to fight when they arrive."

"So, we just need to hold on a day or two?"

"The bad guys won't make it easy, ma'am." The NCO wrung more water over her head and let out a luxuriant sigh. "Ma'am, stop thinking so much and sleep. That's an order."

Those were the last words Nadja heard for several hours.

———

When Nadja roused herself about an hour before dark, there was the faint sound of commotion in the distance, and, looking about, she realized she and the two Marines were nearly alone at the tank. Save for a few sentries, their hosts had disappeared.

She left her two fellows to sleep—they richly needed and deserved it—and after slipping on her boots she walked toward the gentle tumult. Nadja Bikram always prided herself on her good physical condition, but her every muscle now ached and trembled in ways she'd never imagined possible. And she felt as if she could sleep another month. Her curiosity and her deep need not to again become stowage wouldn't allow that. So, she carried on.

144

She found the warriors gathered near the narrow mouth of the wadi leading to the tank, their mounts picketed nearby. Some of the fellows seemed on guard, some ate and socialized, but most rested. It wasn't immediately clear, but their numbers seemed to have increased. There were many friendly greetings as she moved among them, and one of the warriors well known to her, one of Black Flower's band, who Gunny had nicknamed Daphne, took her in hand and led her to where Stig had positioned himself high on a rock outcropping a hundred or so meters ahead.

Her friend Stig showed all the signs she'd come to associate with weariness among Lacertians, but he greeted her affectionately where he sat, taking her on his knee. She'd become accustomed to being treated like a child by her large hosts, but her recent spate of helplessness on the trail still stung, and she felt herself blush.

"*How many will come?*" she asked her friend. Nadja often had seen Gunny playfully tug at their hosts' large canine teeth, and suddenly her hand had a life of its own. She didn't know why she did it, but before he answered, Stig gave an affectionate growl to her jostling of his tooth.

"*I don't know, but many. Half of their army at least.*"

Numbers were always dodgy with their friends. It took a bit of time for her fully to decipher the conversation that followed, but a swift calculation in her head told her that Stig expected at least twelve to fifteen hundred warriors would oppose them. But that number might be greater.

"*But we are well prepared and rested,*" he said, "*and they will be weary.*"

Nadja was no Gunnery Sergeant Nice, but she had a solid understanding of numbers and land warfare. Even if Stig's forces were well prepared, they numbered fewer than 500, probably closer to 400. Such odds were not in their favor. She thought to confirm more of Gunny's estimates. "*And how long before the rest of your army arrives?*"

"*It arrives when it arrives, Nadja. We will stay safe until then.*" A sweet Lacertian smile cracked his tired face. "*We have to win. Greta said she would cook and eat both my arms if I let anything happen to you.*"

A gust of laughter escaped Nadja, a storm that raged more fiercely when it occurred to her that Greta likely hadn't been joking. A warm hand touched her.

"*You humans are amusing. When you think something is funny, it's like you have dust in your lungs you can't get out.*"

She stemmed her laughter and looked to her friend. "*I'm not worried about myself. I'm worried about you and your warriors. Gunny agrees with your estimates. If the enemy is no more than you say, you will prevail. But I'm worried what will happen if there are more of them."* She shook her head and mentally chastised herself. Stig was a brilliant combat leader who didn't need her advice or her grousing. She found herself backpedaling. *"Stig, I'm sorry. It's not my place...."*

"Nadja, don't worry. Don't worry at all. We will win this conflict, not because our numbers are greater, but because our cause is just, and because our enemy does not know right from wrong."

And there it was again, hidden within his words of deep beauty and nobility, that ineffable something that confounded and confused her. As simple as her friend's words seemed, there was something hidden in his words that she was not getting ... some nuance that she might never fully understand. She leaned forward and put her arms around his enormous neck and pulled him close.

"When will they come?" she asked after a brief time.

"They are here now."

Nadja stood and peered over the boulder that formed a parapet at the front of Stig's observation post. It took several minutes in the fading light, but she finally discerned the comings and goings of warriors in the desert before them. Most obviously were well-hidden in the rough terrain that formed this part of the desert, else Stig's scouts would have ascertained their true numbers.

"Will they attack soon?"

Stig stepped closer and peered after her. *"Only if we're lucky. The advantage then would be ours. Likely they will wait, rest, and attack at first light, hoping to overwhelm us in one mighty rush. Nadja, I must talk with those waiting. Go eat and rest. You will know when danger comes."*

For the first time, she noticed a group of officers had assembled below, but rather than depart immediately, she turned back to Stig. There was a question she hadn't yet asked. *"Why did you bring us with you? Why didn't you leave Gunny, Spiros, and me with the band?"*

There was that smile again. *"Nadja, there are no secrets at the gathering. We knew you were trying to find your way home. Black Flower agreed to send you with me, so I could help you. After we defeat Black Rock and recover your companion, I'll help you find your way home. I promise."*

She stepped in and put her arms around the giant for a hard squeeze before departing without further word. Her stomach was growling, and her spirits were roiling. Never since her arrival had these people felt so thoroughly and completely human to her. *They are so much like us,* she

146

thought as she paced back to the tank. *Only, they are the better angels we seek to be rather than the mundane creatures we truly are.*

28: Travois

'How good are you with a pistol, ma'am?"

Nadja raised her head from where she packed their medical equipment. She'd set the alarm in her tablet to wake her an hour before dawn only to find the Marines up and moving around by then and the sounds of Stig's war party rumbling to life in the distance. The three now scrambled to move their field hospital a few hundred paces east, to a spot closer to where the fighting would commence. It was something they should have done the night before.

Gunny, sidearm in hand, regarded her carefully.

"Lethal ... why?" was Nadja's only reply. It was true. She was an indifferent marksman with a rifle, but skill with a pistol was one of her vanities going back 40 years.

Gunny stepped closer and shoved the weapon and pistol belt into Nadja's hands. "There are a hundred and two rounds left, including what's in the magazine, and there's one spare battery. You remember how to arm the battery?"

"I do. Perfectly." She took the proffered weapon and strapped the belt around her waist. "I think you're a better shot, though."

"Ma'am, no offense. But you can't carry one of these big bastards by yourself. And me and Spiros need someone to cover us when we're hauling back the wounded."

The wisdom of the gunnery sergeant's words was obvious. Nadja was strong, able to lift nearly twice her body weight and carry it for kilometers. But she'd seen Gunny several times in her horseplay with the Lacertians lift one of the 300-kilogram warriors from the ground. It wasn't easy for her. It usually required both Gunny and Spiros to maneuver the wounded to the infirmary. But they were far better surgeons and vastly more proficient orderlies than her.

Either way, there was no time to argue. Nadja shouldered her bags. "Alright, let's get it to the front. Where's Spiros?"

"He'll meet us there. He's trying to find his old mount to recover a bag of roots."

The two women set off into the half-light at a quickstep.

Gunny already had spoken briefly with Stig that morning, and his answer was clear: There would be no quarter asked and none given. He'd seemed indifferent to their surgical efforts. "All will fight to the death," he'd told the NCO. It was their way of war.

The humans thought differently—not necessarily that it would matter. They were three and had never plied their healing arts in a proper battle before. How they intended to play litter-bearer, security force, and surgeon to hundreds of fighters all at the same time was something they had not yet discussed among themselves or otherwise worked out, but one way or another, they would do all those things. Their friends on the battle line were risking far, far too much for them not to try.

"Here, Gunny!" they heard as they reached the mouth of the wadi. Spiros came jogging up. "I think the shit is about to hit the fan," he said excitedly.

He pointed them to a space inside the wadi mouth, where he'd set up an impromptu aid station. It was within 200 meters of the front rank of Stig's troops and had a dozen pallets set out for the wounded. The lance corporal already had begun grinding roots, and several dozen flasks lay in careful rows along the nearby cliffside. Each obviously was filled with the life-saving "good stuff" they would need for their day's work. The three immediately fell to further preparations.

A blood-curdling scream followed in the distance, beyond the narrow defile that formed the wadi mouth. It was unlike anything Nadja previously had heard on the planet, but oddly the import of the cry was clear to her. In a land where no one had lips, this was the bugle call that signaled the start of battle. She immediately rose.

By reflex, Nadja checked the weapon holstered to her side. Since the development of the Christine Power-Cell centuries before, firearms of all sizes essentially were railguns, firing projectiles of various calibers through a system of magnets in an upper-receiver that was powered by an enormously potent CPC battery in the weapon's handgrip. The weapon in her hand was light and deadly, and each of the two batteries available to her could be modified into powerful explosives with the twist of her wrist.

"Stay here. I'll be back in a minute." She jogged forward through the wadi opening a hundred meters or so, far enough to catch sight of the ominous spectacle hurtling toward them.

Stig's mounted defenders were arrayed five deep before the entry of the wadi—likely many more were concealed at various points in the heights flanking the battlefield—and through the narrow gaps between their ranks, Nadja saw an enormous horde of riders sweeping through the desert toward them. It was somehow horrific and delightful at the same time, as if she'd been swept up in some fantastical cinema production. It was all so alive and real and dreadful.

Prying her eyes loose, she turned and dashed toward the aid station, screaming at the top of her lungs, "They're coming!"

The gathering rumble of the hurtling enemy steeds reached a crescendo at the precise moment Nadja reached the aid station, and the horrific thunderclap of the two armies crashing caused her to whip about and backpedal several steps before she collided with the two Marines. The three stood shoulder to shoulder for some seconds viewing the grisly spectacle of carnage before them.

"OK, let's go," said Nadja after the thunderclap ended and the first screams of pain and agony began.

Gunny paced immediately to her right. "Don't forget, ma'am, headshots. If you shoot center mass like you were taught, it won't do much. These guys' hearts and lungs are distributed throughout their torsos. They are wicked durable."

Nadja hoped it wouldn't come to her shooting anyone, but knew it could. As a State Department officer, she legally had no business involving herself in the internal conflict of an alien planet, but these were unusual circumstances. The time for pearl-clutching about breaching some non-involvement protocol was past. Instead, she reached down emotionally and, in the words of an ancient holy book she'd once read, she girded up her loins.

They didn't have to go far. As the three moved forward from the wadi mouth on tremulous feet, the line of battle shifted toward them, and at one point several minutes after the initial charge, they thought it might break altogether. But Stig's cavalry held, and 30 minutes later the battle line slowly recoiled as the defenders pressed the enemy back into the desert. The shifting line of warriors left behind it scores of injured, dead, and dying when it moved.

Discerning friend from enemy was much easier than Nadja had first feared. The fighters of Black Rock wore ramshackle armor and appeared to be smeared in a black oil that gave off the scent of rancid vinegar. Those warriors they avoided, both living and dead, and the Marines were soon shuttling injured back to the aid station.

After they moved their first 10 casualties, Spiros stayed behind as surgeon, and Nadja assisted Gunny with further evacuations. The wounds were simply dreadful, but from time to time one or more of the warriors would somehow lumber to their feet or knees and in some way lurch or crawl back into the fray. In a very intimate way, they all knew it was fight or die.

Nadja's first moment of terror came when an enemy warrior sprang to life as she and the NCO hustled one of Festus's companions back to the rear. Hardly breaking stride, she drew the pistol fired once, and returned it to its holster, her only injury the sudden shock of how easily she'd accomplished the terrible and terrifying task.

Twice more in the next 20 minutes she was forced to defend herself or Gunny, once from another revived enemy casualty and a second time from a warrior who somehow had waded through the press of battle and gained the rear. Both warriors fell with a single shot to the head.

"You're good at that, ma'am," said Gunny during their first pause. "Why don't you keep watch for more injured, and I'll step back and help Spiros. He's got to have close to 40 patients by now."

A tired Nadja nodded. "I'll give you a holler if I need help."

She didn't like feeling at loose ends. The humans so far had avoided moving too close to the battle line for fear of becoming casualties themselves. But as the fight raged barely 100 meters distant, more and more injured warriors fell back. The battle seethed, the screams continued, and several times she needed to shoo off riderless mounts that either blocked her view or merely strayed too close for safety.

It was then something occurred to her. The mounts were large, but normally docile, and she'd become quite adept at handling them. Running forward, she stripped the tack and saddle from a downed beast and with a few broken spears began to weave a harness. In less than 10 minutes, she had a simple travois and five minutes later had corralled and calmed one of the frightened and skittish animals and rigged the new implement to it.

With her heart in her throat, Nadja raced the animal to within a few meters of the front line, grabbed the nearest hand that was visible on the ground and pulled. The warrior, who she did not know, was half conscious and godawful heavy, but it took her only minutes to drag and roll her onto the travois. It was another few minutes to lead the animal back to the aid station.

"Fuck me. Why didn't I think of that?" came Gunny's voice as she approached. The NCO helped her offload the patient.

"This is high-level, State Department thinking, Gunny."

She returned for another and then another, and once Nadja found her rhythm, she was veritably running the mount back and forth with her makeshift ambulance, so caught up in what she was doing that she nearly forgot to be afraid. But the heavens smiled upon her, and she did not again have to draw the weapon at her side.

After nearly three miserable, bloody hours, the fighting ceased as quickly as it had begun. It was carnage. The line of battle had shifted over the course of the conflict, leaving dead and wounded in its wake. But the area in which the two armies had last clashed, the arc of space roughly 150 meters outside the wadi mouth, was the spot most heavily contested. There, the bodies of the dead and wounded, both friend and foe, were heaped higher than her waist in places.

Nadja wanted to cry, but then something occurred to her.

Absent were the victory shouts and hoots from Stig's army. They held the field of conflict and at least for the time were victorious. But there were several minutes of stunned and exhausted silence, even among those doughty warriors, before the first faint peeps rose to the heavens. And some minutes more passed before the warriors screamed victory from the depths of their throats.

There was no time for her to think more, and she was back to work. This time, she was joined by hundreds of hands as the army began to disentangle the dead from the living. The enemy wounded were dispatched without mercy, but the wounded of Stig's war party were borne quickly and carefully back to the aid station by their comrades.

It took nearly an hour to clear the battlefield, and when she got her first good look at the aid station afterward, she was appalled. There were well over 100 casualties, of whom the Marines had treated perhaps 30. A certain amount of dragooning clearly was in order, and Nadja grabbed the nearest 20 warriors, sending some for water, setting others to grinding roots, and employing the rest as her orderlies to help her separate the wounded into various categories. Those with simple wounds were treated by their fellows. The rest waited for the humans.

By the time the heat of the day approached, the hospital was humming along as best as it was able.

"*I understand you're the new commander.*" The voice was Festus who, when she turned to regard him, was being treated clumsily for an ugly slash on his muzzle by a fellow warrior.

"I see Stig on his mount over that way, so I'm sure he still commands. But if you want to wait, I can take a look at that cut for you."

"No. It's a simple thing. There are many injuries more deserving."

"I'm sorry you're hurt, but am glad you live. Will the enemy attack again?"

"*Yes,*" he said. "*They must.*"

"Then why did they fall back this time?"

Festus gave a Lacertian version of a derisive snort. *"A few small war parties of ours arrived and gathered together in the hills nearby. When they attacked the rear of Black Rock's army, his monsters lost heart, and their attack faltered ... but they cannot afford to fail again."*

The reason for the enemy's zeal had become obvious by that point. If Black Rock's forces did not manage to wrest the tank from Stig's war party before the rest of the southern army arrived, it would be a catastrophe for them. That essentially was what concerned Nadja now.

"You lost many warriors this morning," she said. The implications were obvious.

"Yes, Nadja. The enemy arrived in far greater numbers than we thought they would. But we have had reinforcements, and the enemy's losses this morning were severe. We will prevail."

She'd finally had enough and reached over and took the needle and thread from the hand of Festus's comrade. It took her but a few wordless minutes to complete what the inept Lacertian had started. *"You will look as beautiful as ever."*

"That's unfortunate," the officer replied without a trace of humor. *"But thank you, for all of this. Many will live who would have died."*

"How long before the enemy rallies?"

"Soon," he said and patted her affectionately on the shoulder. *"I saw you taking risks earlier. Be safe."*

After the officer had departed, Nadja took her first proper break and downed as many greens as she was able. It looked to be another scorcher, and as she reached into a nearby bag to fetch out her cloak, she wondered what she might do to best help Gunny and Spiros at their tasks.

At that moment, the rallying cries again went up. The next attack was coming.

29: Onto the Heights

The wadi in which the tank was located emptied to the east through a narrow defile about 20 meters long and wide enough for about five animals to pass abreast. Once outside that wadi mouth, the opening gradually widened, forming a natural funnel that merged into the desert beyond. It was in that funnel that the morning's battle had been waged.

The place now looked like a different terrain entirely. In addition to the many dead warriors of Black Rock's forces, scores of dead beasts lay bloating in the sun. Stig's men left most of those in the piles where they lay, but they'd dragged more than a dozen to add to those nearest their new front line, which they'd established about 80 meters east of the wadi mouth.

Nadja had kept a casual eye on the war band's preparations, and it took her no time to discern what they planned. Stig had lost many troops, but rather than thin his ranks, he opted to shorten his line, pulling his fighters back about 100 meters from where they'd been arrayed in the morning, and place them on foot with the animal carcasses as impromptu barricades. In that position, their battle line was flanked to the north and south by the stone cliffs and outcroppings that sided the funnel.

The plan seemed an attempt at blunting two enemy advantages. The Lacertian steeds were swift runners and overwhelming in a charge, but they were very poor jumpers, and the advancing animals would need to weave in and out of the bodies scattered across the battlefield. There would be no great irresistible rush of mounted warriors as there had been in the morning. Rather, Stig's troops would meet the enemy with spear and sword at the makeshift wall and very possibly force the enemy to abandon their mounts as well.

It was a wise move, which hopefully would further diminish the enemy's advantage in numbers. With the shortened battle line and the narrowness and high stone walls of the funnel, the enemy would be able to bring only a small number of their total force to bear on Stig's forces at one time.

Of course, the disadvantage of the defenders' position was that it gave them only a slight opening through which to fallback if hard pressed. If the enemy could push Stig's defenders hard enough, such a strategy might prevent them from making an orderly retreat through the narrow defile into the wadi behind them. They could be pinned against the funnel walls they hoped to defend.

That scenario could be catastrophic, especially given the aid station was located at the immediate west of the defile. A moment of deep concern shot through Nadja. No. There would be no time to move the wounded farther from the fighting now. The casualties would have to trust to the strength of their fellows to hold the line and carry the day.

The enemy attack came minutes later, but without the overwhelming rush and cacophony of the morning's battle. After a quick shout to Gunny, Nadja was back at her travois and again evacuating those most seriously wounded.

Her efforts were short-lived.

As in the first attack, the initial charge of the enemy forced the defenders back a way. That was when things changed. From that point, the battle line did not rebound in the direction of the enemy as it had in the morning. Within 40 minutes, the ranks of the defenders seemed to strain and groan as the attackers brought up more and more and more troops, not to flank the defenders, but simply to drive them back by raw numbers and the weight of their bodies.

By the end of two hours constant, bloody, bitter fighting, the rear rank of Stig's soldiers was just scant meters from the wadi mouth. The enemy advance stalled there, because as the defenders fell back, their line shortened, leaving more of their warriors to push against the attackers from behind. Finally, the sound of combat so diminished that Nadja, from where she was situated near the aid station a mere 30 meters behind the defenders' last rank, scrambled aboard the back of her mount and, standing at her full height, peered into the fray.

Before her, she saw over the tops of the warriors' heads the bizarre sight of a reverse tug-of-war as both sides pressed so hard against one another at the wadi mouth that it rendered the front ranks of each incapable of even lifting their weapons to strike at their foes. Instead, the front ranks snapped and snarled and gouged at each other, with only an occasional warrior able to wriggle free a weapon to smack at an adversary. For the first time in their combat, the sounds of growling and screeching drowned out the clash of weapons.

There was little for Nadja to do during this brutal and savage pantomime, so she watched.

The defenders had perhaps 200 warriors on their main line of battle. The remainder of Stig's war party was deployed along the rugged cliffs and rock outcroppings that sheltered the wadi. As the enemy advance

155

stalled, Stig's men above continued to hurl down stones and arrows, but to little apparent effect upon the armored and helmeted enemy.

What came next should have been predictable. For all their size, the Lacertians appeared to be serviceable climbers, and the sounds of battle soon could be heard on the rock walls above. The enemy intended not only to overwhelm the defenders below, but with Stig's men pressed back against the wadi mouth, they were unable to stop the attackers from climbing the natural cliff fortifications on the outside.

The army of Black Rock intended to overwhelm the entire area by raw numbers.

The moment she realized that fact, Nadja turned to the sound of scraping rock and saw a knot of enemy fighters half-scrambling, half-falling down the rock wall near where the Marines labored. Loosing a scream of warning, she leapt from the back of the mount and at a steady combat walk, drew the pistol, took aim, and released a series of rounds.

The first two shots were wasted before the third caught an enemy warrior on the side of the head, felling it instantly. To her shock and surprise, she witnessed Gunny crouch, rush, and in one well-practiced move seize an enemy by both thighs and lift and flip it to the ground, where Spiros expertly drove his curved blade into the back of the invader's neck. (Clearly the Marines' earlier wrestling with the members of the band had been more than just horseplay.) The last standing enemy warriors were set upon by one of the invalids in Gunny's care. The patient felled one attacker before Nadja dispatched the second with one well-aimed shot.

All the patients in the aid station were badly injured. Some were missing limbs, others stood at death's gate. But the "good stuff" worked wonders. Throughout the day, a score of casualties had struggled to their feet to rejoin the fray. The warrior now leaning against the wall was missing its lower left leg and part of the opposite hand, but it began hopping, using the stone wall as a support, toward the sound of battle.

Nadja stepped forward and did something that at any other time and any other place she would have found unimaginable, horrific. She gently placed herself under the warrior's good arm and acted as its crutch, leading it to the battle that raged fewer than 50 meters distant.

"Gunny, I don't think we're going to be getting anymore wounded. Arm yourselves," was all she said.

"Aye-aye, ma'am," said both Marines in unison.

The few minutes it took her to guide the warrior to the battle line showed her things were beginning to deteriorate. Stig's men were beginning to give way, and the last rank of them was five meters into the narrow defile that formed the wadi mouth. Projectiles no longer troubled the enemy without, and stones had begun falling on the defenders from above.

The enemy had begun to seize the high ground, and for all Stig's encouragements and screams of defiance, which she could clearly hear on the battle line ahead, this might be the very end for them.

She leaned the warrior on the hunched and straining shoulders of the rear rank of defenders, on what looked like an enormous scrum for rugby football, and the Lacertian leaned in and bunched his good leg and one arm in Sisyphean effort with his fellows. Nadja turned, ducked her head to avoid a flying rock, and fled back the direction she came.

Several more badly injured fighters stumbled along the short path from the aid station to the battle line. Nadja corralled these and screamed for the Marines to follow her.

She'd always been a good rocker, and though it had been years since she'd done any real climbing, the cliffside on the west of the wadi mouth was only about 20 meters high. The day was hot and miserable, but not the scorcher that she'd foretold. Taking a careful grip, she stretched her arms and legs as far and as fast as she could safely climb. Below, she heard scrambling that she couldn't discern as human or Lacertian. It didn't matter. They needed bodies up top. If they didn't clear the heights to either side of the defile, it was all over—it might all be over either way.

Minutes later, she was peeping over the top of the rock. Fully 30 enemy warriors had gained the heights, slain its defenders, and were now hurling stones down onto Stig's men below. With two great pulls, Nadja was up. She immediately drew the pistol and felled five enemy in five careful shots. Black Rock's warriors, at first startled, turned to rush. Only a dozen meters or so separated them, but Nadja was able to get off four more shots, felling three of her attackers. She pressed forward to give those behind her space to ascend and triggered two more rounds.

By that point, the nearest of the enemy was nearly within sword's reach, but an enormous form flashed past her as the first of Gunny's patients entered the fray, taking down the nearest two enemy in a swirling pile of flesh and screams. Nadja triggered off four more rounds, felling three more enemy.

But then the most shocking thing happened. The remaining enemy, who numbered nearly 20, broke and ran. Two simply backstepped carelessly off the cliff to drop the 20 meters into the defile floor below. The others ran, scrambled, and fell eastward and disappeared over the lip of the cliff.

She'd never seen such a thing from a Lacertian, and Stig's words came to her. *They don't know the difference between right and wrong.*

But it wasn't over. What Nadja saw on the clifftop was so disheartening as to make her despair. Scores of enemy fighters swarmed the heights in every direction, battling the defenders and looking as if they were winning. Worse, a handful of enemy continued to pelt Stig's troops in the defile from the far side of the gap. She didn't have enough rounds to stop them all.

"Shit," she said aloud. Turning, she saw Gunny rising from the cliffside. She snatched the spare pistol battery from the pistol belt and handed belt and weapon to the Marine. "Gunny, clear the other side of the defile."

The Marine gripped the weapon and carefully opened fire on the attackers opposite them.

Nadja then cautiously crossed the 20 meters to the eastern cliffside. The enemy ranks below were legion, and she nearly forsook her hastily acquired plan. No. It was this or nothing.

Carefully choosing a target about 75 meters behind the front ranks of the two competing armies, she gripped the battery, flipped the safety, turned the top counterclockwise once, and pressed the thumb-sized white indent until it turned red and vibrated. Taking careful aim on an enormous bronze-shouldered warrior near her chosen mark, she gave her best toss, turned, hit the deck, and screamed.

"Grenade!"

———

It was a fully charged battery, and the yield was as powerful as she'd anticipated—the blast radius was about 50 meters—but there was no way in hell a single such weapon should've turned the tide of battle, at least not by itself. It killed or injured scores of enemy warriors, but most importantly, it stunned hundreds and broke up the logjam at the wadi mouth.

The first two or three enemy ranks, which before had the strength and weight of many hundreds of their fellows pushing behind them, suddenly no longer had that overwhelming pressure at their backs. Stig's warriors went over the first enemy ranks like an enormous wrath, hacking and cutting, before piling into the injured and stunned ranks of enemy soldiers behind them.

It was at that point the panic began.

As individuals, many of Black Rock's warriors had strength and courage—Nadja had seen that fact for herself—but collectively they didn't know right from wrong. There was not the solid sense of community, loyalty, ethics, and decency in them that bound together the members of Stig's war party or those of Black Flower's band. Black Rock's poor benighted creatures were like "the Others" on the inside.

With their sudden momentum, Stig's 200 warriors went through the enemy ranks like a bulldozer, slaying hundreds and driving the rest into the desert. In less than 10 minutes, the battle was all but over.

Nadja and the Marines sat on the cliffside and watched the mopping-up activities below. The three wounded Lacertians, who had joined them there, already had gone below to join in the fray. Gunny finally got around to asking the question—or, rather, to making the statement.

"You could have given a girl a heads-up on that, ma'am."

"I didn't want you talking me out of it."

"Are you sure that's what it was?"

Nadja regarded the gunnery sergeant. "No. No, I wasn't sure what I was going to do until the moment I did it."

"That's good situational awareness, ma'am," said the NCO, slapping her back. "But we should get down. There'll be wounded, and most of these knuckleheads are useless with a needle and thread."

The hours after they lowered themselves from the rocks were spent in surgery. Thankfully, there were far fewer casualties than there had been from the morning's conflict. Deaths were another matter. More than half of Stig's large war party lay dead, and several warriors with whom the humans had become close were lost, including Festus and Gaspar.

But Stig's scouts assured him the enemy truly was fled, leaving behind many of their mounts and most of their supplies, and over the next hours allied troops began trickling into camp. About 30 minutes before sunset, the main body of the army arrived.

The southern army had won the battle at the tank.

30: Nothing Else Remains

'How is this not a demotion?"

They had spent much of the evening resting and rehydrating with Stig and his troops near the waters of the tank. Their friend had met with the overall army commander, Black Thorn, soon after his arrival, and the general had spent long minutes listening carefully to Stig's report before pronouncing Stig a great champion. The commander then thanked him and the others of the war party for their great courage and fortitude and for what clearly was an important victory.

Black Thorn's healers now tended the wounded, but there was no ceremony for the dead. Funerary rites in Lacertian society seemed to consist of excising heel spikes of the fallen for use as arrowheads before leaving their remains in the desert for the elements to take. The humans earlier had gone out with the survivors to lay out their closest comrades. It took but a few minutes.

Stig now commanded his original war party of which only 14 remained, a number that included Stig and three of Festus's fellows. It was that fact that chapped at Gunny's ass.

"Gunny, you know better than anyone their way of war is different. With these guys, most leadership positions are situational. Stig led the attack against the tank, because he was there and stepped up, and warriors followed him because they saw something in him. Come next big fight, it likely will shake out the same way."

The NCO nodded philosophically. "Especially with a big win under his belt," she admitted. "Still doesn't feel right."

"He seems pretty happy with the whole thing," said Nadja.

"True, ma'am. He was looking mighty harried these last few days." The Marine reached over and tossed a cloak over Spiros. The young Marine was always the first to sleep. "What's the next move?"

Nadja couldn't hide a smile. She was accustomed to relying on Gunny Nice to read the direction of the wind. "We'll find out for certain when Stig gets back from the leaders' meeting, but the army can't stay here long. There's plenty of water, but like you said yesterday, not nearly enough grazing. Like as not, they'll do like they did last time and break up into smaller parties and push the last five or six days to Black Rock's fortress."

Gunny leaned back. "I thought I heard Stig say something like that earlier. They're not worried about splitting up the army?"

"I don't think it'll be like that. They'll probably move in companies of a few hundred. But it shouldn't matter. Stig's pretty convinced they broke the back of Black Rock's army here today, and Black Thorn's patrols are out running down those that got away."

"I don't know either, ma'am. They have pretty good intel, but it ain't perfect. Otherwise they would've had a better idea how many troops this guy had access to."

There was no way to dispute the Marine's words. All involved in the campaign originally had thought Black Rock's total forces to number no more than 2,000, of which he might field half against them to slow or stop their march northward. But according to Stig's own estimate, the enemy had sent slightly more than 2,000 against them at the tank that day, a godawful number of warriors. The total number that'd marched south from Black Rock's fortress may have been as high as 2,500, and it was unlikely the villain had deployed his entire army.

"You know how these guys are with numbers," said Nadja. "Either way, there's almost no grazing where we're going, and Festus's buddies said there are only a few undependable tanks."

"There isn't going to be a siege, then?"

"I don't know how any of this'll work, Gunny. Black Thorn has a supply caravan about a day behind him, but even with that, there's no way they can stage a multi-month siege and not starve to death themselves, which leaves...."

"A direct assault."

"Yep. And the way Stig describes Black Rock's fortress, it is damn-near impregnable."

Really Nice began chuckling quietly. "They've done pretty good so far ... especially with keeping you around to bail them out."

"Let's not talk about that. I'm going to be filling out paperwork explaining that little stunt until the day I retire."

"Little stunt or not, ma'am, it kept us alive."

"I'm not convinced of that." Nadja had been convinced of that fact at the time, else she wouldn't have tossed an explosive, though she'd later had second thoughts. "The main army didn't show up for a few hours, but reinforcements started trickling in right after Stig's breakout. I'm sure these guys would've fought their way to victory somehow, even without my ... nudge."

"Your 'nudge' had the same explosive force as a Mark-126 grenade." Gunny sat up from where she lay stretched on her sleeping pallet. Her next

161

words sounded incredulous. "Has no one mentioned a word about that to you?"

"They're pretty smart folks, but I think Stig and his troops had their hands full at that moment. None has ever seen or heard an explosion, and I'm not sure they're even asking why the enemy buckled when it did. Somebody might put two and two together one day, but I'd just as soon they never figure it out."

The emotions that played across the Marine's face were obvious even in the gloom of the night. "No. I agree," she said finally. "Let sleeping dogs, and all that."

"Speaking of sleeping," said Nadja, "I'm not sure I'm getting any tonight."

"Still spun up from the fight?"

"Very," she replied flatly. Somehow, Nadja had made it through the entire day's battle, and her work in the aid station after, before leaning against a boulder and having a fit of the shakes. It hadn't lasted long, maybe 20 minutes, but she'd been a little jumpy since. She'd told herself it was her reaction to the cool air after sunset, but that wasn't true.

"Ma'am, the jitters after a fight are normal. Hold on." The Marine got up, went to their packs, and returned in a few minutes. She reached out her hand. "Take this and slide it between your cheek and gums."

The item was small, barely a sliver. "What is it?"

"Tiny little slice of root. It does wonders. Greta sometimes gives them out when one of the gang has to go under the knife. It isn't a narcotic, doesn't diminish pain, but I tried them a few times when I was first here. It calms you down, but I have no idea why ... or how."

Nadja did as she was instructed. "Eww...," she puckered.

"It's bitter," Gunny said with a chuckle. "But don't chew it. Just hold it there for 15 or 20 minutes."

"So, it does what?"

"Dunno. Calms you down. And there are no side effects, no withdrawal, no cravings ... nothing."

"Placebo?"

"On this rock? Everything is real here."

———

For the first time in so long she couldn't remember, Nadja slept until she woke up. Her first thought was of Gunny and her miracle root cure. She was 40 percent certain the Marine was just pulling her leg. It was the kind of thing folks in the military did. But she put that thought aside—this was Skiathos.

It was perhaps an hour after sunup when she first cracked an eye, and the Marines were nowhere to be seen. Likely they were off bathing, eating, or on some other morning business. The quiet clank of metal on metal and the subdued sounds of animals drinking and milling about said the army slowly was rumbling to life. If her guess was right, some already had departed north.

She popped her head up and looked around. Not 15 meters away, Stig sat on an enormous rock cleaning and polishing his armor. His back was to her, and as she watched he cheerfully exchanged chitchat with passing soldiers.

She got up and ambled over, taking a seat next to him on the boulder. A sack the size of a ripe melon lay between them. Through its half-open top, she saw what looked like bones. It took her a moment to realize what was within, a sack full of heel spikes for making into arrowheads. She wondered if they were…. She saw Stig was regarding her carefully, his gaze inscrutable.

"Are these from the other day?"

"Yes, from our companions in the fight."

She knew the custom, but was still taken aback. *"Not from the enemy?"*

"No. Black Thorn would not have given me those. The spikes of the enemy aren't special in that way."

"Black Thorn gave these to you as an … honor?"

"Yes," he said. *"It is a great honor, one not often given. I hope never to have another."*

"But you were all very brave, and you fought valiantly."

A shy look crossed his face, but he gestured enthusiastically. *"Yes. Songs will be sung of it, like those you and Greta like to watch at the gathering."*

"I hope so," she said with a laugh. *"When do we march for the fortress of Black Rock?"*

"We are third in order and will begin our march at sunset. You will have plenty of time to rest until then."

"You said the fortress is very strong. How will you attack it?"

"I don't know the details, but Black Thorn is an experienced and cunning warrior. He has bested many enemies and has stormed many fortresses. He will lead us to victory." He gave her a long look. *"But you must be careful. Festus told me of the risks you take, and I have seen them too."*

163

"You shouldn't worry so much about me. You know I'm not a cub."

"Of course, I know that, Nadja," he said gently. *"But if we can't protect those who are dear to us, then what are we?"*

That lump in her throat that sometimes formed when she spoke with her friend returned. She leaned close and again put her arms around his neck for a long squeeze. As was so often the case, his candor and kindness both disarmed and emboldened her.

"Where do we go when we die?" she asked in a burst of curiosity.

He gave her what seemed a look of confusion, for he didn't speak for nearly a minute. *"You know that,"* he said at last. *"You went with us yesterday. When we die, the sand and the wind and the predators take us, and nothing else remains."* He reached in the bag between them and withdrew a 25-centimeter heel spike from the bag. *"Except for these."*

"And there's nothing more?"

"What else would there be? .... Does something remain of your people?"

"I don't know," she said honestly. *"We don't have heel spikes."*

"No. You don't. Nadja ... you seem sad. Don't be. I don't fear death." He touched her shoulder affectionately and held up the spike between them, the thing that was to become a lethal arrowhead. *"And if what remains of me, after I'm gone, gives those I love some small chance at life, it fills me with great, great happiness."*

"I'm not sad," she said with a smile. And she wasn't. She unexpectedly felt very good. *"Right now, I'm hungry. Wait here, and then you can take me to find food."*

She hopped up and stepped back over to her bags. It probably wouldn't be a bad idea if she put her britches on now. Not that she was worried about what Spiros would see—they were long past that—but an impulse gripped her. Out of nowhere, she thought of how disconcerting it would be if a skiff-load of stuffy and officious State Department officials swooped down and saw her in her glory. The notion gave her funny bone a near-lethal whack. It was thoroughly irrational, but she laughed so hard that she was still laughing when, an hour later, she and Stig finally ate.

31: A Familiar Face

The three humans managed to grab some sleep during the day, and just before sunset, a company of warriors headed by Stig struck its laborious course northward. The night was dark, at least to Nadja's eyes, but the pace was easy and sedate. They would travel night and day, pausing to rest during the worst heat of the day and whenever necessary to spare the animals. The goal now was not speed, but to conserve the army's strength.

As Stig had promised, Black Thorn was a thorough and careful general. The first war party he'd sent out was 500 strong, and its duty was to comb the earth along their path and to root out enemy patrols and scouts, as well as to ride down any stragglers from the army Stig's party had routed the day before.

The general's advance force was brutally efficient, and for the first day and night, there was no sign of anything along the company's path, not even wild animals. Not that it would have mattered. Stig led 300 warriors, and under his command every soldier was alert, outriders rode constant circuits, and scouts ventured out north, east, south, and west.

"Do you think we're going up in elevation?" Nadja asked on the morning of the second day. She thought they might be, but on Skiathos the telltale signs weren't there. Higher elevation meant neither thinner air nor lower heat.

Gunny replied. "The map says we are, ma'am. We haven't gone up too much, but sometime tomorrow the grade will be noticeable."

"But it won't get any cooler," Nadja grumbled.

"Actually, it should, ma'am. Dr. Sokay said elevation has negligible effect on air temperature up to about 7,000 meters, but locality matters. The desert is a convection. When we get in the mountains, it'll be noticeably cooler."

Spiros let out an audible sigh, followed by an uncomfortable cough. "Oh, shit ... did I just show weakness?"

"It's OK this once," said Nadja.

"Don't get me wrong, either one of you," Gunny continued. "It's still going to be hotter than shit up there, but the days of 55 degrees in the shade are behind us for now."

"I'll take that," said the lance corporal.

"Me, too." Nadja turned several times in the saddle before speaking again. "There is nothing for vegetation around here. There's even less than before." She shrugged. A high desert was still a desert, she supposed. But on most every terrestrial world, there was a close correlation between elevation and climate. The disparity now was disconcerting. Perhaps the lack of vegetation was due to the soil? Their path since leaving the tank seemed nothing but stone. They certainly trod upon rocks now. And it was flat, unbelievably flat in every direction.

Spiros heard the noise first, followed by Gunny. The two lit out to the northwest, whooping and hollering. Glancing up, Nadja realized her ears did not deceive. It was a skiff, a Navy skiff, gliding to the desert about 200 meters ahead. For just a moment, a mere flash, Nadja imagined her pompous and officious supervisors stepping from the cargo door and scolding her for days before having had a bare butt in public. She goaded her mount after the Marines, and the ridiculous vision vanished.

When the skiff touched ground, the three pulled their mounts to a stop at a safe distance and dismounted. Spiros was laughing, and Gunny was all smiles. Scant seconds later, a helmeted figure slid from behind the door-gunner and jogged in their direction.

It was Sgt. Lyn.

The young NCO ran forward 30 paces, stopped, jumped in the air several times squealing, and resumed her pace.

"They teach them that at NCO academy these days," whispered Gunny.

"Ma'am, holy shit! … Gunny, holy shit! Spiros!" The young woman hesitated, her emotions on high, but apparently not knowing what to do next.

Nadja saved everyone the embarrassment and stepped forward and put her arms around the young sergeant. "Don't think you're getting this every day," she told the young woman after a tight squeeze.

"No, ma'am. How are you here? How are you together?"

"Long story," she told Lyn firmly. "You need to tell me. What happened to the Marines, and to the platform?"

The young woman regurgitated the events of the ill-fated ambush in about three minutes, after which Nadja began to pepper her with questions.

"Fatalities?"

"Not a one ma'am. We were shot to shit that day. Evans lost an arm, Donnelly a leg, and your pilot didn't notice that you were missing until 10 minutes into the fight. Damage was so bad to the transports it took us most the day to limp back, suborbital the whole way. Then we were a half day even finding the platform. Whoever it was who attacked us, hit them the same time. Chief Eddy hid her on the edge of one of the charged layers at about 50 kilometers up. We've been hiding ever since."

"Recent enemy contact?"

"We get an active ping every once in a while, like they're looking for us. But Chief moves us every now and again to throw them off. And Dr. Sokay modified some of her drones to look around, give us some eyes below. Most got shot down, but the hottest activity for our unpleasant friends seems to be in this general area. We saw your transponder ping yesterday a few times, and then it lit up like Christmas about an hour ago. We scooted straight down. Ma'am, we really need to get out of here. This area is popping with enemy activity."

"Please tell me you got a message off to Fleet at Clem's World."

"We've learned to adjust for their ground transmission jamming, ma'am. But I'm not sure about Pinpoint. Chief said the platform put out a distress signal the second they came under attack, but he isn't sure it got through. They're probably jamming that still. We haven't gotten anything from Clem's World since we lost you."

"Fuckers," Nadja whispered. "So, we may or may not be getting naval support soon, depending on how long it takes for Fleet to realize they haven't heard from us."

"That's our thinking, ma'am."

Nadja pulled out her tablet. "Are your reports up to date?"

"Yes, ma'am."

"Go ahead and synch tablets. I'll read them later. Log everything from mine when you get back. Hey, Spiros, go grab the survival kit off the skiff."

The young Marine disappeared at a jog, that hitch in his step still obvious, and Gunny went with him.

Lyn cleared her throat. "Uh, ma'am. Are those friends of yours?"

Nadja saw the company had come to a halt, and Stig and several others were walking sedately in their direction, leading their mounts. "They are very good friends. That one in front has kept Gunny and Spiros alive for the last seven—almost eight—months."

"Oh, shit, they're big," the woman whispered.

"They won't hurt you, sarge. Gimme your tablet." Nadja stared at the young woman's tablet, thinking what she should do next.

Spiros came jogging back. Gunny was again behind him, but this time loaded down with gear.

"Gunny, what are you doing?"

"Ma'am, don't make me cite regs to you. Spiros is a gimp, so he's going back. And either both you and I are getting on that bird, or both of us are staying here and going after Wray. I'm not letting you gallivant over hell's half-acre by yourself."

Optimally, either Nadja or Gunny should go back to the platform to run things. But Lyn and her team had kept everything in order since her absence. And somebody needed to make sure Nadja didn't go into heatstroke again. She relented. "OK."

Gunny turned to Spiros. "You're getting on the bird, and … uh," she wagged her finger back and forth between the two of them several times, "I don't want you thinking this last seven, eight months means we got this special thing going on. Next time I see your boney ass, you better be clean-shaved, in a fresh uniform, and with a regulation haircut. That's an order."

"Aye-aye, Gunny."

"Lemme see that tablet, ma'am." Gunny took Lyn's tablet and began filling forms.

"You don't really need to give me a hand receipt, Gunny." The young woman seemed confused. "Wait. Dr. Wray is alive too?"

"Lyn, I am taking one of your door guns, spare barrel bag, 5,000 rounds of 7 mm, 500 rounds of 10 mm, six grenades, four spare batteries, and the skiff's survival kit and emergency radio. Oh, and give Dr. Bikram your rifle and pistol."

"Just the pistol," said Nadja as she relieved the young sergeant of the weapon and all her spare magazines.

"Just the pistol. You can draw a new one when you get back." Gunny signed the hand receipt and gave the tablet over to Nadja. "What sort of leader would I be if I went off and got myself killed and stuck you with the bill for all this crap, Lyn?"

"Is Dr. Wray still alive?" Lyn repeated.

"Maybe," said Gunny. "We'll find out and be in contact until we do. Any signs of his transponder?"

"No, Gunny. We think he turned it off."

The senior NCO twisted her lips for a moment. "If he was in any real trouble, he would've reactivated it. In that case, you would've picked up on it. Unless he didn't come this way … or he's dead.

"Nah," Nadja muttered as she wrote furiously on Lyn's tablet, occasionally flipping to a new document. "He's alive. Cause if anybody is going to kill that miserable sonofabitch, it's going to be me."

Nadja had said those last words with far more venom than she'd intended and glanced up to see Lyn regarding her with wide eyes and an open mouth. Likewise, several times the young sergeant had glanced warily toward the advancing Stig, who was now within spitting distance.

"We'll be ready to go soon," Nadja called to her enormous friend before turning back to Lyn. "I just thumb-signed a form giving Alex Payton permission to go over all of Gunter Wray's files. Have Sgt. Bisbee give him one of the analysts to help. Have them go over everything, including Wray's personal files and communications. There is something not right with that guy, and I want to know what." Wray had something to do with these attacks. It was an awareness that had been building in her, but now she felt it in her bones.

"Aye-aye, ma'am."

"Gunny and I will be in touch if we need anything, but maintain radio silence on your end. If you lose contact with us for more than a week, move the platform to the most secure location you can find and wait for naval support. Tell Chief his priority is to get the troop transports up and running and fully armed. Everything else, but platform security, goes on the backburner. I just signed a document giving you authority to do what you think is necessary."

"Aye-aye, ma'am."

"Have the Marines on standby. If we need you, we'll need you quickly." Nadja took a nervous breath. "Have you deployed the satellite net?"

"No, ma'am."

Nadja pressed her thumb to the tablet screen, authorizing the document. *This is the one that's getting you fired, Bikram*, she thought to herself. But, treaties or not, she needed to know what was happening on the planet. "I just gave Chief the order to auto-deploy the net. Don't let it interfere with anything else you're doing to keep the platform secure."

"Aye-aye, ma'am." The young sergeant hesitated, looking once nervously at Stig, who now knelt next to Nadja and regarded Lyn curiously. "Ma'am, you should take a few of us with you."

Nadja smiled. "Sarge, I got my friend here and 300 of his best and most heavily armed buddies to pull security. Besides, Gunny's got my back."

"Yes, ma'am."

"OK," Nadja concluded, "there are some files in the synch for the linguistics team, including scans of what I think is a language alien to Skiathos. Make sure they get those and all my notes. Give everything else to Alex. As for you, get Spiros back to the platform in one piece and he owes you a beer." She'd noticed the young lance corporal several times eyeing Lyn furtively, a silly grin on his face.

"But just one," interjected Gunny, "and then straight to the infirmary."

Sgt. Lyn looked back and forth between the two women, a sudden and irrepressible smile on her face. "Everyone will be very happy to hear you're safe. Do you need anything else?"

"Nope," said Nadja. She usually wasn't the emotional type—this planet was doing something to her—but she gave Spiros and the sergeant a quick arm around the shoulder that might have been construed as an embrace. "Now get out of here and stay alert."

After Spiros made his hasty goodbyes to Stig and the others, the two young Marines jogged to the skiff, which lifted off moments later and cut a low course westward across the hills, before accelerating rapidly skyward. The sudden change in their fortune left Nadja light headed and somewhat giddy, and she leapt when Stig stepped up and put his hand on her shoulder.

"Why didn't you go with them?" he asked.

"We need to recover the last of our number from Black Rock."

"Of course," he said, patting her arm softly. *"I shouldn't have forgotten that. But couldn't you travel there with Spiros? It looks very swift."*

"It's not safe in that direction right now. And anyway, I'd rather travel with you," she said, rubbing his hand in return. *"Let's get going."*

It took less than five minutes to help Gunny stow their new gear and to get back on the trail to the fortress of Black Rock. There still were at least three days' travel ahead of them, and Nadja had a great deal about which she needed to think.

32: The Fortress

S ometimes things just disappeared on the frontier.

Real tragedies didn't occur often, especially given how remote some regions on the edge of settled space were, but from time-to-time a ship would disappear, or a mining outpost would go dark. There was almost always some explanation: human error, mechanical malfunction, the malice or cupidity of passersby. The answer nearly always was something simple, something clearly legible.

But it wasn't unheard of for things simply to vanish, to fall from the charts with no explanation. Everyone knew the story of the *Prima Nocta*, a pleasure ship that specialized in ferrying the soon-to-be wed on their last carnal cruise about the cosmos, before consignment to the constraints of connubial bliss. The faster-than-light bacchanalia had disappeared without trace when Nadja was still in college. The *Balustrade*, a naval support vessel, had dropped from the literal and figurative radar not many years later. During a short, three-week jaunt to join a new battle group, the vessel simply had vanished in a puff, and not so much as a trace of ship or crew ever was seen again.

And who could forget the outpost on Dewey IX, the research and planning station so often likened to the lost settlement of ancient Roanoke? For the past 15 years, stories and tales spun wildly about the missing 200 workers and dependents, who simply had vanished from the place with no signs of violence or foul play. Food was still on plates, vehicles were parked in their bays, weapons remained in the armory unfired. Not a single log, whether personal or official, had hinted at any threat. The crew of the resupply ship that first had discovered the mystery declared the station normal in every way—absent the people.

Sometimes things just disappeared.

That fact was one of many things Nadja and Gunny had discussed as the company had wended its way to the fortress of the villain Black Rock, and it was a topic that had continued for three days after the whole of the southern army arrived and the siege began.

Someone wanted the survey team gone.

At that precise moment, Nadja Bikram wasn't thinking of Roanoke or of missing ships—though such thoughts weren't far from her mind—rather, she was thinking of roots, and about what possibly might be on this planet that was worth killing over.

"You know, ma'am? I think the lads are going to pull this off."

Gunny's words drew Nadja from her thoughts. Glancing over to where the NCO leaned against the saddle beside her, Nadja wondered what had prompted the comment. Gunny had spent most of the morning and much of the preceding day watching the fortress through the powerful optics she'd detached from the light machine gun they'd commandeered from the skiff.

"I mean, it looks impressive, damned impressive," the Marine went on, "but take a look at the ground running up to the base of the lower tower. What do you see, ma'am?"

The two humans were sitting on a rise about a thousand meters west of the base of the fortress. In the broad and stony field before them, the warriors of Black Thorn were hard at work in their thousands preparing equipment, constructing siege engines, and fashioning ladders to launch an attack.

Nadja took the optics Gunny offered and peered through them. She first used the powerful lens to examine the length and width of the impressive fortress. The gigantic stone fortification was nestled in the hollow where two small mountains met in the foothills of a broader range. A single enormous tower, with numerous walls running from it, guarded the fortress's base, and a series of ramps, walls, and towers climbed the steep mountainside above it. The highest and largest tower, an imposing central keep, rested on a wide recess in the mountains about 200 meters above the plain below.

There only seemed to be one entrance to the entire fortress. To the north of the base tower, a broad stone and earthen ramp wended its way past the tower to a thick gatehouse in the next highest wall. The gate appeared constructed of the light reed or bamboo material Lacertians glued and laminated together to use for those tasks for which humans might use wood. The gate in question was about five to six meters high by as many meters wide and was riveted throughout with what appeared to be thick iron bands.

The structure, rather, the series of structures that constituted the fortress was a work of great skill and beauty. The walls were of solid dark stone, towers were pocked with arrow slits and topped with heavy battlements, and ramps and walls were supported by carefully crafted arches.

Arches! That architectural device had not been developed on old Earth until Roman times. And it was yet another example of the "nothing to see here, move along" approach by which Wray had crafted his reports, attempting to portray Lacertian society as being barely in the Bronze Age.

172

She stilled her anger with the man and lowered the lens to the area below the base of the lower tower that Gunny had directed. After about two minutes of scanning, she shook her head.

"I don't see anything, Gunny."

"That's my point, ma'am. Look again."

Nadja again raised the optic.

"See it? About 50 meters in front of the base tower … see that slight rise in the dirt that runs parallel to the mountainside?"

"Uh … yeah. What is it?"

"If my guess is right, and I think it is, that used to be a short and thick curtain wall, ma'am. The kind of thing a smart military architect would use to keep siege engines from approaching the fortifications."

Nadja pivoted the optic left and right. "It's hardly noticeable in some places."

"Exactly, ma'am. A few hundred years ago, that might have been an impediment two or three meters high to prevent attackers from pushing up a siege tower. Now? Nothing. The whole place is like that. Some of it's well cared for, like that main keep up on top. Some of it's been allowed to go to shit, including that little curtain wall at the base."

Nadja smiled at the Marine. "So, you think that's where the main assault is going through?"

"I dunno. Black Thorn's troops are putting a lot of energy into preparing siege equipment, but if they break through there, they still have to fight all the way up to the top of the fortress. Either way, Black Rock screwed the pooch on letting that wall deteriorate."

"What other weak points we looking at, Gunny?"

"Glad you asked that, ma'am." The NCO motioned to the most northern portion of the fortification. "See that little section a couple hundred yards to the north, just above the bottom of the main keep? Looks like it's built straight into the rock?"

Nadja had to pull up the optics and took only a quick peep at the area in question. "Yeah, looks sort of like … I dunno. You think they're building something there?"

"I don't think so, ma'am. In fact, just the opposite. See how the side of the mountain bulges to the west? I thought at first that structure was just an old fighting position for firing on enemy troops trying to breach the main gate. But it's too high for that. No. I don't think anyone in the upper fortress can see around that bulge in the northern mountain, and some years back they put a little turret there to spot anyone trying to climb that side of the mountain so as, you know, to keep an attacker from climbing over the top and dropping down on the fortress from above."

A pulse of surprise hit Nadja. "Seriously? Are they that good at climbing?"

"Our friends? You've seen 'em climb, ma'am. They certainly ain't mountaineers. But as big as they are, they're at least as good as the average human at scampering up rocks. I think that's what the structure is for, to spot and maybe shoot climbers off the rocks, and I think they abandoned it years ago, let it go to shit like the rest."

"Have you seen anyone manning it?"

"Ma'am, Black Rock's got a whole boat-load of soldiers in there, hundreds, maybe more. I haven't seen one in that section." Gunny gave a smile. "But I have seen a few of Black Thorn's officers giving that place the eyeball."

"You think they're going to try and climb up and let themselves in?'

"They might, ma'am. It'd be dangerous. If they can get into that section, they could probably follow that path that runs from that spot all the way to within jumping distance of the upper keep—I can't tell if the path goes all the way down. Get 50 or 75 warriors up there, and you'd have a chokehold on the upper fortress. But it would be win or die. Because there is no way in hell they could stage an orderly retreat back down the cliff."

By that time, the Marine had recovered the optic and again was scrutinizing the fortress for weaknesses.

Nadja settled back to ponder Gunny's words. She'd always fancied she understood things martial, but Really Nice had a rare gift for seeing things around them. The Marine already had calculated that Black Thorn's army was larger than Stig first had declared. It probably was closer to 3,500. And she'd even estimated, given the supplies that arrived in the caravan, that the army had about five weeks to stage the attack and depart before mounts started dying and the entire army was in jeopardy. Both projections later had been confirmed by officers Nadja had spoken with on Black Thorn's staff.

She began to think Gunny was right about their friends' chances of success. Rather than the disordered rush she first had expected, the campaign under Black Thorn was smooth and well organized, supported by careful logistics and prudent planning. There was even a field hospital with a squad of doctors for treating the wounded, and a company of a hundred or so engineers overseeing the erection of war engines. There was nothing slapdash about this.

"Shit!" she heard Gunny spit. "Shit!"

"What?" Nadja sat up, suddenly alert.

"I just saw somebody," the Marine half whispered.

"Who?"

"A person."

"A per… Wray?!"

"No, no." She handed Nadja the optic and pointed to the fortress. "He's gone now, but look at that line of battlements at the base of the main keep."

She took up the glass and began to scan. "OK, umm … I don't see anyone. Well, there are two Lacertians there."

"Near the stairs?"

"Yup."

"He was just to the right of them."

Nadja looked longer. No trace of a human was visible, but she did not doubt the Marine for a moment. "What did he look like?"

"Fair skin, light hair, a bit of fuzz on his face. He looked fit and wore those black wraparound glasses spec ops douchebags wear. I'm pretty certain he had a rifle slung across his back, either that or a radio antenna poking up. I stared at him for a good three seconds before it registered what I was seeing."

"Just the one?"

"I only saw one, but about the time I realized what I was seeing, he turned and then suddenly ducked out of sight, like somebody said something to him. God, what I wouldn't give for a squad drone right now."

Nadja's mind raced. Cubs who are not cubs. "What the fuck?" she whispered.

"My words exactly, ma'am."

"What do you think, Gunny? Should we relocate? Stay out of sight?"

"Nah, ma'am. We haven't exactly been high profile since we've been in camp. And we're a least a klick away from those guys. Unless they use optics and actively look for us, they won't see us."

Nadja nodded. "Still, let's keep wrapped up. No use giving it away." The women had little to do in camp but think, plan, and watch the fortress, and they had abandoned their fatigues and taken to lounging about their small pavilion wrapped head-to-toe in their cloaks, like two princesses from ancient Persia.

"That's easy to do, ma'am." The Marine looked straight at her. "What's your best guess?"

"As to what's going on?" She blew a raspberry and shook her head slowly. Finding another person there should not have come as a surprise, but it took a moment to steady herself and form her words. "Pretty obvious we're not dealing with aliens. That's been mighty clear for a while given Wray's bizarre antics."

"Could he be dead, ma'am?"

"You mean now that we know there are other humans on the planet outside our survey team?" Nadja leaned into the saddle and thought. Such a thing was possible. She generally was not the vindictive type, but might she be working out her fury on a dead colleague, because she had no one else to blame for their plight? "I guess it's possible one of our attackers was marooned and then picked up by a band and stuck in with its cubs, but it doesn't seem likely."

"Why not, ma'am. It happened to us."

"That's the point, Gunny. It's just too much of a coincidence. I mean … it's a miracle you, me, and Spiros survived. And Wray went walkabout of his own free will in a place only about a hundred klicks from where Black Rock raided and took off with a smelly cub who was not a cub."

"So, he's probably here?"

"I think so. But it doesn't matter at this point. Somebody is out to erase us, and everything in the reports Lyn logged says this area is ground zero." She paused to think and mouth a few greens. The heat of late morning was just arriving. "Look, that dick Wray did everything he could to make this project as uninteresting and unappealing as possible. In hindsight, that should have been obvious. But no one presumes a project head, especially someone with his credentials and his ego, would sabotage his own project. Next, Melissa Downey bucks the guy and comes to do linguistic research in an area we now know to be Grand Central Station for our attackers. You and your team get blown out of the sky, an event your attackers staged to look like an accident, and then Wray disappears in the same area a few months later—why, I have no idea. But in rapid succession, the search party for Wray is attacked, the platform is attacked, and a person, probably Wray, gets scooped up and dragged off here to Fortress Black Rock. Where we find…."

Gunny nodded. "Where we find a human, who is not supposed to be on the planet—probably one of our attackers."

"There has to be something on this planet worth going to all that trouble over. Really. I think it's the roots."

Gunny sat chewing on Nadja's words for long moments before speaking. "Ma'am, those things are fantastic, remarkable. If we would've found something like Greta's roots even a hundred or a hundred and fifty years ago, we would've been rich. But there's nothing I've seen those things do that the most basic Marine infirmary can't do better."

Nadja shrugged. "Maybe there are applications we haven't seen. I got to talking to one of Black Thorns surgeons yesterday. You know what? I'm half convinced it's the roots that generate the EM field that kept jamming our transponders. The field seems only to occur in places where there are greens. And it never occurred to me to mention at the time, but Greta showed me how to dig for the roots. The roots and greens are tied together somehow. They're the basis of life for the folks in the band, as near as I can tell the basis of the Lacertian economy. Greens are about the only thing their animals eat."

Gunny had turned to regard her carefully. "What's your point, ma'am?"

"My point is that … look, I assumed the Lacertians' great health and long lives are somehow tied to their very nature. But what if our friends on this planet live long and healthy lives because of something the roots give them, either directly, or indirectly through the greens? Wouldn't such a discovery be worth killing over?"

"How…?"

"I'm grasping at straws here, Gunny. I don't know if any of that is true. But unless there's buried treasure on this rock somewhere, there's precious little else I can think of to explain why someone would act so recklessly."

They sat in silence a time longer. Gunny continued her observations, and Nadja mulled and pondered, attacking their problem from every angle. Should she just write off Wray? Retreat with Gunny to the platform? Come back when naval support arrived?

Under a best-case scenario, a naval relief force would show up any time. But that all balanced on whether the platform's original distress signal had gotten out. It was three and a half weeks for a Pinpoint message to travel to Clem's World, about the same time it would take a Navy relief force to make the return trip. Seven weeks. Roughly that amount of time already had passed.

But if the distress signal had not made it through, Fleet headquarters at Clem's World might not notice that the survey team had gone silent for many weeks more. And if they did notice, such an event might not cause immediate alarm. Communication glitches happened sometimes. Once alarm did register, it might be days more for the Navy to decide what to do and to prepare a relief mission.

No, they simply could not depend on a best-case scenario. They were on their own, and all the while their secret enemies were searching high and low for the platform to erase all evidence of their crimes. Nadja couldn't just wait around, and for the umpteenth time in recent days, she scolded herself for not having gone back to the platform with Lyn and left the search for Wray to others.

Nadja Bikram was like a dog with a bone sometimes, and she knew it. It was one of her worst character flaws.

But what could she do? Even on the platform, her options were limited. It would be nearly a week before the satellite net was fully deployed, presuming their hidden enemies didn't shoot them down as they deployed. And might their foes be able to trace the deploying satellites back to the platform? She didn't think so. The shrouding on the platform was good, and Sgt. Lyn and Chief Eddy wouldn't be so foolish as to stay in one place.

If she only knew more, could somehow …. "Gunny?"

"Yes, ma'am."

"We need to get into that fortress."

"We do, ma'am. I'm working on a plan as we speak."

Neither Nadja or Gunny Nice had spoken of entering the fortress before, presuming that if Black Thorn and his men succeeded that Gunter Wray would be released into their custody. Now it was important. At least one of the enemy was in the fortress, and Nadja intended to learn what the man knew, one way or the other.

"Come up with anything yet?"

Gunny reached down into the bag between them and pinched a green. "I got a few ideas, ma'am. How good of a climber are you?"

"Back when I was doing it regular, good … very good, in fact. You?"

"Like a mountain goat."

33: The General

Gunny's first idea was a good one, and Nadja was upset that she hadn't thought of it herself. She and the Marine NCO had been communicating with the platform at random times during the day in short encrypted data bursts sent on rotating frequencies. Even the best military cryptologic equipment would have a demanding time tracking their origin and interpreting their content.

In the burst she sent at noon that day, Gunny had requested access to Dr. Sokay's geological drones. Nadja knew from Sgt. Lyn's earlier reports that nearly 20 were still airborne and fully operational, and three of those were within eight-hours flight time of the fortress. Using a second burst, the geologist directed the three slow-moving and high-flying drones to stage a near simultaneous low-level flyover of the fortress, snapping multi-spectrum scans of the structure from different angles as they went.

The flyover would not be until later that night, but it would be their first real look at the enemy, and hopefully it would give them an idea of how many humans were in the place and how they might best be dealt with. It only then had dawned on Nadja what a threat their human enemies could pose to Black Thorn's army, if they chose to do so. Likely or not, such a contingency was another good reason to deal with their human enemies swiftly.

After the worst of the heat, Gunny continued her surveillance and Nadja went on a walk-and-talk to the area where the general kept his command tent. When Nadja had last seen Stig, her friend had told her a meeting of the commanding general and senior leaders would take place the evening prior to the attack on the fortress. Gunny's estimate was that preparations for the assault on the lower fortress were nearly complete and that the attack might be launched as early as the next morning. Given the army's need for haste, this likely would be the night the general briefed his officers.

Nadja now was voracious for information on the attack. As much as the idea churned her stomach and sat her heart to racing, she and Gunny needed to get in the fortress, the sooner the better. The two humans had no idea how to do that effectively and safely until they knew Black Thorn's battleplan.

She found Stig sitting with some of his comrades near the general's tent, laughing and joking. It seemed the most natural thing for her to join them, and she was soon the center of attention. Only two of Stig's companions were known to her, but all were friendly and curious. Nadja had long-since determined that the existence of other worlds and other races was common knowledge among them—though she had yet to meet anyone who had seen such a being—and no Lacertian she had met was frightened or startled at her presence.

The air was just beginning to cool when the gathering broke up, and she found herself alone with her friend.

"Will the attack begin tomorrow?"

"I think so. Black Thorn will inform us all after dark and give us our orders. I look forward to it."

She'd come to find candor worked best with Stig. *"Gunny saw a human near the high tower today, but it wasn't the person we seek."*

"Another of your kind? Is this one known to you?"

"No. Remember I told you things aren't safe for us right now?"

"I do. Are you at war with another band?"

She hadn't thought of it in quite that way. *"Yes, and the humans inside don't know the difference between right and wrong."*

Her friend gave a noticeable shudder that she'd come to associate with him giggling. *"They are certainly in the right place then."*

"Stig, they are very dangerous and have very powerful weapons."

"How many are they?"

"I don't know. We think there may be a few, and we're trying to find out."

"Nadja, I'll make sure Black Thorn and the rest of the fighters know. But if the other band is few, there is nothing to worry about."

"Perhaps you're right." Maybe she was being overly cautious. *"But I'd like to go with you to the meeting anyway."*

Stig gestured his assent, and less than an hour later officers began to gather at the large tent that was Black Thorn's command post. Once all were assembled, including about 30 officers and a few warriors that comprised the general's staff, the general arrived and almost immediately began issuing his plan. The pace of speech between Black Thorn and the others was swift and curt, but Nadja followed the gist of the meeting easily.

The two main assaults would commence at dawn against the fortress's main gate and lower tower. It was these assaults that the general was confident would seize the lower fortress. A third group, consisting entirely of archers, would deploy that very night under cover of darkness to take up positions on the heights to the south of the fortress. And as Gunny had predicted, a fourth assault would take place the following night. Taking full advantage of the distraction caused by the continued assaults on the lower fortress and gate throughout the day, a small company would scale the mountain north of the city, gain access to the abandoned fortification she and Gunny had surveilled that day and, if successful, form another breach point on the upper fortress, ferrying more warriors into the fray as they cleared the way.

It was bold. It was audacious. It was the type of pluck and mettle she'd come to associate with the Lacertian way of war.

Once the plan was laid out and Black Thorn patiently answered the questions of all assembled, the general gave out task assignments, giving half a dozen officers command of specific units. For each assignment, the general sought the consensus and opinions of the assembled officers. Three times there was discussion, and on one occasion the assigned officer deferred the command to another. The commander then asked for a volunteer to lead the first wave of troops up the northern mountain to open the assault on the upper fortress.

It was the most dangerous command, and it should have been no surprise to Nadja when Stig stepped forward.

"*I will,*" said her friend.

The general regarded Stig a long moment. "*Does anyone question the right of Stig of Black Flower's band to take this honor?*"

None objected.

"*Stig, choose your party.*"

34: The Ascent

I t was a peculiarity, one uniform throughout the settled worlds, that human height was still reckoned in feet and inches. No one had ever explained to Nadja why that was so. Most everything else was calculated in the metric system, a way of weighing and measuring that had been around well over half a millennium. Scientists, of course, measured things in all manner of batty ways, especially when calculating and cogitating sciences that had been pioneered by other races. But this one thing was unique.

At five-foot-eight, Nadja was hardly a runt, but she was a bit on the shortish side by modern standards. Unquestionably, by any standards, she was fit and strong. Centuries of genetic engineering had done much and continued to do more to ensure such outcomes. The bell curve of male and female strength and endurance, for example, very nearly overlapped. Most champion weightlifters were still men, but only most. Most Olympic-level long-distance runners were women, but only most.

Gunnery Sergeant Really Nice, who topped Nadja by only an inch, was herself a hair or two shorter than average, but she was a physical phenom, the recipient of the very best genetic tweaking the government had to offer. And at that moment, as Gunny pulled herself up the side of the mountain from which she, Nadja, and four others were suspended, she was as she had promised, a veritable mountain goat.

Contrary to how the wall they now scaled looked from below, it wasn't a tremendously challenging climb, not for someone with any experience. The first 50 meters or so from the plain could've been completed by any agile hiker, the next 50 meters by any fit climber with even the most rudimentary skills, and the third 50 meters were well within Nadja's skillset even now, nearly 10 years after her last real climb. The last stretch, the final 50 or so, would have been an ascent to take seriously even in Nadja's climbing days, especially climbing in darkness as they were. But Nadja inched along steadily and confidently, coached in hushed whispers by Gunny, who was on lead above.

It had taken some arguing, but Stig finally had allowed the humans not only to join his company, but to ascend first. The idea that the humans also had enemies in the fortress above was a compelling one for their normally over-protective friend and an easy one for him to appreciate. Their final and winning argument had been a combination of climbing skill and total zeal. The Lacertians at best were only average climbers, and none had looked at the wall before them with great enthusiasm. Gunny had vowed to lead them to their goal.

Of course, that didn't matter for most of the warriors, because Stig's plan had never envisioned everyone climbing, not really climbing. Only a small handful truly needed to ascend. Those who achieved the heights first would lower a rope, to which would be attached a contraption that resembled a long cargo net, which the advance party of climbers would then haul up and anchor in place. Once the first hundred and twenty or so warriors were up, they would clear the route to the keep and make room for the next company. It was devilishly simple and bloody clever.

Their real advantage in this dreadful ascent was the commotion afforded by the assault below. Early that morning, Black Thorn's army had begun its attack on the lower fortress, one that was bloody, but brilliant. After an unrelenting day's battle, the attackers had overrun the lower tower and had fought their way up the first set of ramps to the foot of the second level. Even now, the battle raged, and most of Black Rock's forces were concentrated on containing the breach.

The greatest danger of the plan was that Stig and his company might be detected by the fortress's defenders. The abandoned observation point to which they now climbed was itself within clear view of several positions in the fortress, and only a narrow trail scratched into the side of the mountain ran from that spot to the upper fortress. The roughly 200-meter trail was terribly exposed and provided little or no cover to those on it. The last 100 meters of the path would put the attackers within easy range of any archers in the keep.

And archers were not the only danger. The drone scans they'd obtained of the fortress the night before were brilliant in their detail. They showed in addition to several dozen Lacertians that there were five humans in the main keep, at least four of whom were armed. If Gunny or Nadja discharged their firearms too early in that first assault, it almost guaranteed those within the keep would return fire. Such an outcome would be a slaughter for Stig and his men if they were caught exposed on the trail.

Nadja had cursed herself for not having brought a few Marines to the fortress as Lyn had advised, and she and Gunny had kicked around the idea of ferrying down a squad to aid in the assault. But the chance of detection was too great. Hidden weapons of some type (probably shrouded enemy ships) had destroyed two of the drones they'd used for recon the night before, but thankfully only after the drones had accomplished their mission.

No, the two humans needed to move like church-mice until they were able, alone or with the help of Stig and his company, to breach the keep and engage those within at close range. If Wray was there, they intended to take him into custody. Whether he was there or not, this would be their first opportunity to confront and hopefully capture one of the enemy. It was a dicey and dangerous plan.

The problem immediately in front of Nadja was the last five meters of the climb. The bottom of the observation post, some sort of decking, extended more than a meter out from the cliff face, a gap that moments before Gunny had wriggled up and over. The angle of the slight overhang didn't trouble Nadja overly much. With the Marine's help she should have no trouble. But the condition of the deck did cause her some apprehension. Up close, even in the dark, it was far more dilapidated than they'd presumed. Gunny's scant weight on the thing had forced it to utter something akin to a death rattle.

The situation troubled her more with each centimeter she moved closer to her goal, and by the time she reached the deck she needed a dozen breaths to steady herself. After a couple of tense and precarious reaches, and a vigorous 20 seconds of squirming on the deck's lip, she felt Gunny's strong hand on her wrist, and the Marine more-or-less lifted her to the top.

Nadja's heart raced as her additional weight caused the deck to emit an unholy caterwaul, an experience from which she needed a minute on solid rock against the cliffside to compose herself.

"There is no way our friends are climbing up on that," Nadja whispered breathlessly to the Marine.

In theory, how the decking might support more weight would be for the third climber to decide. Next up was Conchita, one of the engineers. (Gunny's nicknames were growing more eccentric.) Her task was to assess the deck, make any repairs necessary, and ensure the climbing net was securely fastened to the cliffside.

As the engineer approached from below, Nadja and Gunny knee-walked toward the edge of the deck, probing and testing the material in front of them. The section farthest from the cliff was almost entirely of the hardened pseudo-wood these folks used. There was no way for the two humans to repair the rickety thing without perhaps dropping it on the heads of the four climbers below, but neither would it support Conchita's 300 kilos.

In the end, they whispered to the four climbers below to brace themselves. When Conchita came within reach, Nadja slid onto the wobbly deck on her belly, Gunny holding her legs, and the two spent the better part of five minutes grunting, hissing, and wrestling to help the scampering and panicky engineer up and onto the stone ledge nearest the cliffside, inadvertently demolishing much of the deck in the effort. The three sat after for some minutes more, catching their breath and bracing themselves for a further effort.

Conchita clearly found the episode harrowing, but was soon at work with her bag of tools, shoring what was left of the deck after its thrashing. Below, the remaining three climbers, Stig at their lead, remained pressed against the wall. Aided by Nadja's whispered directions, the last of them ascended 20 minutes later, and the party went about their work of pulling up the cargo ropes and securing their position.

The ascent had been quicker than they'd imagined, but also had caused far more noise than Nadja had hoped. However, it appeared the small party somehow had avoided detection. With a quick word to Stig, the two humans secured their gear and gingerly began to make their way southeast along the rough and narrow pathway toward the keep, serenaded by the sounds of the battle below as they went.

It took about five minutes of careful, stop-and-go walking to reach a point with an unobstructed view of the keep that also afforded some cover behind a curve in the path. Had they continued along the cliffside, the path would have taken them left before dipping slightly and making a right hairpin turn to the base of the keep. That walk would have taken another 150 meters to complete, but from where the two humans crouched, the keep was only about 40 meters distant across a deep gorge. The distance was an easy shot for Gunny's light machine gun and not a difficult one for Nadja's pistol.

They waited and watched. What they would do next was unclear. If all went well, members of Stig's company soon would start stacking up behind them. Until then, the light wasn't optimal, but Nadja could make out everything around them with reasonable clarity.

There was nothing to see.

In addition to her own enhanced night vision, Gunny had the advantage of the night-vision setting of her optics and after fewer than 30 minutes spoke. "That trail ahead is a lot shorter and wider than I thought it would be," she whispered.

"Meaning what?" responded Nadja in her lowest murmur.

"While we're waiting on the troops, I could slip down and take a listen. There's nobody outside, and the lowest arrow slits on the keep are only about four meters up. Might be able to hear something."

The idea wasn't terrible. It would require Nadja taking the machine gun to provide security. Not her strong suit, but at less than 50 meters there was no missing. And she was intimately familiar with the weapon after three days on the trail being drilled by the NCO.

"Go," Nadja whispered.

It took the Marine less than five minutes to creep to within listening distance of the nearest arrow slit, carefully and quietly picking her way as she did. By that time, Nadja could hear the first of Stig's company gathering behind her. All were aware of the need for silence, and the rundown condition of the trail likewise forced the giants to choose their footing carefully.

All the while, Nadja scanned the area and kept her watch on Gunny, who some minutes later quietly began to shimmy up the wall to a place nearer the arrow slit. The dark was not an impediment to Nadja's vigil. The optics were top-of-the line, and the area around the keep was like broad daylight through the lens. But there was nothing, not a sight, not a peep, only the sounds of weapons and wailing wafting up from below. Had the humans in the keep fled in anticipation of the fortress falling? Or was the keep empty but for five humans, the rest of Black Rock's soldiers having gone below to enter the battle?

There was no way of telling. The drone scans from the night before had pointed out several hidden passageways and ramps within the mountainside, including one that led to a large chamber on the far side of the two peaks. Some sort of escape passage? It may have been. The passageway did lead in and out of the keep, which Black Thorn's officers had told her was Black Rock's personal stronghold.

And where was the villain Black Rock? She'd heard news of him since her arrival, but hadn't caught sight of the fiend. One would think he was the Devil.

Time passed, and Gunny shifted from the first arrow slit to the second and then back again. There was no high-sign or indication from the Marine that she'd heard anything of note. Another 30 minutes passed, and there was a gentle touch on Nadja's shoulder. Stig.

"*It's time,*" he said in his lowest voice. His company all had made the ascent.

Nadja duck-walked to a nearby boulder and rested the short barrel of the machinegun across the top. It was an advantageous position she'd noticed earlier and wondered why she hadn't moved sooner. It afforded the warriors room to pass and was a steadier support for the gun than her own arm. She re-sighted the weapon, finding Gunny below, and the warriors soon were whispering by, their pace accelerating as the trail widened to the left.

A sudden hiss of gunfire and the nasty sound of rounds hitting flesh and stone erupted around her as the thin plume of a railgun's barrel flared from the arrow slit nearest Really Nice. Nadja squeezed off a burst of machine gun fire, but stilled her hand at the audible sound of Gunny's screaming, "shift!"

35: The Keep

Nadja held her fire, and in a flash, the Marine below leapt and ran, and leapt and ran. With each leap, she deposited a casual, but precision, something within the first two arrow slits. Nadja didn't need to hear the explosions to know the NCO had tossed a grenade in each, before dashing at full tilt around the corner to the front of the keep, heading for the structure's heavy front gate.

The battle was on, and Nadja emptied a half magazine of machinegun rounds into each arrow slit before rising and joining the flow of bodies down the trail. Her first step very nearly took her off the cliff, but an enormous hand grabbed her and lifted her from thin air. Somehow, she was back on the trail and running faster than her body knew how. As she staggered, she careened off several mammoth forms before smacking the cliffside on the left with her right shoulder, spinning, but not falling, and bounding on at a breakneck pace after finding her footing.

By an agency not her own, her hands busied themselves loading a new magazine onto the top of the gun, and she heard another explosion not far to her front. Somehow—she wasn't sure how—she was dashing along the northern wall of the keep amid a crowd of clanking and heavily armed warriors and soon rounded the corner toward the keep's gate.

The sound of screams and steel told her Black Rock's forces were near, dreadfully near, and off to her right there was a commotion as Stig's company ran against something on the only ramp that led down from the fortress's top level. Their enemy somehow had arrived.

She couldn't concern herself, not at that moment, and after taking a hard left up the stairs to the keep gate, she almost immediately came under fire. By some miracle, she was untouched, but the sudden burst of speed that pushed her through the gate shoved her a bit too hard, and she soon was staggering head-over-heels into a darkened room and onto the deck. Rounds whizzed overhead, and by reflex she rolled in the direction of a familiar voice

"Ma'am, cover fire!" Gunny screamed desperately.

Nadja rocked to her side, chambered a new round, and fired on full-automatic into the darkness in front of her, hitting she knew not what. As she fired, there were two gentle tugs at her belt, followed seconds later by another explosion, this one so close it was deafening.

Somehow, her eye found the optic, and three illuminated figures appeared before her on the far side of the long and dark room. She recognized none of them and began casting short bursts of fire toward each. One adversary went down immediately, and a second dashed off around a corner to the right. The third continued to fire at her from behind a column, and Nadja squeezed the trigger of her automatic weapon until that person's shooting stopped.

There was silence in the large central room of the keep, and the only sound came from the brutal fighting outside. Her now shaking hands loaded another magazine, a task for which the large open gate provided the faintest light.

"Eleven o'clock high, ma'am," she heard Gunny whisper.

Glancing upward through the optic, Nadja saw not a second level, but a narrow opening in the ceiling, some sort of murder-hole placed by defenders to guard the keep's front entry. She stood, stepped swiftly to a position beside a thick column on her left, and gently squeezed off a short burst of rounds at the opening from her raised weapon. Through the optic, she saw Gunny step forward, leap, and gently toss another grenade into the opening, before dropping to the ground, grabbing Nadja, and spinning them both behind the thick column.

The explosion was again deafening.

"How many are there?" Nadja asked over the ringing in her ears.

"I don't know, ma'am," the whispering Marine laughed. "More than we thought."

"Oh … shit." Nadja this time remembered to lower her voice. She raised the machinegun optic to her eye and began slowly to scan the room.

Gunny continued, whispering in her ear. "I'm pretty certain I got three with the grenades I tossed through the windows, one with a pistol after I blew the front door, and one more after you came into the room."

"One on the far side of the room," Nadja whispered back. She tried to pop her ringing ears. "One by the column on the far left. And another one ran either up or down the stairs."

That was seven adversaries down, two or three more than they had first anticipated. And an eighth had gotten away from them. There was no hint how many enemy may have been lurking in the murder-hole into which Gunny had tossed the grenade. There could be more.

Nadja bent over suddenly and vomited, after which a hand gently patted her back.

"Give it a second, ma'am."

"You should take the long gun," Nadja whispered around the raw bile in her throat.

"Ma'am, I snatched up one of their rifles and a night-sight. You go to the right until you hit the wall, and I'll go left. Shift left and shoot anything that isn't me. We'll meet on the far side of the room."

Gunny was gone, and by reflex Nadja mirrored her, heading hard right to the wall, her weapon covering the empty space to her left as she moved, before pivoting left and heading into the length of the room and away from the front gate. No targets presented themselves to her optics, and she met Gunny on the far side of the enormous chamber near a wide column, the very one she'd punished in shooting her second assailant. The woman she'd shot was down but continued to move weakly on the floor.

"Watch the stairs, ma'am."

Thanks to the drone scan, the layout of this section of the building generally was clear in Nadja's mind—the murder-hole had been a surprise—and she knew there was only one way in and out on this side of the room, a set of up-and-down stairs to her right. She took a knee, her eye still at the gun's night-vision optic, and guarded the portal.

Behind her and to the right, someone not Gunny said something angry but unintelligible.

"You're the silly pig-fucker lying there bleeding out your asshole," said the Marine quietly in reply. "How many of you are there?"

Precious little of the short conversation between Gunny and the stranger was audible to her, but Nadja could tell from the sound that Gunny probably was staunching the woman's bleeding, searching her, and binding her in some way while they spoke. The exercise took less than five minutes, a period of time in which the tumult of battle outside grew significantly. There was something afoot, a substantial change in the bloody and wretched struggle for control of the fortress.

Gunny again was beside her, speaking quietly. "Wray was here," she said, "but he's probably gone by now, out that underground passage to a skiff on the far side of the mountain."

Nadja hesitated. What the hell? Should they...? "How long ago?"

"She says 10 minutes. Apparently, he and two others abandoned them here." Gunny slid something small into her hand. "The mic's on mute."

It took some seconds for Nadja to fit the tiny headset to her ear. The first words from the device were a panicked babble from a pair of voices, male and female.

"How many more of them are here?" she asked the Marine.

190

"Other than the two with Wray, three are upstairs, and there's one more down below in the lower fortress. The guy below is apparently their boss."

"Shit," whispered Nadja. The tunnel in question was more than 500 meters long. They might still rush to catch up, dispatch the two with Wray, and … what?

A deep voice in the earpiece decided for her. "Light 'em up," it said.

The thump of automatic weapons erupted upstairs, and Nadja heard the unmistakable smack of bullets on flesh through the keep's open gate. She stood, leveled the weapon in front of her, and spoke. "Upstairs," was her only word.

A hand gently slowed her, and something tugged at her belt. Gunny was again in front of her.

"I just took your last grenade," she whispered. "Same as last time. Wait for the blast, go hard right, I'll go left."

"Shoot anything that's not you," Nadja agreed with a nod.

The two soon were creeping up the high steps, the optics on their weapons guiding their way. The drone scans said the room above was very much like the one they had just left, high, broad, and deep, a chamber that was impressive even by the standards of the enormous inhabitants. When they reached the landing above, Nadja waited for the explosion. The earpiece in her right ear had gone silent.

She'd had close-quarters combat training in the Navy, but that was decades ago. And though Gunny had walked her through the drills during recent days, it wasn't muscle-memory for her as it was for the Marine. There was a tremor of self-doubt in her spleen before the grenade detonated in the room above, and she was up the stairs in a bound.

Rounding the corner from the landing at a fast walk, her weapon at a high-ready, she immediately encountered a man, and her weapon erupted in her hand. The man disappeared from her optic, and she kept walking, taking two strides before she remembered the threat was on the far side of the room to her left. Without breaking forward momentum, she swung her weapon left just in time to see a gout of flame and hear a swarm of hisses and pings around her.

It was all she could do to keep from making the rookie mistake she had below and burning off an entire magazine at once. Instead, she recited a 40-year-old mnemonic, 'fire bursts of six to nine,' in her head, squeezing and releasing the trigger with each new recitation. She soon rounded the corner of the room, moving at a careful, but rapid walk, now firing nearly straight ahead, and doing her best to force the two shooters on the far side of the room to keep their heads down.

It only worked partly. Their enemy's rate of fire diminished as she advanced, but they were well-concealed behind what looked to be a fallen column. Sooner or later, either she or Gunny would take a round, and there would be no one there to pull them out.

There were plenty of thick columns in the room behind which to shelter, the floor before her was smooth, and there was just enough light from the arrow slits behind their opponents to make out their movements unaided.

In an act of pure pique, Nadja squeezed the handle of the machinegun and detached the battery. Running forward as fast as she was able, she armed the battery, counted to three, and tossed the explosive the last five meters toward the enemy, before ducking behind the nearest pillar and screaming.

"Grenade!"

She was just able to make out the panicked scrambling of the two shooters before the explosion ripped through the room, knocking the wind from her and rendering her nearly deaf. She didn't lose consciousness, but it was a moment before she was able to rise discombobulated from the floor.

It took her another moment to realize there was slightly greater light in the room than before and seconds more to see the exploding battery pack somehow had blown some masonry from one of the arrow slits, widening it significantly. From the sound, the battle outside had reached a fever pitch.

She lifted the rifle and scanned the room and jumped when she saw Gunny stepping from behind a column.

"Check the two against the wall, ma'am," said the Marine, a hint of a wince in her voice.

A quick glance told Nadja the two were very dead.

"You hit, Gunny?"

"Just a little skin off the top of my arm, ma'am. Thanks. It was that guy you got right inside the door. It slowed me down." The Marine moved toward the arrow slit, laughing wickedly. "You know, if I'd known there were that many of them in here, no way in hell I would've come in the building."

It really was a miracle they were both alive. Nadja wanted to laugh, to join the Marine in the lark of it all, but she bent over and puked again instead. There was a nasty burning in her right arm and her right hip and side.

"Oh, crap," Nadja moaned. She found herself supported by the Marine, who leaned her against the large stone their opponents had used as a defensive position. She felt the Marine's hands swiftly run down her body from head to toe, probing here and there until Nadja several times flinched.

"Oh, you're fine, ma'am. You got a couple nicks and cuts and some stone or bullet fragments in your skin. 'Fight bites,' we call 'em. You can't go through a firefight without getting scuffed up a little."

"Why am I just feeling it?" Nadja new the answer before she'd finished speaking.

"Adrenalin, ma'am. You might even have gotten those downstairs and not realized till now." Gunny fumbled about. "Here. Take a nip of the 'good stuff'. I'll clean your cuts later."

Nadja took a pull and then a second from the bottle of bitter delight the Marine had offered and then joined her over by the opening in the wall to get a glimpse of the battle below.

36: The Champions

The widened arrow slit showed them the battle was now desperate for Black Rock's forces. Fires illuminated the fortress high and low, and in their light a battle raged a hundred meters below. Black Thorn's troops had made huge gains and were now clearing ramps toward the upper fortress as fast as they could throw the defenders from the battlements.

Just beneath the window, the fight was fevered and savage. Stig and 80 or so of his warriors held the five-meter-wide ramp that was the only way onto the top level of the fortress. Bodies were everywhere, in some places three deep, and though Stig and his attackers had no success in forcing the defenders downward, they kept the route sealed. Along the trail from the climbing net, Black Thorn's reinforcements hurried in twos and threes to join the fray.

Was it enough? The desperation and fury of the enemy fighters below was tangible, so tangible she could almost smell it in the air.

"The tunnel through the keep is the only way out," whispered Gunny. "And Black Thorn ain't taking no prisoners."

"Shit," Nadja muttered, not for the first time recently. But for the first time in days, she decided to forget about Gunter Wray. And she also opted not to interfere in the fight below.

She'd meddled in their friends' affairs before, but her last act had been one of desperation, when her life and the lives of the Marines were on the line. Right now, a victory for Stig and his allies seemed if not certain, then very nearly so. Did it matter whether some of the enemy warriors slipped through and skulked away? It shouldn't, but by reflex, Nadja felt herself gripping the machine gun in the low ready, as if she were about to take a firing stance.

"Ma'am," whispered Gunny, "there's no way we can fire from here without killing some of Stig's troops."

Leave it to the Marine not to overthink or overanalyze things. The woman was right. From the angle of the window, they just as easily could kill friend as foe. With a sigh, Nadja let the newfound bone slip from between her teeth. As much as she cared deeply for these folk (far too deeply by State Department standards), this was their fight.

But unexpectedly the tide took a strange turn. More of Black Thorn's men arrived to help hold the ramp, their numbers increasing by the minute, but from below, something enormous waded through the ranks of the enemy, pushing and shoving up the ramp, as if merely wading through a calm mountain pond.

She'd suspected Lacertians continued to grow throughout their lives. All those she'd met with the black cowls of older adults, even sweet and studious Gaius, were noticeably taller and broader than the average. This was different.

Black Rock was simply leviathan.

The enemy general appeared to be a full head taller than Stig, who was large by the standards of his people, and towered head-and-shoulders above his own troops. The villain was 10 feet if he was a single inch and was equally as broad and powerfully built.

"Christ," Gunny hissed.

It took the monster but minutes to ascend the ramp, several times grabbing and tossing aside his own warriors, and he was soon within a few meters of the battle line, where now a hundred or more of Black Thorn's fighters held the high ground, with Stig in the middle of them.

If the battle had been desperate and savage before, now it was frenzied. The enemy warriors, hard-pressed to advance up the steep ramp against Stig's fighters, now found themselves beset by enemies above and their own wicked master in their midst. The fiend seemed just as likely to slash or cut his own troops as he did those of Stig, and soon the battle line began to resemble that of the fight at the tank a week before. Those to the rear pressed forward so hard that fighters in the front ranks of either army had a tough time swinging their weapons.

But somehow it all slowly worked to Stig's advantage. Every minute of gridlock was a minute where another handful of Black Thorn's reinforcements arrived. Soon they numbered 150, with more coming, and the cruelty of Black Rock became so great that his own soldiers began to buckle and to fall back in terror.

For the first time, Stig's company began to push the wretched and battered troops of Black Rock down the ramp. It was mere steps at a time, but by the morning's first light an hour later, they'd shoved the enemy 20 or more meters down the ramp.

His army folding and near collapse, Black Rock unexpectedly began snatching up his own troops and hurling them far into the ranks of Stig and his companions. Miraculously, the gesture appeared to slow their advance, at least momentarily, as soldiers in the rear ranks of Black Thorn's forces were compelled to battle enemies dropped among them. Seeing an advantage, the fiend snatched and hurled even more of his fighters, at least

30 in little more than a minute, before plunging into the battle line for the first time. Black Rock was soon hurtling through the attackers in what was clearly a desperate bid for freedom. The scoundrel was abandoning his army and saving his own neck.

The breach in the lines soon closed behind him, but through his immense size and lumbering strength, Black Rock managed to drive his way over the top of the ramp and to the very steps of the keep, a small knot of his companions by his side. A score of Black Thorns troops, Stig among them, gave chase, and the battle resumed on the steps of the keep, outside the view of the two humans in the level above.

Nadja turned at a sprint and headed to the stairs on the far side of the chamber, Gunny by her side. The morning's light through the arrow slits guided their course, and in less than a minute she and the Marine were midway through the bottom level. Near the door, Nadja saw Stig in a desperate battle with Black Rock, a contest so one-sided that it appeared like one of Gunny's many wrestling matches with her Lacertian pals.

But this was deadly serious. Thirty or more times the two warriors' swords met, and each clash seemed to rock Stig to the core. Black rock was strong and remarkably quick. Several times he grabbed Stig and attempted to toss him aside, only for Stig to find his feet and reengage.

Nadja watched helpless and mesmerized 10 meters away, her weapon raised as if to shoot, but uncertain whether she should, or whether she could without endangering her friend. The battle before her was a maelstrom.

Once again, the swords of the two titans met and Black Rock reached to seize Stig with his free hand, but instead of hurling his opponent away, the villain dropped his now parried sword, snatched a long dagger from his belt, and plunged it deep into Stig's armored breast before tossing the warrior to the ground five meters in front of Nadja.

There was no time to scream or cry out. As Black Rock strode toward her, Nadja centered her weapon on the malignant creature's forehead and squeezed the trigger.

Click.

She hadn't replaced the weapon's battery.

But then the most remarkable thing happened. Before Nadja could grab her pistol, before Gunny could even raise her weapon, Stig's body erupted from the ground, his torso whipped, and his legs pinwheeled so swiftly and wildly that Nadja wasn't sure whether they'd moved at all. Suddenly, Stig was in a fighter's crouch to their left front.

The monster Black Rock stood motionless for but an instant, took two shaky half-steps to the rear, and fell flat on his back, thick black blood oozing in great spurts from his deeply severed throat. It was some moments before Nadja realized that the razor edge of one of Stig's heel spikes had cut the creature's thick neck nearly through.

Stig slumped back onto the ground, and an ugly wheeze erupted from him.

The fighting was done at the door, and all Black Rock's companions were dead on the steps. Nadja dashed to Stig, abandoning her weapon, and soon was cradling his enormous head in her arms. It was only then she realized the stumps of two arrows also protruded from her champion's chainmail armor. For the first time since arriving on this wonderous and wretched planet, she allowed a deep and painful sob to escape her throat.

"Ma'am," said Gunny, taking up a position on Stig's left, "I keep telling you. These guys are like old bicycle innertubes. Keep patching 'em up, and they keep chugging along. If you wanna kill one, head, neck, or armpit. That's the best bet."

Nadja stared at the NCO, unable to suppress her shock.

"Ma'am," the Marine said evenly, "I know he looks like hell, but these aren't fatal wounds. Stig'll be fine in a few days. Now, help hold him steady while I work these things loose. I've got some root paste on me and a few more bottles of the 'good stuff.'"

Nadja eased her friend to the ground and helped Gunny with her preparations. Several times Stig tried to speak, and after a few minutes he reached up and touched her arm.

"*Nadja, you and Gunny shouldn't have put yourselves in danger,*" he whispered faintly.

"*If we can't protect those who are dear to us,*" she replied, taking his hand in hers and reaching out to caress his muzzle, "*then what are we?*"

———

It was again as Gunny had promised. It took about 40 minutes to properly treat Stig's wounds, and within an hour he was able to sit up and, within a brief time more, to totter to his feet. His first act was to sway over to the body of Black Rock and remove the felon's head, which he deposited on the ground near the remains of the keep's front gate.

By that time, the battle for the fortress was nearly over, and a now exhausted Stig slid down the doorframe to take a seat next to his trophy and to watch as events concluded. Nadja could tell it troubled her friend not to be with his troops, but as always, the warrior took the circumstances stoically.

The two humans tended to their own minor injuries, including a wicked patch of missing flesh over Gunny's right bicep and a dozen painful slivers of rock or metal stuck in the hides of both women. The Marine recovered the injured mercenary from where they'd left her hours earlier and brought her near the light cast by the gate. The unconscious woman was badly injured, but still alive.

"She gonna make it?" Nadja asked the Marine after a brief time.

"She'll make it, ma'am. I gave her a dose of BECC from the med kit and cleaned her up some. Might even be walking in a few days or a week."

Might the woman's friends come looking for her? Nadja thought not, but it might be just as well if those people thought her dead. She needed time to talk to this woman and to get some answers. "Let her sleep for now, Gunny. But disable her transponder, if she has one. After that, why don't you take the radio outside and send out a burst to let Lyn know we're still alive."

"Will do, ma'am. If you don't have anything else pressing, you might search sleeping beauty's buddies before they start bloating and stinking. I'll move them outside later."

It was a good suggestion, and Nadja again faulted herself for not thinking of it first. She went to those nearest and recovered weapons, comms, and any information devices they had. None had any sort of identification. The bodies upstairs were much the same, yielding nothing of great interest beyond a few tablets and a map she would go over later.

When Nadja got back downstairs, Gunny had news.

"Got a data burst from above, ma'am. It's a few hours old." There was no smile on the Marine's face. Both knew Lyn would not have broken radio silence without a good reason. "There's a ship in orbit."

It clearly wasn't good news, but Nadja had to ask. "Navy?"

"No, ma'am. But otherwise unknown."

"Shit," Nadja whispered yet again. It just kept coming and coming. She found herself leaning over and staring at the ground, her hands on her knees. If their adversaries had gotten reinforcements, Nadja and those she was trying to protect might royally be screwed.

"Ma'am, I saw Black Thorn below just now. I think he's heading up."

The two humans moved to the keep gate, and indeed Black Thorn was approaching. The general saw Stig, who attempted to stand, and rushed up the stairs to his side. The injured warrior's reaction was typical Stig.

"Pardon me for not rising," he said to his commander.

Their conversation was rapid and fluid. Nadja caught little of what went between the warriors for the next several minutes. Clearly, Black Thorn was happy, a joy that bordered on giddiness. And from the words Nadja understood, the officer heaped praise upon Stig and his men. In return, Stig lifted the severed head of the villain Black Rock and presented it to Black Thorn. Three times the general refused the offer before finally taking the token reverently into his arms.

As such things were in their society, the ceremony was short. Black Thorn turned next to Nadja and spoke slowly in simple words.

"Thank you for being an ally," the general said, *"and for the healing you have provided to our hero. We have something for you."*

The commander motioned to his officers, and two of them brought forward a human male. The man was stripped naked, but—save for copious cuts, scrapes, and bruises—appeared unharmed. He obviously was terrified and babbled a few words when brought through the gate. Gunny stepped forward to take the man and quickly bound his wrists in cord.

"He is a wicked thing we found among the wicked," the general continued. *"Do with him as you wish."*

Uncertain what to say, Nadja thanked the officer before adding, *"General, I can't punish him until I return him to our band, but once there, he will face the harshest punishment."*

Her words appeared to satisfy Black Thorn, who remained buoyant and lively. After a battle lasting a single day and night, he and his men had abolished a great evil that long had afflicted their land, a terror that had lasted perhaps for thousands of years. They had every right to their high spirits.

It dawned on Nadja that for these folk, this was an age of heroes, a time of legends.

"You are always welcome in our land," the general said. He turned, gave Stig an affectionate touch on the shoulder, and went onto the keep stairs, the great head of Black Rock lifted high above his own.

The explosion of cheers from the troops assembled outside was louder than a grenade.

37: New Arrival

Despite all that was transpiring, the two women felt compelled to rest, and Nadja and Gunny took turns grabbing a scant bit of sleep while the other tended to Stig and watched the prisoners. When Really roused Nadja three hours later, it was hot, and Stig's fellows from Black Flower's band had returned to tend to and dote on their leader.

Happily, the group still numbered 14—apparently only the hardiest and luckiest of the original band remained—but it soon became obvious something small had changed. The troops always had been deferential to their leader; now they were positively reverent. All things considered, it seemed understandable.

As always, Gunny had news. "I separated the prisoners, ma'am. Beauty is still sleeping, but the bloke's calmed down enough to talk, if you're of a mind to have a few words. Says his name is Eric and that he's some sort of assistant project manager."

The two women spoke for some 30 minutes and developed a list of information they'd like to glean from the prisoner. It had been years since Nadja's 18-month turn as intelligence officer, and she'd never received training in interrogation.

"You're a charmer, Gunny. Why don't you do the talking, and I'll take notes. I'll chime in, if anything occurs to me."

They proceeded without further word to where the man was leaned against one of the room's thick pillars.

"You're Nadja Bikram," the man said, before they'd even reached him.

She took a long look. Her memory was good, and the face was familiar. The voice helped. Eric what? ... Ganz. They'd met at a conference seven or eight years before. The exact details of the man escaped her. He had a doctorate in something from some no-name university. They might even have a few mutual acquaintances.

"Eric Ganz," the man continued, as if it wasn't an attempt to curry favor. "We...."

"Direct all your comments to Gunnery Sergeant Nice," she said, cutting him off. "I'll let you know, if I have any questions for you."

The man complied meekly, and Gunny began peppering him with questions. It appeared the NCO had at least some training in such matters. The questions were orderly and systematic, starting with the man's basic data and moving to his most recent activities and the activities of those nearest him in his organization. Afterward, Gunny began questioning him about the organization of which he was a member.

An hour into the questioning, things began to take shape.

Nadja had never heard of Elphinstone, Ltd., but that didn't mean anything. The company had maintained a facility on a mountain plateau near Black Rock's fortress for more than six years, a place so secretive that none of the work conducted within was shared outside of the facility. The hundred or so scientists and technicians at the site had run across some rather fascinating properties of a local tuber, which seemed to exhibit biomechanical properties.

"So, what?" Gunny asked. "It makes you live forever?"

The man gave a confused look. "No ... no. The thing is a matrix for some sort of naturally occurring nanite. It's almost like raw biomatter that thinks. The thing can fix cells, mimic proteins and enzymes, neutralize toxins, and clean your body down to the cellular level. Best of all, it can even reset your body systems and coach your own cells to do all manner of things. It's a wonder."

It all hit Nadja like a tidal wave. She'd always been a good biochemist—it was the nature of her work. Why hadn't she seen this? It was nothing short of a wonder that humans could eat, digest, and be nourished by food on Skiathos. How had it not occurred to her how unlikely it would be that a single medication would weave such miracles on humans and Lacertians alike?

How had recent events so addled her mind? Was it just the heat and the stress of their situation?

The point that Ganz was driving at now was obvious. One of humanity's oldest miracles, the development of the Clemence Acclimatization Process, the process that made interplanetary travel possible, was a godsend and a curse.

Despite the speculations of early human novelists, homo sapiens simply were not built to travel from planet to planet. Primate physiology was too fragile and the conditions, even from one terrestrial-type world to the next, were far too varied for survival on a new world to be feasible without careful and thoroughgoing intervention.

Genetic manipulation was an accepted part of life, but CAP was different. Even Nadja's trip to the relatively welcoming climes of Skiathos had required a long and discomforting process that had prepared and altered her body for the diverse physical, chemical, and biological differences of the world. One such process was a burden on a human body, but each successive CAP treatment increased the likelihood of a variety of catastrophic and systemic breakdowns in the recipient.

Far worse, CAP readjustments that allowed humans to live in more hostile environments changed human physiology so radically that they virtually guaranteed a one-way ticket to a new world. Most humans lived in a small core of carefully terraformed worlds for the very reason that such places did not require CAP to travel from one world to the next. But worlds suitable for such terraforming were vanishingly rare, and humans had turned to CAP to enable them to live and work in preexisting planetary ecosystems.

The long-promised pill that would allow simple and pain-free travel to any world even vaguely suitable for human life? Was this it? Were the roots the answer to such a dream?

The good people at Elphinstone, Ltd. seemed to think so, and they were willing to kill government agents to make that dream a richly lucrative reality. It was on that very topic Gunny now questioned Eric Ganz.

"Beyond the research team, how many security personnel?" Gunny asked the man.

"I ... um. That's really not my department ... I," Ganz stuttered. It was the man's first outward sign of evasiveness or reluctance.

The Marine leaned forward. "You were here with at least 11 of them," she said in a stern voice. "This ain't the fucking time to play coy. How many security personnel are there?"

"Around 40."

"Counting the ones that were here last night?"

"Yes," he said with a nod.

"How many vehicles?"

"Other than the station itself, there are 15."

"Fifteen?" Gunny gave him a strange look. The number seemed high. "Who flies them?"

"Some are used directly by the security teams. Mm ... m ... most are flown by wire." This line of questioning clearly had touched a nerve. Eric Ganz's voice had pitched up an octave and several times had cracked. All of a sudden, he turned away from Gunny. "Nadja, I swear, I had nothing to do with the...."

Something inside her snapped. This was the man's second attempt at appealing to their previous acquaintanceship. That he might not directly be responsible for the attempts on their lives and the murder of others meant nothing. He conspired with those who did. That was enough.

Nadja spoke for the first time since Gunny's interrogation began. "You can call me Dr. Bikram, or you can call me ma'am. But we are not friends or colleagues sunning ourselves at some symposium. You and your asshole friends have killed Marines, have killed scholars working on this planet, and have tried to kill me, Gunnery Sergeant Nice, and the rest of us. If you ever speak to me on such familiar terms again, I will shove my thumb into you and keep pressing until I find something soft, and then I will rip it out! *Do you fucking understand me?*"

It wasn't clear to her when exactly she had come to her feet, but Nadja soon found the NCO leading her away from the frightened and naked man on the floor.

"How about you sit and chat with Stig awhile, ma'am," Gunny said gently. "I'll let you know what shakes loose."

At any other time, Nadja would have resisted with teeth-bared, but Really Nice had located all her buttons and knew how to work them. So, she acquiesced and soon found herself slumped by the keep gate with Stig and his gang. It was not a scorcher, but it was a fearsome hot day, and over the next hour or two they wiled away their time playing a game on the floor that required hopping different colored rocks around a board scratched in the stone.

Those moments were so mellow, she allowed herself to drift off for a time. She'd have to start planning and worrying again soon, but for a short while, everything seemed right again. There was something about these folks, something about being in their presence.

"*When is the army leaving?*" she asked sleepily after a while.

"*The first will leave in two or three days,*" Stig responded. "*Black Thorn is thorough. Even now his men scour the land looking for hidden enemy. Once he is certain, the army will go as it came.*"

She presumed that meant in small companies, a notion that made perfect sense. "*When will you leave?*"

"*I will heal for a few days, and then we will help you return to your band.*"

Nadja hoped they might be able to spare Stig the trouble. A plan had begun formulating in her head, based on the information they already had recovered from Ganz. She now knew the approximate location of the Elphinstone facility—it was about 20 kilometers east of the fortress—and if enough of the satellite net was online, they might be able to locate it more precisely. If push came to shove, and the facility was shrouded, she and Gunny could hike there and get eyes on.

The platform's armaments were robust, but mostly were designed for defense, to defeat incoming weapons. But there was one battery of orbital bombardment weapons aboard that likely could hit and destroy any facility they could find. The targeting of such an attack wouldn't have to be exact, but it would require a fair degree of precision.

And there was the ship in orbit with which to contend. It was unlikely just a passerby. She had to presume it was more Elphinstone people, but there was nothing yet in her plan for that.

She shook her head, got up, and stretched. With the help of two of the warriors, she spent about an hour moving the bodies of the dead mercenaries outside. Rather than bury them, she opted to follow Lacertian custom and leave them exposed for the wind, sand, and predators. There was no ceremony. Her only mourning was that the sorry and worthless lot had nothing to provide the living, not even heel spikes.

By the time Nadja returned to the keep, Gunny had finished with the prisoner.

"Thanks for doing that little chore, ma'am. Ganz just fleshed out some details," the Marine told her. "The only interesting tidbit was about Wray. Like you assumed, his job was to make sure the survey came up with nothing and just went away. Apparently, there was quite a bit of money that changed hands."

"Then why did he flip out?"

"Because he really did flip out, ma'am. Ganz says the whole Elphinstone research team was stunned when their security people shot us down back when. Wray slowly unraveled and headed down planet-side to … well, who knows. The Elphinstone people sent Black Rock to round him up, and Black Rock, trustworthy lad he was, was holding Wray hostage and shaking Elphinstone down for weapons. That's what Ganz was here for, to negotiate Wray's release."

"Wait. Hold on. Why did they care what happened to Wray? And how did they communicate with Black Rock?" There was something funny. Was Ganz a linguist? She couldn't remember that small tidbit.

"This guy isn't certain about that first part, ma'am. He thinks Wray may've had something Elphinstone wanted, or maybe he had something on them … something he held over their heads. The other part is easy. Ganz is a systems guy, develops communications AIs. He developed one they could use to communicate with the Others, who they call the 'Friendlies.' It was the Others that Elphinstone was working with, and it was their language Ganz used to communicate with Black Rock."

"That all makes weird sense," Nadja muttered finally. "It's all like some sort of bad old movie."

The Marine chuckled. "Wray can explain the finer plot-points when you finally get your hands around his neck. Any notion of a plan on what we do next?"

"Sort of," she said with a laugh. "Send out a burst to Lyn. If there's a satellite in range, get a picture of the spot Ganz pointed out as their base. It's probably shrouded, but we might get lucky. Have Chief make sure the planetary battery is fully operational and have him begin to move the platform into position above us. Oh … and, um, tell Lyn to stay quiet as a mouse. I don't know what to make of the new ship up there. One thing at a time."

"You really gonna drop a house on these people, ma'am?"

"Yup. I will drop a whole damn mountain on our new friends at Elphinstone, if that's what it takes. And try and get some rest. If the satellite photos don't pan out, you and I are hiking up to that plateau tomorrow."

38: The Facility

In the end, Nadja and Gunny took the hike. The satellite photos revealed no enemy base, but the analysts on the platform were convinced from the shadows cast by nearby terrain features that something was shrouded nearby. But "nearby" wasn't good enough for a good targeting lock.

So, they hiked.

A still-weakened Stig was, for the first time since Nadja had known him, deeply intransigent. He could not go himself, but insisted the humans take six of his warriors. His final winning card was that, if Nadja and Gunny refused the escort, then Stig would follow behind himself, on hands and knees, if necessary.

They'd relented.

If truth be told, it was another good idea. Black Thorn's riders were still combing the countryside, so there was no telling whether stragglers from the defeated army might still be at large. Such desperate characters could be a danger, even to the well-armed humans. And there had been no sign of the Others—that fact had occurred to Stig, who suspected the great might of the southern army had frightened their hereditary adversaries away. Still, Ganz had revealed an important nugget: The Friendlies, as he called them, were on good terms with the Elphinstone people and sometimes were to be found near the facility.

No. In the end, having the company of six strong warriors, who Nadja and Gunny both knew well and trusted, was a great comfort, one that further ensured the success of their mission.

And despite the danger that still loomed over them, the extra company wasn't without its fringe-benefits.

Molly, as Gunny referred to her, wasn't the chattiest Lacertian Nadja had met, but she was a gifted and energetic raconteur. Most of the way along the narrow and torturous path the Marine had charted to their objective, Molly gabbed on about her various adventures, victories, and occasional setbacks. The stories, or at least what Nadja could understand of them, were funny and charming, and Molly had an almost human way of pausing for effect or sometimes waving her arms to paint the scene. It was lovely.

Of course, Molly wasn't female, any more than Stig, Black Flower, or Festus were males. It was just the magic of naming things. In a time in

206

human history when gender differences had never been so narrow, there still existed notions of what was masculine and what was feminine. How could it be any different?

There was nothing even slightly feminine about Nadja's sweet Greta, save what Nadja herself had written into her friend's story. But the love, tenderness, and deep motherly warmth she felt from Greta was real, as real and honest as the earth beneath her feet. She'd never share such feelings with anyone, but she'd never foreswear them either, any more than she ever would stop seeing in Stig the strong, loving, and patient father she'd always needed.

There was such a great power in naming things.

Molly kept Nadja entertained throughout most of the day, and it wasn't until about an hour after sunset that they reached their destination, a ridgeline above and some kilometers distant from the plateau where the Elphinstone facility was located. It took them scant minutes to recon the area and hunker down to wait. Their new perch was a good vantage point, one outside the security grid Elphinstone monitored, and it afforded them a view of the facility, which, from that angle, was partly visible despite the distance and the place's vast shroud.

To Nadja's surprise, there seemed to be little going on there. She'd envisioned at least some sign of heightened security. But according to Ganz, most of the facility's 15 modified and automated skiffs were searching for the platform. And Gunny's interrogation of the man had revealed that a deep rift had developed in recent months between the scientific and security departments at the facility. Might the folks below be oblivious to what had transpired at the fortress on the previous day?

By that point, Nadja didn't care. She'd found their enemy.

"How long before the platform is on station, Gunny?"

"About three hours, ma'am."

That would be about two hours before sunrise. "That'll give the gang below something to talk about with their morning coffee," Nadja observed with a chuckle.

The plan was simple. Gunny's first act upon spying the Elphinstone station had been to plot its location and send those coordinates in a burst to Lyn on the platform. With the help of Ganz, Gunny had programed one of the radios they'd recovered from the security guards with the frequency used by Elphinstone's facility managers.

Just past dawn, Nadja would issue a simple ultimatum: Surrender the codes by which Elphinstone controlled its modified skiffs, deactivate all their communication jamming equipment in the system, and then prepare to be boarded by the Marines. Nadja was willing to fire one warning shot to hurry the manager's thought process, but that was all. If the codes weren't surrendered and jamming stopped within 10 minutes, Nadja would order the facility flattened.

About the ship in orbit? Well, she was still working on that.

Over the next hours, the warriors squatted quietly in their dozy twilight, and Gunny snoozed in fits and starts near the radio. Nadja couldn't sleep. Several times she allowed herself to imagine a shadow was one of the Others come to eat her, but such moments always ended in a laugh. The warriors all had assured her they could catch the scent of the Others from far away—it was the stench of death—and she knew she merely was letting the stress of the moment toy with her.

No. The weather was mild and the next hours were remarkably bearable. At just past sunup, she nudged Gunny, who immediately alerted the platform they were up and rolling, and then went through the ranks and gave each of the gang a playful pat on the neck. It was time.

"You ready, Gunny?" she asked the NCO minutes later.

"Go, ma'am." The NCO would be in communication with the platform throughout.

Nadja plugged in and activated the Elphinstone earbud and spoke. "Bravo 2-6, Bravo 2-6, do you copy?"

To her surprise, a sleepy and somewhat angry male voice was on the other line within seconds. "Who the hell is this, and why are you calling so early?"

Nadja gave Gunny a nod, and the NCO sent a burst to the platform. Before Nadja could respond to the man on the line, Gunny mouthed a silent, "shot over."

"Kim Nesbit. This is Nadja Bikram, commander of the Skiathos planetary survey team. You've got exactly 10 minutes to turn over the control codes of all your aircraft and to shut down all communication jamming equipment in the system, or I flatten your entire facility. If you need any convincing, look out your window to the east."

"Who in the fuck...?" the man snapped.

"The person you've been trying to kill, you moron." She'd promised herself she wouldn't lose her temper, but her words and tone were nonetheless harsh. "Now look out the fucking window!"

Inertial bombardment systems were among the oldest and technologically simplest weapons ever devised by humans. The projectile that a minute later struck to the east of the Elphinstone facility was merely an enormous metal dart, one nearly 10 meters long and half a meter thick, that transferred the inertia it had picked up while falling into the hard earth with which it collided.

The weapon didn't have the energy it would have if dropped from higher in orbit, but Chief had calculated the yield of the single dart to be nearly one-eighth of a kiloton. The impact when the weapon struck was terrible, buckling the hard soil from point of impact for hundreds of meters in every direction and sending out a shockwave that Nadja and her team felt seconds later, even 15 kilometers away. The people at the Elphinstone facility would have felt the strike in their nose hairs.

"Mr. Nesbit," she said into the communicator, "you've got seven minutes."

"Look … uh, Nadja … there has to be some sort of…," was the man's panicked reply.

"Shut down jamming and send the codes out on this frequency. Bikram, out." She muted the speaker on her side and ignored yet another enemy's use of her first name.

Gunny regarded her with a faint smile, as if wondering whether Nadja might not blink. The Marine said nothing.

And there was nothing to say. Nadja had only the faintest wisp of a plan about how to deal with the ship in orbit. Ganz had known nothing about it. The resupply ships they received were infrequent and always shrouded.

But Nadja still felt a sudden sense of relief. This part of their ordeal was over, one way or the other. She knew from experience that a station like Elphinstone's would require hours to be fitted to move. And though firing the battery had narrowed the places the platform might be, it still would take many hours for Elphinstone's ships to find it. The people on the plateau below had less than seven minutes.

Nope. The Elphinstone people would surrender or else.

Two minutes before the expiration of the deadline, Gunny, her ear still on the radio headset, called over. "Jamming's down, ma'am, and the codes just came in."

"The second Lyn confirms and changes the codes, have her get the Marines down here. Tell Chief to hold fire and send out a distress signal on Pinpoint."

"Aye-aye, ma'am."

Nadja hadn't needed to issue those last orders. Everyone knew their part in the plan. It was just her ever-present anal retentiveness.

"Codes are changed, ma'am," said Gunny with an enormous smile "Marines are on the way, and distress signal is out."

Nadja smiled back. "Well, I guess we just need to wait for our bus."

———

Their bus was two Navy skiffs from the platform that had been fitted for cargo. It took a little convincing to get the warriors to pile three-a-piece into the cramped vehicles for the short hop to the Elphinstone facility, but they ended up being enviable fliers, and it was no time before the party neared the enormous structure, it's shroud now partially deactivated.

It was Nadja's first good look at the facility, which was a newer and larger version of the old Navy platform Nadja's team utilized, only deployed planet-side to make it less conspicuous. The place must have cost a fortune. It wasn't the first time Nadja had considered the enormous sums of money at play. The cost of shrouding one single skiff like those Elphinstone used to hunt them was considerable. The entire site must have represented many billions of credits to the company's investors. Big stakes.

The Marines had landed and the situation was well in hand by the time Nadja's skiff arrived, and they were herding the first of the staff to a holding area to be counted, identified, and searched. Nadja refused to allow the frightened people to take anything but the clothes on their backs, not even a toothbrush, and they soon would be ferried under guard up to the platform and placed under lock and key. She had no idea how events on Skiathos would play out before the courts, but she was determined that no one would profit the value of so much as a single mustard seed for the work done at the Elphinstone facility.

The only things of value that would leave this place were a handful of items for which Nadja had assigned a small team of naval personnel to search the place, including the installation's data-core.

Lyn met them at the landing zone.

"Any trouble?" Nadja asked the woman.

"Some of the security guys got a little frisky, ma'am. We had to put two down."

"Any injuries on our side?"

"No, ma'am, but six or eight hostiles are holed up in a security block on the north of the facility. Sgt. Bisbee has the area cordoned off, and Sgt. Matthews is up with Alex Payton trying to get their boss to talk them out. Apparently, they don't think you're serious, ma'am."

Nadja sighed. "They'll find out. Get on the wire and tell Bisbee not to take any risks. If these assholes want to stay, that's on them. And what's Alex doing here?" Nadja hadn't wanted any civilians on the ground.

210

"You said you wanted the data-core, ma'am. He's the guy that knows that stuff."

"Alright, let's walk. I don't want to be on the ground more than an hour."

The first Elphinstone skiffs were powering up to begin ferrying the prisoners to the platform. The people, many still in their pajamas, were moving down the broad ramp from the facility's belly. Most apparently had never seen a Lacertian. Each was struck dumb by the sight of Nadja's six companions, who were amused at the sight of so many humans and began cooing and barking in curiosity. The pleasant sounds were decidedly hostile to the untrained human ear, and a panic nearly ensued.

"Just get them all down to the landing zone, Lyn. And is there any sort of duty roster or crew manifest for this lot?"

"Alex, ma'am," said Lyn as she and her squad began to hurry the civilians down the ramp. "Top of the ramp. Private Nunes will show you the way."

Nadja didn't bother to silence her Lacertian friends—let these people be afraid for a while—but she did several times have to corral the curious warriors, who were captivated by a place unlike anything they'd ever seen. Their dialogue now was an admiring flow of peeps, whirrs, and hisses. Molly would have many new stories to tell.

Two minutes of walking found them at what appeared to be an operations center. Next to Sgt. Matthews, a man, who from the voice was Kim Nesbitt, was on a commlink attempting to convince someone to surrender. Alex stood nearby. Having been on the ground less than 30 minutes, the young man already had two large data-cores stacked on the floor beside him.

She ignored Nesbitt for the moment and pointed to the cores. "Alex, is that all of it?"

The lad stepped forward and unceremoniously threw his arms around her. She had to choke back something. On her and Gunny's walk from the skiff, busy Marines had flashed broad smiles at them. It was good to be among friends.

"Easy, there, buddy," she whispered.

"Yeah, Nadja. It's good to see you," the young man said in a voice thick with emotion. "Those are the only data cores, but they are something."

"Good to see you, too. Get those downstairs and see Petty Officer Shedd. The two of you need to make sure everything on the list Gunny sent you is on the skiff before we go. And … oh, is there a crew manifest?"

The young man passed her the tablet in his hand and departed after another short embrace. She gave the tablet to Gunny.

"When we go down, make sure everyone is accounted for, one way or the other. When we get this lot back to the platform, separate the leaders and the security personnel from the rest. Isolate that lot, one to a room. I don't want any of them having a chance to get their stories straight."

"Aye-aye, ma'am. We should have space on the foredeck, if we double and triple bunk the others."

Nadja whispered her next words. "And don't let it be widely circulated, if this bunch decides to stay behind. I don't want the people in custody blaming everything on whoever isn't present."

"Aye-aye, ma'am."

"Mr. Nesbitt," Nadja barked. "How many are holed up?"

"Uh … eight, I think. They're just being stubborn. If I could…."

"Tell them we are leaving in 50 minutes, with or without them. Give up their weapons and come out, and they'll be treated fairly. Either way, in 55 minutes, I'm dropping a full battery on this place."

The man gave a look of shock and disbelief. "But…."

"Tell them now," Nadja insisted.

Nesbitt relayed the message, and Nadja yanked the comm from his hand.

"Let's go," she said.

On the way down to the landing zone, she continued to discuss matters with the gunnery sergeant, pausing only long enough to corral the warriors when necessary and allowing them each to take a small souvenir.

"Am I forgetting anything, Gunny?"

"As long as Alex has the material you asked for and all our people are accounted for, I can't think of what, ma'am. If any of these people are foolish enough to stay behind … I'm with you. Screw 'em."

"Are we going to be out of here in 50 minutes?"

"Give or take a few minutes. Enough of the Elphinstone vehicles have been recalled that it shouldn't be a problem. Shouldn't take more than three trips, if we pack 'em in nice and tight."

Sgt. Matthews had been walking beside them, casting a wary eye at the warriors the whole time. "What's the hurry, ma'am?"

"I'll brief you all in full once we're back on the platform. For now, I just don't intend on giving these people time to do anything stupid." Nadja had been able to come up with a single flimsy and half-formed plan to deal with the ship above, one she hadn't even shared fully with the gunnery sergeant. Once again, she was winging it.

On the LZ, Gunny gathered the squad leaders, and within five minutes, vehicles were being loaded and the first groups of prisoners were being ferried to the platform. The entire thing was hasty, and Nadja had to trust to the zeal, professionalism, and skills of her NCOs to get it all done.

It was best she stayed out from under foot while they worked, fielding questions only as they arose. For a time, she leaned back into the comfort of the warriors and spent some minutes chitchatting with them as events proceeded. All throughout, she thought about the problem in orbit over their heads.

As the last wave of skiffs loaded, Nadja composed a short message and sent it in a burst from a radio on one of the Marine transports. She'd seldom been so nervous. The message, which went to Chief for later redelivery on her command, might be the biggest gamble she'd so far taken on the planet.

The only folks left on the ground after that were Nadja, Gunny, Stig's troops, and the Marines under Sgt. Lyn and Sgt. Bisbee.

"Lyn," she said, "have Bisbee and her Marines pull back to the LZ. We're bugging out the second Gunny gets a headcount."

"Aye-aye, ma'am." The Marine was on the radio immediately.

"Got a plan yet, ma'am?" asked a smiling Gunny.

Nadja pointed up at the great monolith that was the Elphinstone facility, a place so secret none of its work had been transferred or replicated elsewhere. "Ganz gave me the idea. With that hunk of metal flattened, the only thing left of six or seven years of priceless Elphinstone research is in those data-cores Alex took up. We got a distress signal off finally. Until help arrives, those data-cores are the only leverage we have. And I'm not giving whoever is in orbit a chance to stop us or to salvage anything."

A light went on in Really Nice's eyes. "Oh, good plan, ma'am ... if it works."

"If it works," Nadja repeated with a laugh. "Here comes Bisbee's squad. Have everybody mount up and let me know when we have an accurate headcount."

Five minutes later, Nadja was again in the cargo skiff with Molly and two more of her enormous friends.

"All accounted for, ma'am," came Gunny's modulated voice through the vehicle's headset.

"All vehicles, let's roll," she radioed the pilots of the final four aircraft to depart the LZ. It had been one hour and two minutes since she'd arrived at the facility. "Marine 3-3 and Marine 3-4, ascend to 50 and offload, but stay clear of the trajectory of the incoming battery fire."

As the Marines ascended, the two remaining skiffs circled north and then west. She needed to make sure this was done. Nadja cleared her throat and switched over to another frequency, the one used by the platform's weapons desk, and quickly signed on.

"Chief, all PAX clear. Adjust fire. Fire for effect, over," she said, after once more clearing her throat. *This is the one that's getting you thrown in jail, Bikram*, she couldn't help but remind herself. But there was no other choice—hopefully, this would give them some small leverage with those in orbit. Besides, a powerful corporation seldom knew punishment outside of profit and loss, and she was determined no one would get rich from this wretched place.

"Fire for effect, out," she heard from Chief's gravelly voice.

Two minutes later, what had been a partially shrouded facility on the plateau below was less than a twisted wreck, as the Elphinstone research facility and several grid squares around it were obliterated.

"Jesus," she heard from the pilot before a shockwave rocked the vehicle, sentiments echoed from the other skiff through the auxiliary radio channel. Molly and her companions contributed admiring purrs from the cramped cargo area.

"End mission," she signaled to the platform. "And, Chief, have comms transmit that message to the bogey in orbit. Don't forget to ping it off a satellite."

"Roger, Six."

"Six, out."

Nadja tapped the pilot. "Let's get out of here. Those grid coordinates I gave you shouldn't be more than a few minutes out.

She had to return Stig's warriors to their leader.

39: Goodbyes and Hellos

T heir goodbye barely lasted 15 minutes, little more than the time necessary to drop off the boisterous and elated warriors and to recover Ganz and his injured companion. As he had planned, Stig already had returned to the tent they'd all shared at the camp of Black Thorn. Their friend was looking much healthier, and he and several hundred others were there to greet the two skiffs and to say goodbye.

Nadja didn't want the episode to be an ordeal, but she had no idea if she might be back tomorrow, next year, or never again, and she wanted her goodbye to be sincere. She and Gunny went around to those closest to them first and exchanged affectionate touches and familiar squeezes.

When she got to Stig, she felt her heart flicker, and for the first time, her eyes rained more than just mist. She pulled her friend close. *"I hope to see you again,"* she whispered. *"Thank you for saving our lives and for protecting us and helping us find our way home."*

"There are no thanks necessary, Nadja." He knelt and stared hard at her, reaching out and pulling Gunny to their embrace when he did. *"You are ours, and we are yours. That's what it is to be the members of a band."*

And that was their goodbye.

Twenty minutes later, the two skiffs were the last vehicles from Skiathos to dock with the platform, which remained in hiding in the upper atmosphere. At that elevation, the platform was buttoned up and carefully pressurized, but on the dock the first thing Nadja realized was not how cool and wonderful the air felt, but how tired she was and how badly she reeked.

"Oh, shit, I smell awful," she said to no one in particular.

"You need a bath, ma'am." Gunny walked up from the next docking bay over. A Marine detail behind her was taking the two prisoners below. "But what you really need is to come to the mess with me right now."

"Gunny…."

"Ma'am, there are shitloads of things to do right now. I get it. But you and me need to go down to an air-conditioned mess, drink a cold beer, and rest our tired and weary bones for 10 or 15 minutes."

"Ah, agreed," she relented.

The two sat for close to 30 minutes drinking beer, chatting, and fielding questions from those who sought them out. Spiros swung by to welcome them back, almost unrecognizable in regulation grooming and a fresh uniform. His stride was normal now that the infirmary's trauma surgeon had removed several weighty pieces of metal that had been lodged deep in his thigh. It was only after the young man left that Nadja realized she hadn't seen Gunter Wray in all the chaos.

"He was on one of the first skiffs out, ma'am, and he's locked up now." The NCO gave her a long look. "Am I safe to let you in the same room with him?"

Nadja began to laugh, a long and refreshing hoot. Now that she had the man in hand, her obsession with getting her hooks into him abated. Someone would have to interview him later as they tried to sort out the dimensions of the Elphinstone conspiracy, but right now it didn't seem pressing.

"I think it's safe, Gunny. But I don't need to talk to him right now. Sgt. Bisbee is still acting as S-2. You and her sit down and come up with a list of personnel who've had the intelligence or criminal investigation short-courses. Then we can come up with some sort of schedule to start interviewing these people. Throw my name onto that list, but you know what … I don't care whether I talk to Wray or not."

Sgt. Lyn entered the mess. "Ma'am, we got a reply from the ship in orbit."

Nadja felt a knot in her stomach tighten. "OK, what do they want?"

"Dunno, ma'am," said the NCO. "The reply wasn't in English."

———

News that the ship in orbit wasn't from Elphinstone was like a death-row pardon for Nadja, who since becoming aware of the vessel's existence had been in turmoil at what its presence might portend.

Not that they were out of danger yet. The message the ship had sent over on multiple radio bands was like nothing else they'd ever encountered, and without more information, the translation AI drew a complete blank. They were dealing with a new species, something that should have been exciting for them. But coming as it did at the end of a miserable ordeal, the fact that the ship had not yet attacked them or exhibited any hostile intent was the only thing that boded well. Then again, it may well be that the new visitor simply had not yet found their location.

They again hailed the ship, bouncing the message from another satellite and sending the same greeting in each medium with which humans and their intergalactic counterparts were accustomed to communicating, including a long burst of mathematical data that humans and others frequently used to signal sentience.

216

There was no reply beyond an additional transmission of the original message.

Next, they thought to try something new. Janet and Ken De Novo had spent most of the last week processing the notes she'd provided them on the Lacertian language and attempting to extrapolate some information from the manuscript for which Gunny had bartered. The item in question had been only partly translated by its original Lacertian owner, but the AI had filled in many of the blanks.

As near as they could figure, it seemed to be some sort of musical construction that relied entirely on rising and falling tones to express meaning. For want of a better description, it was a composition of melodic poetry that might roughly be termed epic. The story the AI translated reminded Nadja very much of one of the many stories she and Greta had watched together at the gathering.

Even with the AI, it took Nadja and the De Novos nearly six hours to compose a message in the strange cant, a missive that Nadja couldn't be sure was not complete gibberish. Their note merely said who they were, what they were like, and that they wished to meet. It was not ideal first-contact procedure, but the survey team was on the edge of known space. They needed at least to establish common ground with the newcomers, before something unfortunate came to pass through some misunderstanding.

Nadja instructed the comms tech to send the message. And then they waited.

And they waited a bit longer. It was the longest three hours Nadja could remember, a period the only saving grace of which was that it provided her and Gunny more time to shower, change, eat, and rest. At the end of that time, they received yet another transmission of the original message and nothing else.

"OK," said Nadja as she stood in the communications section after receiving the message. She had a few moments of indecision before walking over and taking the seat from the comms tech. She composed a short missive in Lacertian and sent it as an audio file on all channels. A response was forthcoming within five minutes. It was quick and to the point. There was a set of coordinates and a short "hello."

"Well, I guess it's a date," Nadja told her assembled staff.

There was no use putting things off. No time had been specified for the meeting, so Nadja merely needed to choose a team. It was her job to go, but she opted not to take the De Novos. Neither had first encounter experience, nor did they seem terribly excited at the prospect of joining the club. Her senior bio-anthropologist was in an impromptu holding cell on the foredeck. But one of his juniors, Devin Erskine, had assisted in diplomatic encounters in the past.

Against her better judgment, Nadja took along Really Nice. She should have left her second-in-command to manage the platform, but if the new race's intentions were hostile, it wouldn't matter much. The alien ship was large and no doubt well-armed. Anyway, Nadja had come to rely on the gunnery sergeant.

An hour later, the three had repaired to the crash room to suit up. The mood was typical of such circumstances.

"You have much time in an EV suit, ma'am?"

"Oh, scads, Gunny."

"How about you, Dr. Erskine?"

"Uh, I've had the basic course."

There was something in the young man's voice, some whiff of vulnerability. Nadja saw Gunny moving in for the kill. Like a wild snaggletooth, the woman was relentless.

"Don't worry, doctor," said the NCO. "Easy-peasy. And don't believe the crap people tell you. Explosive decompression is over in seconds. You hardly feel a thing."

Nadja should have said something, but didn't. She'd made the same ugly jibes and taunted the same naive rookies more times than she could count. Given the precision design of their suits and the rugged construct of the skiffs, it was unlikely they would have any problems. The only real danger was contamination from their soon-to-be hosts, and they had a legion of protocols in place for such things. Still, she cut the rookie some slack.

"Devin, the suits are just a precaution. We're not going EV, and the skiffs are in great trim. Don't get your heart to racing. Hey, Gunny, you mind if I fly?"

"If you're rated, ma'am."

"I am."

The three stepped out of the locker area, and the deck boss gave Nadja the maintenance log of the skiff they were taking. She gave it a review. It was as she'd promised Devin. The record was spotless beyond scheduled maintenance. Chief's crew had even done preflight checks. Nadja gave the vessel a once-over anyway before signing the dispatch log and returning it to the boss.

"OK, children, let's go."

Their new friends already might know their location, but Nadja opted not to broadcast it. She took the skiff for several hundred kilometers through the same charged layer in which the platform was concealed before dropping into the lower atmosphere and reemerging under the coordinates indicated by the invitation.

The ploy turned a 20-minute flight into an hour, but it was worth the trouble. When the skiff entered the vacuum of space, a large vehicle that had detached from the main alien ship was at the prescribed coordinates. Nadja signaled their presence and maneuvered to what appeared to be an airlock.

"Oh, jeez, Dr. Erskine," she heard Gunny mutter. "There's a bag in your seat for that."

The whirr of a small suction device was soon audible in the cabin behind her as Gunny no doubt cleaned the refuse from the zero-gravity cabin. Nadja took her time docking. They weren't on a time schedule. Ten minutes later, their minor mess contained, the skiff bumped lightly against a large pad that, like those used by many races, looked to be some sort of universal coupling and locking device. It seemed a good sign.

"Button up," she said, releasing herself from the seat harness and floating free from the cockpit. "Gunny, wanna give Devin a hand to the airlock?"

The skiff, in fact, was fitted with its own airlock, suitable for only one person at a time. Five minutes later, Nadja, the last through the lock, stood on a deck of perfectly generated gravity about equal to the pull of Skiathos below. A short causeway led them to a secondary lock, and then, finally, to a small room of a general type Nadja had seen many times. On one side of the room was a clear material. Obviously, their new friends used visible light—or they surmised from their presence over Skiathos that humans did.

Gunny checked the tablet on her wrist. "Right mix of oxygen, tolerable radiation, and the bio filter says we are in a room that is 100 percent sterile. We can unbutton any time you're ready, ma'am."

The three popped their helmets off and waited. Several times a warm sensation passed over them. Their suits' sensors said there was nothing about which they needed to worry. Their shy new friends were simply taking little probes to figure out what they were dealing with. Nadja would have done the same.

After 10 minutes, there was a faint burp in the air, as if someone had broken squelch on a finely tuned microphone.

"Ahh … I guess they want to talk more," Nadja whispered.

Moments later, a single voice greeted the three humans. English long had been the lingua franca of the known worlds, but many other tongues persisted within human society. To their surprise and delight, they had travelled thousands of light years to be greeted cordially and politely by an alien speaking heavily accented, but otherwise thoroughly unimpeachable, Spanish.

40: Subedar

T he lounge of the naval cruiser *Subedar* was large and comfortable by the standards of a warship, and after nearly an hour Nadja finally had persuaded herself to sit back and enjoy the place. They very soon would be breaking orbit, and she would be leaving Skiathos, probably forever.

Her meetings and conversations over a three-week span with the new race they'd encountered, who referred to themselves (half-jokingly, she thought) as *los cojos*, the Lame Ones, had been among the most fascinating of her life. This new people had indeed met humans before. Half a millennium before, when humans first had ventured to the stars, they had done so in one enormous, audacious wave, peppering the heavens with humankind. The humans with whom *los cojos* were familiar inhabited several score worlds a thousand or more light years distant, many months travel by the fastest FTL drive, in the heart of a great star cluster that was home to 27 spacefaring races.

Even now, word of this momentous discovery was being transmitted back to settled space. It was humanity's first encounter with one of their ancient cousins, and it heralded extraordinary things.

Nadja had liked their new interlocutors from the first meeting. The Lame Ones, whose true physical form she'd not seen beyond their small and many-armed EV suits, were brilliant, inquisitive, and—much to her delight—possessed a wicked sense of humor. By the end of her first encounter with them, they'd already attained a mastery of English sufficient to make a few bad puns.

They also were an advanced and highly benevolent society. So benevolent, in fact, that they had negotiated a system of protectorates over all non-space-faring races within their far-flung corners of the cosmos. For *los cojos* and their spacefaring neighbors, the isolated planet they referred to as Las Arenas was a protected world, one that in ages past had experienced much interference, but one whose natives now were protected by agreement of all. So benevolent were *los cojos* that they would pardon a single unwitting transgression against the isolation of the planet, but only one.

Thanks largely to the decency and kindness of this new folk, the first encounter had gone remarkably well. After three weeks of meetings, she'd just finished her initial report for her supervisors back at State when the

Subedar arrived at the head of a small taskforce. The platform's initial distress signal had not gotten through, but a conscientious duty officer had taken note of the survey team's failure to make routine communication and had been persistent in not letting that fact go unnoticed.

A board of inquiry had convened almost the moment Nadja had emerged from the CAP recovery module, which readapted her system to a standard environment, and had gone on the last 16 days. It had not been an inquiry into the actions of Elphinstone, per se—Nadja already had submitted their report on that subject to both Fleet and State via Pinpoint— rather, it was an investigation of Nadja and her dropping a nearly one-kiloton payload on an Elphinstone research base, killing nine.

Nadja wasn't sure whether she currently was under arrest, but she'd been sequestered and incommunicado for the last 16 days as the proceedings wended their tortuous and wretched path. No, she couldn't claim it was all misery. As a naval officer and later while in her job at State, she'd sat on such boards and knew the rules and procedures better than most, and the advocate she'd been provided, a studious and solemn lieutenant commander, the type who inspired confidence, was both experienced and able.

She wasn't sure how the board would decide and wouldn't find out for a week or more, but she sensed it was a flip of a coin whether they would convict. Either way, her days at State were over.

A familiar voice inserted itself into her thoughts.

"Dr. Nadja Bikram," it said sweetly.

Nadja stood and offered her hand. "Hello, Gunny. They got you on *Subedar*, now?" It was great to see the NCO again—when last she'd heard from her former team, they'd still been on the platform—and it was her first time seeing the Marine in dress uniform. It had never occurred to her what a fetching woman she was.

After shaking Nadja's hand, the Marine joined her on the lounge's broad and comfortable bench. "She's the biggest ship in the group, ma'am. The Marines and naval personnel are here. The rest are billeted on the other vessels."

"How was CAP for you?" Nadja had emerged in record time with none of the aches and general sense of malaise she'd experienced in previous Acclimatization Procedures.

"I was last off the platform, but first through CAP ... except for Spiros. They kept us both an extra 36 hours just to make sure things were on the up-and-up. Must still be a little of the 'good stuff' in our systems."

"There might always be, Gunny. But let's keep that between the three of us for now, at least until this Elphinstone mess is cleared up. I'd just as soon they believed their data-core and all the samples of Skiathos root were destroyed planet-side."

The gunnery sergeant nodded. "Spiros is a smart kid, but I'll remind him to play his cards close. But ... um, now that word about this stuff is out, won't the government push to get access to Skiathos?"

"They might, Gunny, but I doubt it. No one wants to alienate our new friends. They're amiable and generous and simply have far, far too much to offer. Just the new long-range communication technology they've already agreed to share will change the way we do business. It puts Pinpoint to shame. *And* they're leaving a permanent observation station near the planet just to make sure there won't be any more incidents."

"That makes me happy, ma'am," said the Marine with a solemn nod.

"You said we're all onboard?"

"The last few are still going through CAP, but we're all accounted for."

"The platform?"

"Abandoned, ma'am."

An unexpected twinge passed through Nadja. She hadn't been on the vessel long, but it had served them all ably. Still, it was old and likely should have been made salvage years ago. "Oh, wait ... how's Chief Eddy taking that? It was his for what, 11 years?"

Gunny made an innocent pooh-poohing sound. "Oh, he was a little emotional but took it like a pro. His next berth will likely be bigger and better."

"Please tell me they didn't make him strip her down."

"He volunteered, ma'am. Said he could do it in a third the time, which he did. Then he floated her out to the asteroid belt and scuttled her himself."

"The man is a professional," Nadja agreed.

"He'll probably be doing some hard drinking over the next few weeks, but he'll be OK."

Gunny had raised an interesting point. The three and a half weeks back to Clem's World was a trip too short to merit Hibernation. Nadja would have to figure out some way to while away the hours. "What'll you be up to for the duration?"

"The ship doesn't have much room to train, ma'am. Other than the gym, I have the Marines on their extension courses. Well, that and a little free time. They deserve it." Gunny winked. "I've got a sweet collection of vintage movies. You like Bogart?"

"Not usually, but I've seen *Casablanca*, I dunno … five times."

"I have that," said the Marine with a sweet smile. "Play it again, ma'am?"

Nadja couldn't help but laugh at the tepid joke. "I'd actually love to … assuming I'm not in shackles for the rest of the trip."

"Oh, shit. I didn't want to ask. How'd that go, ma'am?"

"Not as bad as it could have," Nadja replied. "Believe it or not, there was actually some chubby bald civilian there the first day sitting at the long table with the board. The putz never introduced himself, and I thought for the first hour he was some sort of Defense Department civilian."

"He was what? … State?"

Nadja barked a contemptuous laugh. "The guy's a program manager from Hewitt, Daftar, and Proud."

"HDP? The defense contractor?"

"Yup." Nadja couldn't control her mirth.

"What the hell was he doing sitting on a Navy board of inquiry?"

"That's a very good question, Gunny. It was the first thing I brought up once I realized who he was. I'm not convinced the members of the board realized the importance of where the guy was sitting … or, at least I want to give them the benefit of the doubt. He went and sat in the rear after, but I moved that he be ejected from the proceedings."

"What did they do?"

"Oh, he bitched and moaned, but I had a right to limit the proceedings, and the board chair sent him out."

The Marine seemed flabbergasted. "How does something like that happen?"

"Gunny, who knows? So many officers go to work for companies like HDP after they retire that it's a little too cozy. I tried not to think too much of it. Things were pretty much by-the-book after that."

"What do you think he was up to?"

"What? Trying to make himself out to be a member of the board?" Nadja thought. "I suppose the obvious—just trying to influence the proceedings, shape the narrative in some small way, maybe get a glimpse at my testimony."

"And HDP is tied to Elphinstone, how?"

"My advocate did a little research. Ship's data-core says there was no such thing as Elphinstone, Ltd., before eight years ago."

Gunny nodded. "And whoever paid the bills had a lot of money sunk into that project."

"Yeah, a fortune. Elphinstone is probably some HDP subsidiary hidden behind 20 or so layers of shell companies. After weapons, pharmaceuticals are their biggest business."

"You know what, ma'am, HDP also has an office on Clem's World. They do a lot of business with the Navy there."

Another fit of laughter hit Nadja. "Yeah … uh, the guy … Wentworth, whatever his name was, asked to come back in and give a statement a few days ago."

"What would he possibly have to add?"

"Oh, I think he phrased it as some sort of victim or witness impact report. It's not real clear how he got the authority, but he must have spoken with the Elphinstone people in holding. The story he wove painted a vivid picture."

Somehow, the Marine's look of shock became even greater. "Go on."

"If you're to believe this guy, I went native … or rogue. He used both words. But I went rogue, raised an army of savage brigands, raped and pillaged my way across the countryside, defeating several armies along the way, overthrew the rightful king, and then turned my cruel hordes on a hapless band of innocent researchers."

"That sounds like a fair assessment of events, ma'am. But, look, why didn't you call any of us as witnesses?"

Nadja waved her hand lightly. "I could've called witnesses, but the tribunal admitted your written statements without cross examination. My advocate thought it was our best avenue forward."

"Your mouthpiece like your odds?"

"*He* does. I think it's about 50-50."

"I'll bake you a cake, ma'am."

Gunny abruptly went to her feet as a man walked toward them, Fleet Captain Carl James, the relief force commander and captain of the *Subedar*. Nadja had met him only briefly since boarding.

"Gunny, this is the lounge. You don't have to snap to." The man wore a broad smile and extended a hand to Nadja. "Dr. Bikram, may I join you ladies."

After Nadja's handshake and short nod, the man grabbed a chair and pulled it closer. Gunny resumed her seat, now sitting in a position approximating attention.

"I'm sorry I haven't had a chance to stop and chat since you've been onboard."

"We've both been a little busy, captain," Nadja replied. "Though I was a little surprised you didn't chair the board of inquiry."

"That would've been the custom, doctor," he said. "But I opted to conflict myself out."

Nadja gave the man a sideways look. "Have you and I met before?"

"You used to command *The Dread*, didn't you?" was his only reply.

The man suddenly looked familiar to her. "I did."

"My brother Dennis was your helmsman. You were his first skipper out of the academy, and he always spoke glowingly of you."

Nadja laughed. "I thought that nose looked familiar!"

"We both got the family crest," said the captain with a vigorous nod.

"How is Dennis? Did he make admiral? I remember that was his dream."

"You know, five years ago they offered him a star, but he took retirement instead."

"To do what?" The Dennis James Nadja remembered was Navy to the bone.

"He's a poet now."

She gave a laugh of pure surprise. "You're kidding me. Dennis?"

"Yes, ma'am." The man again nodded. "You're a Californio too, aren't you, Gunny?"

"I am, sir."

"I read your file," said the officer while gently shaking a finger at the NCO. "From up near … Saint Pete, right?"

"We have a farm there, sir."

"Right." He passed his friendly gaze between the women. "Dennis is living with our folks down near Doña Ana."

"Near the park, sir?"

"Exactly. Mom runs a small outfitter, and dad's a hunting guide. If either one of you ever wants to take a moose, that's the place to go. They even have a poet-in-residence to memorialize the occasion."

Nadja couldn't get over it. Dennis was a fine officer and now a poet. She continued to laugh.

The captain suddenly was serious. "I'm sorry I sprung that board on you so quickly," he said sincerely. "I could've waited until we got to the rear, assigned you a proper attorney and gave you more time to mount a defense. But Slawomir is one of the best and smartest officers who's ever served under me, the kind of leader under whom I'd proudly serve, if circumstances were reversed. And … and things are different on the settled worlds. Out here on the frontier, officers and crew understand that sometimes you have to make tough decisions, and sometimes you have only yourself and those few around you to depend on to survive."

Nadja had been wary of the circumstances, but she now realized the captain had done her an enormous kindness in rushing the proceedings. The officers of a frontier command were those in the best position to understand the circumstances that she'd faced.

"And don't worry about that nitwit from HDP," the officer continued. "Nobody takes him seriously out here. There are no thumbs on the scale. The members of the board will treat you fairly, whatever the outcome."

The man stood to go, and the two women joined him, Gunny again at attention. As they again exchanged handshakes Nadja spoke.

"It was good meeting you, captain. And give my best to Dennis."

"Call me Carl," the man insisted. "And every Tuesday and Friday when we're underway, I have a little soiree at 2000 hours for senior staff in the captain's mess. I hope to see both of you ladies there, regular."

"You can count on it."

After the man departed, the two again sat.

"So," drawled Gunny, "not going to jail?"

"It sounds like my odds are a little better than I'd imagined, but I'm still not taking bets." Nadja glanced at her watch and stood. "Come on. That catwalk runs the length of the foredeck. Believe it or not, there's an observation deck at the bow. We can watch as we break orbit."

Gunny joined her walking. "It sounds appropriate. Are you missing our friends too?"

Nadja had to remind herself that Gunny and Spiros had spent much longer with the warriors of Black Flower's band than she had. Their feelings for the folk ran deep and strong. She knew her own sadness at leaving them soon would abate, but wasn't certain she had the strength now to speak of her sweet Greta and Stig.

"I stepped off a cliff," she said instead.

"Ma'am?"

They walked several more paces at a leisurely gait.

"That night at the keep. I took a position on the trail near a boulder, and when I got up to run, I stepped right off a cliff. One of the warriors, I never learned who—it could've been one who died that night—snatched me out of thin air and put me back on the trail. Did so without breaking stride or uttering a word." She took several long breaths. "The event completely slipped my mind in the rush of things, and I didn't remember it until sitting in that stupid fucking hearing the other day, listening to someone drone on about nothing."

"Our friends are like that," said the Marine, "casually selfless and protective."

Nadja wasn't sure she could come up with a better description. "Well, I learned one thing from that entire episode. I am not a warrior. I couldn't do that every day the way you do."

Gunny gave a sudden snort. "Ma'am, you are a thoroughly gifted fighter, an absolute natural. Give it a little time. You'll fall in love with it like I have. Hell, I'm not sure I'll ever be able to retire from the Corps."

"Oh, speaking of which, my mail caught up with me this morning. Sgt. Matthews wants me to write him a letter of recommendation for officer candidate school. I'm not sure I know him well enough. What do you think?"

"Great Marine, ma'am. I'll probably be cleaning that young guy's office one of these days. But ... um, do *you* still have a job?"

"I'm finished at State, no matter how the hearing goes. Maybe I'll go back and be a full-time college professor."

"Even after that successful first contact?"

"Oh, Gunny ... you have no idea how petty a petty bureaucrat can be until you've worked at the State Department."

"The Marines are always looking for good officers."

That was an idea, thought Nadja. She'd never formally resigned her commission from the Navy and could probably transfer to the Marines. There were no longer age limits on service.

But then, there were the 200 kilograms of roots in the bio-container she'd brought onboard with her hold baggage. She'd always been a good biochemist, and she had friends with facilities and money. With the research files she'd cribbed from the Elphinstone data-core, that magic pill that would allow humans to travel freely between terrestrial worlds might still be a possibility. And who was to say, maybe the stuff was the key to everlasting life after all?

She didn't want to think of that now.

"I'm not sure I'd be a good Marine, Gunny. Maybe I'm too old and set in my ways. Lemme ask you. Do you think anyone will ever pay for shooting down your transport and killing Melissa Downey and your Marines?"

"You mean other than the assholes who pulled the trigger? That's tough to say, ma'am. Like the captain said, things on the settled worlds are different. Once money starts getting spread around, memories sometimes grow fuzzy and opinions begin to change. But I have hopes."

"What kind of hopes?"

Gunny began to laugh. "Remember I told you about my folks? They were always sort of half-ass, more-bark-than-bite revolutionaries. Some of their friends, though. They were serious about bringing accountability to government and industry. I've kept up with a few of them."

"And?"

"And … my last data pack home had everything a would-be reformer would need to crack open the nut that is Elphinstone, Ltd. Whether anything comes of that or not is anybody's guess."

"Gunny…," Nadja began. "What … what do your friends *really* call you, Really … really?"

The Marine's mouth gaped in an enormous smile at Nadja's fumbled play on words. "My closest friends call me Verity, ma'am."

"Verity?"

"My middle name."

Really Very Nice, thought Nadja without speaking a word. The two had reached the observation deck by that time, and the great arc of Skiathos filled the enormous screen before them, a land of beauty and wonder, a realm of noble champions and selfless heroes. A place she and the Marine who stood now beside her had navigated together.

Should she manage to avoid prison, Nadja wasn't sure what the future would hold for her. Perhaps she'd become a poet. Perhaps she'd conduct her own research to unlock the mysteries of the roots. Or perhaps she'd pass that work to someone more qualified and join Gunny in the Marines and travel to worlds unknown.

Whatever she chose to do, she suddenly was filled with a deep sense of hope and optimism and the happy notion that the entire universe lay open before them.

"You know, Verity. I have a strange feeling."

"What's that, Nadja?"

"That this is the beginning of a beautiful friendship."

The End